What others are saying...

"*Picture Imperfect* is a relatable and charming tribute to that transition time in life after college—struggling with romance and the rent, all while trying to find your place in the world and wondering if your passion could possibly pay the bills. Readers will cheer for these three-dimensional characters as they work out difficult family dynamics, go for their dreams, and learn that sometimes veering off course is actually imperfectly...perfect."

~Betsy St. Amant, author of The Key To Love and Tacos for Two

"Misunderstandings, failed relationships, and too much pressure come to a precipice in *Picture Imperfect*. This story will take you on a journey of forgiveness, healing, and seeing things from another person's perspective. A sweet romance from a Christian worldview."

~Kimberly Rose Johnson, award winning author of stories that warm the heart and feed the soul.

"What a delightful, witty read, complete with snappy dialogue, relatable characters, and an on-point message that, sometimes, "perfect" is way overrated. Young women will thoroughly identify with the struggles that Caroline and Andy face, both in their professional and private lives, as they seek to focus on the bigger picture and what truly matters. Be forewarned—on occasion, readers may laugh out loud, as well as reach for a tissue or two!"

~Cynthia Herron, award-winning author of **Her Hope Discovered and the Welcome to Ruby series**

"Clever, fast-paced, sweet, and surprising...everything I like in a romance!"

~Carmen Schober, author of the debut sports romance After She Falls

D1498897

"*Picture Imperfect* by Hope Bolinger and Alyssa Roat is a charming story you'll want to read more than once. I thoroughly enjoyed it."

~Linda Hanna, co-author of Reflections of a Stranger and the Seasons of Change series

"Roat and Bolinger write a sweet romance that goes deeper than simply falling in love. In the characters of Andy and Caroline, we find the gentle reminder that life doesn't always look like we thought, nor is it always perfect, but it can still be beautiful—especially when we let go of our plans to hold onto God's. A thoroughly delightful book in oh so many ways."

~Susan L. Tuttle, author of the Along Came Love series

"Hope Bolinger and Alyssa Roat are not new faces to the publishing world but teamed together as authors they are a pair to watch. Readers will love this newest adventure, *Picture Imperfect*, greedily turning pages to discover if workaholic novelist Caroline and perfectionist artist Andy can collaborate in time to save a beloved non-profit as well as their careers. The writing is clever, the characters well-formed, and the story deep. Looking forward to more fun stories from this writing duo."

~Patricia Lee, author of the Mended Hearts series

PICTURE IMPERFECT

PICTURE IMPERFECT

Roseville Romances Book One

PICTURE

IMPERFECT

by

Alyssa Roat   Hope Bolinger

Picture Imperfect
Published by Mountain Brook Ink
White Salmon, WA U.S.A.

The website addresses shown in this book are not intended in any way to be or imply an endorsement on the part of Mountain Brook Ink, nor do we vouch for their content.

This story is a work of fiction. All characters and events are the product of the author's imagination. Any resemblance to any person, living or dead, is coincidental.

Scripture taken from the Holy Bible, NEW INTERNATIONAL VERSION®, NIV® Copyright © 1973, 1978, 1984, 2011 by Biblica, Inc.® Used by permission. All rights reserved worldwide.

The Author is represented by and this book is published in association with the literary agency of Hartline Literary Agency, www.hartlineliterary.com.

© 2021 Alyssa Roat and Hope Bolinger
ISBN 9781-953957-07-8

The Team: Miralee Ferrell, Kristen Johnson, Cindy Jackson
Cover Design: Indie Cover Design, Lynnette Bonner Designer

Mountain Brook Ink is an inspirational publisher offering fiction you can believe in.
Printed in the United States of America

HOPE'S ACKNOWLEDGMENTS

Just like Andy and Caroline needed help to launch a book, no story is complete without a team of encouragers and readers to aid it in finding a way to shelves.

First and foremost, to my Lord and Savior Jesus Christ. God, on the seventh day, you rested. May we remember that we need to take moments to stop and reflect on your goodness. And even on our days off, you continue to work with us and guide us.

To my crazy co-author who spent way too long giggling with me about cabbage incidents and sparkly pink scrunchies. Sorry I call you way too much when you and I should be working.

To my family for supporting me in my writing journey and having grace with me in the moments of intense hustle that publishing often requires.

To my friends—especially James, Carlee, David, The Merlin Squad, The Pizza Squad, and Sonya—for teaching me to have boundaries with myself and to take moments to step away and rest.

To my hardworking agent Tessa for dealing with the fact I practically send her a book a month. So sorry, and thank you for rooting for me!

To Miralee, who believed in this project and fell in love with the characters, and with whom we got into side-tangents about oil paintings. Thank you for encouraging me to have boundaries and for ushering this project into the world.

To the proofreaders, cover revealers, endorsers, ARC team, reviewers, and readers. You are the backbone of this book. Thank you so much for your honest feedback and willingness to share Picture Imperfect. We would be absolutely nowhere without you.

ALYSSA'S ACKNOWLEDGMENTS

I believe I have been called "about as romantic as a potato." My comfort zone is speculative fiction. Which is why it's funny that I find myself writing romance, again.

I have to thank my parents for showing me what real, enduring love looks like, and ensuring that I have at least one (maybe half?) romantic bone in my body. You two set the bar high.

A shout out to Hope, who somehow got me hooked on this romance thing. I didn't expect to fall this deeply in love with this story. What have we done?

Writing as Caroline gave me an even bigger appreciation for my parents, who always supported my dreams of writing and publishing. Thank you, both of you, for your unwavering love and support.

I also have to thank Katie, the constant witness to my writing crises, deadline stresses, and late-night writing sessions. Thank you for reminding me to emerge from hunching over the keyboard and enjoy the world around me too.

My family, all the many, many of you, for being so supportive. My beautiful sisters Steph and Julianna.

And my friends. Oh, my goodness. The Pizza Squad. The Soddleppoodlert Groodleoodlep. Cyle's Henchfolks. The PWRs. You all were there for us to let us spill tea or to give feedback or to cheer us on.

Thank you to Miralee Ferrell, Jenny Mertes, Kristen Johnson, and Nikki (yes, you still count, you will always be my MBI partner in crime) and all of MBI for this wonderful publishing experience.

And of course, thank you Jesus, for this wonderfully, perfectly imperfect life you have given me.

HOPE'S DEDICATION

*To Grace, a wonderful sister, mom,
and a woman of many talents.*

ALYSSA'S DEDICATION

To my parents, who showed me what love looks like.

Chapter One

CAROLINE PENN WAS *NEVER* LATE.

Never late except for today, apparently.

"Liv! Will you feed Rabbit?" she called over her shoulder, yanking on her black heels.

"Sure," her roommate mumbled as she shuffled out of her bedroom to start the coffee maker. She sleepily pushed her dark hair out of her face and tied her robe around her. "How can you possibly be late? It's still dark out."

"It's that special meeting with Mr. Knox I told you about."

Liv's half-closed eyes widened. "Oh, snap."

"Exactly." *Coat. Keys. Purse. Good.* "Goodbye!"

"Good luck! You'll rock it, you're beautiful, go get 'em!"

The door slammed behind Caroline as she ran down the snow-covered front steps, Liv's overzealous encouragement echoing behind her. Snow. Fresh snow. Not the sludge that had been coating the ground for the past week. *Oh, no. Why, Michigan? Why snow in March?*

By the time Caroline finished brushing the snow off her baby blue hatchback, the sky was starting to lighten. Tinges of orange sprang up over the horizon as she pushed the speed limit as much as she dared.

She took a deep breath and checked her appearance in the sun visor mirror. Good. She could hardly tell she'd been up until two in the morning—if she ignored the dark circles under her eyes.

"You got this, girl. It's going to be great. It will be fine."

She hadn't seen herself working at a nonprofit when she graduated four years ago. Especially not a nonprofit in a mid-sized town in Michigan, copy-editing flyers, web content, and pamphlets instead of the next bestselling novel. But Helping Hope Publishing paid the bills until she finally got that book contract, and at least there was the word "editor" in her title. And maybe, after today, it would be an editor of books.

Why else would Mr. Knox want to have a meeting with her? The promotion had been a long time in coming. Her copy was impeccable, certainly much better than Zinnia's.

Her car skidded on an icy patch. She yanked the wheel in time to keep it on the road, but not before her rear tire churned up snowy sludge from the shoulder, splashing brown slush all over the blue coat of a man walking down the sidewalk with a package under his arm.

She gasped and considered stopping. But no, she couldn't. She was already too late.

"I'm sorry!" she called as if the dripping man could hear her.

Five minutes later, she wove through the cubicles to Mr. Knox's office. When she arrived, a blonde with bright red lipstick stood in front of the door, one perfectly plucked eyebrow raised.

"Are you all right, Carrie?" Zinnia asked, voice dripping with concern.

Caroline clenched her teeth but managed to smile. "I'm fine, thank you. Pardon me. I have a meeting with Mr. Knox."

Zinnia glanced at her watch. The pink band matched her cardigan exactly. "Wasn't that three minutes ago? You look exhausted. Are you sure everything is fine?"

"Yes, perfectly fine. I was just up late last night." Caroline tried to skirt around her coworker.

"Oh, were you working on your little story again?"

"My novel? Yes. Sorry, Zinnia, excuse me."

"Oh, I'm so sorry. I'm in your way. Have a good meeting." She waved over her shoulder, practically sashaying back to her desk.

Caroline knocked on the door a little harder than she intended. "Come in," a deep voice called.

Mr. Knox's office was an… interesting place. Before he started a publishing company/children's charity, he'd spent his time exploring the wilds of Africa. He'd done some sort of relief work, but Caroline wasn't sure what. She did know he'd done a bit of hunting as well. A water buffalo head hung behind him, while a few gazelles and other African creatures were crammed together on the limited wall space. Caroline always felt like they watched her, judging her.

Caroline pasted on a smile. "Good morning, Mr. Knox."

"Ms. Penn!" His words boomed in the enclosed space and his waxed mustache twitched with his smile. "I've been looking forward to talking to you." He frowned at his watch. "Though you're a little late." He threw a hand in the air dismissively. "But no matter. Come in, sit down. We have a lot to talk about."

Caroline took a seat across the desk from him, her ears ringing and her head spinning a bit, as they usually did from Mr. Knox's exuberance.

He leaned forward, his khaki button-up straining against his broad shoulders. "You know we do a lot of charity work, of course. Boys and girls' homes, toy drives, donations back to my good friends in Africa, so many wonderful things. But—" He wagged his finger. "We are a *publishing* house. And you know how much of our revenue for our projects comes from book sales?"

"Forty-two percent as of last quarter, sir."

"Exactly. Unacceptable. Our sales are going down and our donations aren't going up. What do you think that means?"

This was it. "Perhaps, sir, the editorial team needs more help putting out quality books." *They need me.*

He blinked. "What? No, no. What we need are more books."

Caroline's heart dropped. *Is he going to stick me back in acquisitions, reading all those badly rhymed submissions?* "More... books, sir?"

"Yes!" He was back on a roll. "We aren't getting the same quality of writers that we used to, and we can't afford any big-name authors. No, we can hardly afford to pay writers at all. We need a new series of children's books. Something that will bring in profit. Something innovative. Heartwarming. Preferably with gorgeous artwork."

"Do you... have anything in particular you're thinking of, sir?"

"No, but that's why you're here. You're going to write them!"

Andy Jackson was *always* late.

Including today, apparently.

If he'd arrived at the Roseville Post Office five minutes earlier, he might not have had a fresh coat of road paint splashed on his blue winter coat. Road paint, otherwise known as a mix of Michigander slush, fresh snow, and the screech of tire wheels, dolloped wet brown onto the once cobalt jacket.

As an artist, he knew his blues—and knew browns typically didn't quite go with them.

"Who on earth needs to race down an icy road that fast?" Then again, Michigan drivers considered ten over exactly the right speed.

Shivering, he turned the lock of his apartment with his free hand and dropped the wet package on the floor. Too bad he'd borrowed the last of his roommate Elijah's cardboard shipping boxes. True, he could've gone another couple blocks and bought a new one at the post office. But that would have necessitated waiting in a line while smelling of fresh mud and asphalt. And that would also require more money...something he didn't have.

Plus, the contents within would have to dry, and perhaps, if he remembered, he'd get his mother her birthday gift... three weeks late.

He hung his coat on a wooden peg and slumped into a frayed, blue fabric chair. Elijah's. In a lazy motion, Andy's dark fingers flicked the pile of letters on a black side table. Craning his neck at them, he stopped after spying a handful of "Past Dues," and ran his fingers instead through his hair, where they got caught on a curly tangle.

"So much for delivering Mom's birthday gift today. Can't do that while it's still wet." Perhaps he could get it to her when she came up from Tennessee for Mother's Day.

That was, if he could handle her being here alone, after that incident from his sophomore year of high school, and the track record of disappointing her ever since.

Straining from the effort, he reached for the TV remote at the end of the side table. *Come on, Andy, you're only twenty-six. Don't tell me your back is giving out.* Granted, Elijah did run him pretty hard in their pickup basketball game the other day. Even the players seemed to move ten miles an hour faster than usual.

With a bright flash, almost too bright for that time in the morning, the TV flicked onto a scene from *Midnight in Paris.* Not bad for Elijah cancelling their cable four months ago.

He picked through the letters on his table again.

At the bottom of the pile, under an envelope with a "Final Notice" stamp, he found his sketchbook. He plucked out a worn pencil buried in the chair, and he traced the giraffe into Noah's Ark.

The toddlers at the church were going to love this when he added the ideas to the mural he'd been painting for their classroom. A smirk ran up his cheek at the thought of little Ruth in her dinosaur T-shirt asking him to put a T-Rex on the ark next to the elephants and horses.

A couple minutes in, he paused. And frowned at the sketch. Something about the proportions felt off. Oh, well. He shrugged and placed the sketchbook on the table. He'd work on it later.

Digging into his wet pocket, he inched out his phone and scrolled through his Instagram feed until a sudden buzz filled his hand. "Whoa." Nearly jumping, he squinted at the unknown number that crossed the screen.

Maybe Charming Chocolate Factory was getting back about the logo he made them. Not quite the same feel as a physical pencil and paper, but Adobe Illustrator produced work he could almost be proud of.

Speaking of, had he paid the monthly bill for that program?

Shrugging, he slid open the green phone logo. "Hello, Andy Jackson speaking."

"Andy. Clark Knox from Helping Hope Publishing."

The voice blasted through the speaker and he moved the phone away from his ear. Helping who? That didn't sound like one of the companies he freelanced for. "Umm, hi, Clark. How are you?"

"Terrible. Now, I got your work samples, and although we usually only accept illustrator submissions from agents or from illustrators we've worked with before, we have a last-minute need to fill, and your style is unlike anything I've ever seen. It's so, so—" The snapping of fingers came through the receiver. "Hopeful."

Work samples? He didn't send any of his work samples to a publisher. Unless... he sat up in his chair and caught the glare of his computer on a white desk, covered in crumpled papers. *Elijah.* Shouldn't have given him his email password.

"Anyway—"

Andy's skin jolted a little. Clark Knox was still speaking.

"We were wondering if you would be willing to partner with an author on an assignment."

His eyes bounced from the letters to the wet package by the door and then to his computer. "What kind of assignment?"

A children's book.

Not just a children's book. Worse. A *series* of children's books.

Back at her desk, Caroline stared at her computer screen, the cursor blinking over the proof of the brochure she was supposed to be editing. *Writing for children.*

The last book she had written was a thriller back in college. She'd submitted the manuscript to multiple large Christian publishers where her professor knew people, but they said it was too dark. She hadn't had the desire to get rejected again, so she shelved that project.

Too dark. And now children's books.

Sure, she'd learned since her angsty college phase. She gravitated from researching the criminal underworld to world history. She fancied her current project a literary historical work, set in the early Byzantine Empire.

But obscure locales and time periods didn't translate well to children's literature either.

"That must be quite an interesting brochure."

Her blank stare broken, Caroline turned around. "Oh! Miss Evie. I didn't see you."

The white-haired woman chuckled, her bright blue eyes sparkling. "How is my favorite copyeditor?"

Caroline couldn't help smiling. "You're going to hurt Zinnia's feelings."

"Favorite copy*writer*, then?"

"She's that too now. Mr. Knox let another writer go last month." Which made her frown. They'd downsized from five full-time copywriters to one within the last year, leaving Caroline and Zinnia to pick up the slack.

"Oh, pish." Miss Evie leaned on her cherry-red cane. "This office is getting too quiet. You're the only one who has time for an old woman. My son's in his office blathering the ear off some poor fellow on the telephone, so I figured I'd come say hello."

Caroline's smile grew. "It's always good to see you, Miss Evie."

"What's got you staring so hard at that brochure?" She leaned forward, squinting. "Doesn't look too interesting to me."

"I was thinking." Caroline took a deep breath. "Mr. Knox assigned me to write a series of children's books."

Miss Evie threw her head back and laughed out loud. One of Caroline's coworkers jumped as he walked by, the sound of mirth echoing in the quiet office. Must be where Mr. Knox got his volume control.

"Did he, now?" Miss Evie smirked. "He told me he didn't think that was a good idea when I suggested it to him at dinner the other night. Well, look at that."

Caroline's mouth opened and closed. "You... you suggested it?"

"Of course, I did." The elderly lady patted Caroline on the head. "I know what a good writer you are. And you'll write them quicker than any author would."

Caroline glanced back at her computer. The screen had gone dark from lack of use, as empty as her inspiration. *I don't know about that.*

"I told that son of mine." Miss Evie smiled with self-satisfaction. "It would save money to do it in-house, I told him. You've got a good writer sitting right in front of your nose, I said, if you'd ever think to read your own magazines and donor letters. Well, I guess it got through his thick skull."

"Thank you, Miss Evie. But... I've never written for children. I've never had a book published. I don't know what I'm doing. I..."

"Hush, now." She made a shooing motion as she turned to leave. "When God opens a door, you don't ask questions. You just walk through it." She tapped her cane as if that settled the matter. "Now, I'm going to go rescue whoever Clark is talking to."

Caroline was about to turn back to the computer when Zinnia leaned over the cubicle wall. "Carrie, I don't mean to pry, but I couldn't help overhearing. Did you say Mr. Knox is having you write children's books?"

Where is she going with this? "Yes. He just told me."

"Wow." Zinnia crossed her arms over the wall. "That's brave of you. I admire that. I mean, I wouldn't mind it. I've written for children before, you know. I had a short story come out in a magazine last fall. But for you, with no experience..." She shook her head. "I've got to say. I'm impressed."

"Thanks," Caroline said tightly.

"Well, if you need any help, let me know." She flashed her too-white teeth. "I'm always willing to help the newbies."

Caroline bit her lip. Hard. She was hired only four months after Zinnia. Four years ago. *Four years.* Had it really been that long? "Thanks, Zin. Appreciate it."

"Always!" With a flip of her hair, she ducked back into her cubicle.

That's it. I'm writing the best darn children's book series they've ever seen.

Sammy placed his head in Andy's lap. Andy scratched his golden retriever's head and listened to the phone pressed to his ear as Clark Knox went on, through the receiver, about due dates.

"Now, I know the deadline is ambitious." Knox's voice sounded like the color orange, loud and abrasive. "But in your email, you mentioned finishing projects on time or at least a couple days before."

Had he now? Thanks, Elijah.

Come on, Andy, say you can't take the job. You're already behind on a ton of other freelance projects.

"And, I'm not saying that we can't pay you a lot, but we aren't one of the Big Five publishers—"

Say no.

"What do you think?"

No.

He chewed on his bottom lip. "Sure."

Close enough.

Maybe now he'd have enough to pay this month's rent and repay Elijah for paying last month's rent for the both of them.

Sammy attempted to crawl onto his lap, the best a sixty-seven-pound dog could do, and let out a whimper as Knox went on about royalty splits and an advance. Andy patted the dog's spine and worried if some of his snow-slush smell would get onto Sammy's coat. Nothing quite like the odor of wet Sammy. Made all the ladies swoon when he walked into public wearing that cologne.

"Does that percentage work for you?"

"Huh?" The phone nearly fell out of his hand. He gripped it in his slippery palm at the last second. "Sure, that works fine." *I hope he said a high percentage. Why do you always zone out on phone calls, man?*

"Great. Now, I want to swing another thing by you. We're hosting a charity event this weekend. Have a balloon artist and face painter coming out, good stuff."

There was a long pause. "Umm, sounds like a lot of fun."

"Eh, we'll see. Anyway, I know it's last minute, but a caricature artist dropped out on us last minute. Think you could swing by the David Livingstone Center at five on Saturday?"

"Oh, I, uh." Didn't he have a poster he was making for a coffee shop by that day? What was its name? She Brews?

"You ever drawn caricatures before?"

"Sure, but I, uh—"

"We could pay you."

Or maybe he was thinking of the flyer for a local band, The Roseville Rockettes. When was that due?

"Not a lot, of course. We're not Simon and Schuster."

Either way, he couldn't say yes to one more thing.

"And you'll meet the author at the event. Great way to hit things off by drawing her nose extra big. What d'ya say, Handy Andy?"

Oh, right, he had to work *with* someone on this project. Forgot that part. He never was a fan of group projects in high school, college, or really, ever.

Just say no. "Sure, Mr. Knox, sounds great."

"Call me Clark. I'll email you the details. See you at five on Saturday." The phone's receiver clicked.

Andy dropped the phone onto the pile of letters and buried his face into his free hand, the one Sammy wasn't currently sitting on. "Oh, buddy, why did I say yes?" Unpalming his forehead, he saw Sammy crane his neck up at him for a moment and then slump down onto his knee. Oof, Elijah had worked those hard in basketball the other day too. Lots of running.

"I have to make a poster for a coffee shop, fix the logo for Charming Chocolates, get the flyer for that band done, do dozens of illustrations for a children's book, finish painting that room in the Sunday school classroom…" He'd run out of fingers on his free hand. "And now, I'm drawing caricatures."

He draped his head over the chair and moaned. Below, Sammy's ears twitched once, twice in irritation and then lay still.

"At least we'll meet the author and get that part over with." He smirked at Sammy and then the stack of letters. "Let's hope she's easygoing."

Chapter Two

THIRTY MINUTES. SHE HAD THIRTY MINUTES to change, grab food, and rush off to the charity event.

She hadn't intended to cut it so close, but then marketing had a typo in their proposal that had been transferred to the press release, so of course she'd had to track that down, and then Mr. Knox had left emails unanswered to donors, which inevitably fell to Caroline.

Caroline pushed open the door to the apartment. "Liv?"

Nothing. Of course Olivia wasn't home. Olivia had friends.

At least Rabbit would be happy to see her.

She kicked off her heels as she entered her bedroom and tossed her keys on the bed. She knelt next to the elaborate cage against the wall, plastic tubes darting to bedding-filled burrows, a wheel, and plenty of toys. Yes, Rabbit was spoiled.

Caroline reached into the cage, setting her hand in front of the rounded hutch. A small pink nose snuffled out from the bedding. With a yawn, Rabbit pulled herself out of the fluff and climbed into Caroline's hand.

Caroline stood, cupping the dwarf hamster to her chest and stroking Rabbit's tiny head with one index finger. "Hi, baby girl," she crooned. "Wanna have some free time?"

She set the hamster in a ball and closed the lid. As she rifled through her closet for something a little fancier and less business-y, Rabbit bumped into her ankles, squeaking for treats.

Caroline ditched the slacks she'd worn into the office. Maybe she didn't have to dress up to go in on a Saturday when no one else was there, but Mom had drilled into her the importance of appearances. Today marked the third Saturday in a row she'd needed to make a trip in on a weekend to finish a last-minute project. She traded the slacks for a black skirt decorated with tulips, one of her favorite flowers. Maybe that would put a spring in her step.

She swished down the short hallway to the kitchen and pulled out a container of leftover quinoa, chicken, and kale. Only a healthy diet could maintain a busy schedule. She downed the meal cold while scrolling through her phone, checking emails. The endless emails.

Her phone dinged and a text message popped up. She dropped a piece of quinoa into the hamster ball for Rabbit as she reluctantly tapped on the message.

Dad: Any more thoughts on coming home for Easter? Mom misses you.

Caroline clenched her jaw. *Now* Mom missed her? *You had eighteen years to act like you cared, Mom.*

Ding! Another message. When she saw the name, her heart began beating faster. She opened the text.

Clark Knox: WhER r u?

She hated that he had her number. Hated even more his propensity for abbreviations and random capitalization.

Caroline: On my way. I'll be there in 20.
Clark Knox: Make it 10. Need 2 tlk

Caroline bit her lip. She would have to speed.

"Sorry, Rabbit. Free time is over."

Exactly eleven minutes later, Caroline pulled into the parking lot. Late again, the second time this week. Though only quarter to five, vehicles already packed the parking lot. The event didn't officially start until five thirty.

She found a spot at the back, cursing her decision to wear heels. But at five three, she felt the need for that extra height. She'd learned in college a few more inches helped people take her seriously. That and makeup, fashion, anything to help her look older. She'd even mastered the bun, as hard as it could be to tame her hair into submission at times.

She hoped the heels, makeup, outfit, and hair would help her appear like she meant business to whatever artist Mr. Knox had chosen.

She pushed open the doors. To be honest, she didn't want to admit that her attempts to come up with a story were going nowhere. If she looked like she knew what she was doing, hopefully Mr. Knox and the artist would believe it too.

"Caroline!" Heads turned as Mr. Knox's voice reverberated through the open convention center. Caroline winced. He strode toward her, sweeping an arm out toward the booths. "Doesn't it all look wonderful?"

"Yes, sir." She was just glad she wasn't part of the events team. With the banners, the streamers, the colorful booths all with themes representing Helping Hope's various programs, it must have taken forever to create. Although with the way things were going, she might find herself on the events team soon as well. Another job.

"Listen, since I gave you that new assignment on Thursday, I haven't seen a thing from you. I'm a little worried, you know? Deadline is Monday, after all."

First draft due Monday. And it was Saturday already. Only one more day to get Mr. Knox something not completely terrible.

She straightened her shoulders and used her professional voice. "I want to make sure it's the best it can be. I promise it will be on your desk Monday morning."

He didn't look convinced. "Well, I thought you might want a little inspiration. We need a volunteer at the balloon booth." He grinned like he'd announced she won the lottery. "Not animals or anything fancy, we have someone for that. Just helium. But it might give you a chance to work with the kiddos, get some observation in."

Pretty sure helium isn't going to give me inspiration. But if it would give her a reprieve from the possibility of his questioning—

which would reveal her utter lack of anything halfway decent to turn in on Monday—she'd take it.

Twenty balloons later, her fingers already throbbed from tying off the ends, and one wayward balloon floated dozens of feet up in the rafters. She felt especially incompetent next to the balloon animal guy, who whipped out flowers and dogs faster than she could tie one helium balloon printed with Helping Hope's logo.

Caroline spotted her roommate's familiar, tall, thin form strolling by. Olivia stopped when she made eye contact with Caroline. "Hey." Olivia waved, the bangles on her wrist jangling. "Balloons, huh?"

Caroline smiled at a little boy with wild blond curls and handed him the string. "Here you go." He bounded off, calling a quick thanks over his shoulder, and Caroline turned her attention to her roommate. "Didn't expect to see you here."

"Of course. Got to support Roseville's favorite charity." She cocked her head, and her lips twitched in an effort to suppress a smile. "Haven't seen that hairdo before, but it suits you."

Caroline reached up and patted her hair, then stiffened, mortified. It was sticking up everywhere with static. "No," she moaned. "Why balloons?"

Olivia laughed. "Maybe if you take it down, it will smooth out?"

Caroline pulled out her hairpins, stuffing them in her skirt pocket—part of the reason why this was her favorite skirt. She ran her hands through her hair. "Better?"

Olivia snorted. "Um…"

Caroline's eyes darted over Olivia's shoulder, where she spotted Mr. Knox striding purposefully in their direction. *Fantastic.* "I think someone wants to talk to me."

"Caroline! You have to meet the illustrator." Mr. Knox brushed past Olivia. "Come with me."

Caroline tried to keep up with his confident stride, desperately pushing hair out of her face. This was not how she wanted to meet the illustrator. Not how she wanted to display her professionalism.

Mr. Knox glanced over his shoulder and chuckled his booming

laugh. "Looks like the balloons got to you."

She felt her cheeks flush. Everything about this project so far was a disaster. She had a feeling it would only get worse.

The man seated in front of Andy had the largest nose he'd ever seen.

Andy stared at the bulbous snout for two solid seconds, noticing its vast similarities to his dog's squeaker toys at home. If someone were to honk the nose, would the nostrils make a similar sound?

A woman behind the man tapped her foot and balanced a plate with vegetables and dip in her hands. Andy's stomach dropped when he observed the winding line behind her. How long had he taken with this man's caricature?

Andy faced the easel, hand wobbling.

One wrong move, and this black pen could permanently etch something into the cartoon visage of the man who sat before him on a stool. No, he had to get this perfectly.

The man cleared his throat. "I'm sure you're doing a great job. But this better be Mona Lisa level quality for the time I've been here." He creaked the stool when he adjusted his weight. Then the man threw a quick glance over his shoulder at the silent auction. No doubt he wanted to place a bid on an item. Andy had spotted Maldives vacation tickets earlier that he'd love to get for his mom, for all the years she'd invested in his schooling.

If only he didn't have cell phone bills to worry about. When had he last paid those?

Focus, Andy. He returned to the easel and applied a brushstroke to the cartoon chin.

His lips twitched, and he huffed. Nope, that wasn't rotund enough to capture this man's round jaw. He winced and stared at the line. Three more members had joined the queue that wound all the way back to a face painter. She was busy applying a purple butterfly to a young girl's cheek.

He'd have to do a shoddy job. Even though he hated anything less than perfect.

On the table next to the easel that held a bucket with the words "Caricature Donations" on it, his phone hummed. He blinked and tried his best to ignore the emails that said, "Late Notice," and "Water Bill Now Available." And the text messages from Mom.

Dizziness buzzed in his brain like the bees he'd spotted outside the other day, awakened from their winter hibernation. He clenched his fist and tightened his jaw.

You have to finish this. He added a constellation of freckles on the cartoon's forehead. *Look at that line behind him, Andy.*

But the more he observed the train of people that seemed to keep collecting passengers, the more the blood left his cheeks.

Right as he added the finishing touches to the picture, trying to get the bushy eyebrows fuzzy enough, but not too woolly that they'd be overgrown like the hedges outside his apartment complex, a, "Hey, wait your turn in line!" pricked his ears.

He looked up and watched a greasy man barrel toward him. Behind the man, a woman with hair flying in every direction jogged in heels to keep up.

If it weren't for the static electricity hair, Andy would've loved to do an illustration of her. Not a caricature. That couldn't capture the beauty of her high cheekbones, flowery skirt, and defined collarbone. This woman deserved a real portrait by the looks of her.

"I'm not here to get my picture done." The greasy man had turned to a suited customer in line who'd crossed his arms. The suit, two sizes too small, crept toward the suited man's elbows, revealing a purple oxford long sleeve underneath. "Give me two minutes to talk to this guy."

With this, the greasy fellow turned to Andy. It looked like the man's right eye was permanently stuck in a squint.

A large grin split his cheeks. "Glad to see my illustrator for my children's book project in action." He bustled over and stole a long gaze at the caricature.

This must be Clark. The voice did sound the same from their phone conversation, even more filled with gravel now, if possible.

The woman with Clark stood at a distance and brushed out a wrinkle in the flower skirt. Now the tulip at the bottom sat on her leg in a pristine, ironed fashion.

Clark swiveled away from the caricature and almost knocked over the easel with his broad shoulders. "I was hoping to introduce you two before the main auction gets started." He licked his lips and pointed to a stage at the opposite end of the room. "When that happens," Clark eagle-spread his arms, "pandemonium."

Something tells me that this man loves to exaggerate.

Most likely, at the worst, patrons would toss glares at each other across folded chairs as they held up their bidding numbers on sticks.

"Since we're paying you a flat fee for this event, I figured it wouldn't hurt your finances to talk with our writer for the children's book project I'd mentioned on the phone the other day." Clark, now next to the woman, gave her a hefty shove. She almost tripped on her heels and massaged her shoulder. "Andy, meet Caroline."

Caroline clasped her elbow with her hand. She wouldn't make eye contact with him. "Hello."

"Hi." The greeting got caught in his throat, like the hummus from the food table had earlier after he'd arrived at the banquet hall. Had her beauty made his words go all dry?

Thunder jolted Andy from his seat.

Wait no, not thunder. Most of the April showers hadn't started yet. It was Clark clapping. Then, Clark shivered and made jazz hands. "Sparks! I can feel the synergy between you two and know you'll work well together. Can't wait to see what you both come up with." He jabbed a finger at Caroline. "Don't let me down on this."

With another wide sweep of his shoulder that almost knocked into Caroline's clavicle, Clark marched toward a table covered in pies, a man on a mission.

Andy glanced at the caricature and the man on the stool who now had his arms crossed.

Oh well. I guess we'll have to give him a half-done job. Andy signed his name at the bottom of the drawing and tore the sheet from the easel. The man took a long look at the picture and squinted at Andy. Then he honked his nose with his fingers. "A bit of an exaggeration, don't you think?" With that, he dug a twenty out of his pocket, dropped it into the donation bucket, and stormed off toward a table with a silent auction for seasons' tickets for Wolverines games. The caricature flapped like a sail behind him.

"Next customer, please!" Andy beamed at the next person in line, a woman with her silvery hair wrapped into a severe bun.

"I was hoping we could plan ahead." Caroline, beside him, brushed her fingers through a tangle. "That way we can finish the picture book before the deadline."

Andy shrugged and got started on the woman's large forehead on the sheet of paper. "Planning's great, but I'm sure we have lots of time." He gestured to the line, and his lips twitched. "Can it wait until after the auction?"

"I don't think so." Caroline planted her hands on her hips. Behind her, a group of women chatted at the pie table about some paper flower decorations they admired. "I'd like to speak with you, and if you don't mind, I'd like to go out in the hallway where there's no noise, so you're less... distracted."

He hadn't registered the noise in the banquet hall. But now that she mentioned it, a din of conversation did echo around them. The lack of carpeted walls or floors didn't help with absorbing any of the hubbub.

Still, something about the way she said "distracted" prickled his skin. *Does she not trust me to get the job done? Does she think I'm some teenager who can't focus on a task?*

Caroline tapped a foot.

Andy's eyebrows furrowed. *She's not going anywhere until we settle this, is she?*

He sighed and clapped his marker on the easel. Then he turned to the line. "Leaving for a five-minute break. Please make sure to check out the auctions while I'm gone." The crowd dissolved into grumbles and eye rolls. He even heard a voice from the back of the scattered queue say, "You've got to be kidding me! I've been waiting for half an hour."

Thanks a lot, Caroline.

They marched toward the hallway, Caroline ten steps ahead. When he stepped outside, under an archway covered in paper flowers, the buzz of the auction escaped his ears. And Caroline's snarky, "Are you coming?" replaced it.

He held up his hands. "Look, I only came out here so we didn't cause a commotion in front of the line, not to discuss the picture book. From what I could tell on my phone call with Clark, we have plenty of time. Besides, it's a children's book. Aren't those twenty pages?"

"Thirty-two." She flicked up an eyebrow. "And from what I've seen so far, we need every second of planning we can get."

Andy furrowed his brows as a couple in matching green outfits handed their tickets to a woman stationed at a table by the entrance. "What's that supposed to mean?"

"Remember the ridiculously long line for caricatures? I mean, how hard is it to draw a cartoon of someone?"

Heat flared in his cheeks. It took a lot to get him this mad, especially this fast. But in this moment, she sounded like every one of his school teachers wrapped into one flowery skirt.

Especially Ms. Buren… and he didn't like to think about her.

"If you ask me, it seems like you're the kind of person who is obsessed with work and doesn't know how to enjoy life. Here you are at a charity banquet and all you can think about is what's next. Do you ever live in the now?"

She gawked. "Excuse me?"

"You're excused. Now if you'll excuse *me*, I have a caricature of a woman with lovely silver hair that I need to finish."

Not waiting to hear her retort, he marched into the banquet hall and got lost in the noise.

Chapter Three

CAROLINE NEVER WANTED TO SEE A blinking cursor again.

She shut her laptop and picked up a pen and paper instead. She had been up since five, trying to yank words out of her brain and onto the screen. But everything she wrote sounded terrible. She now had nine discarded drafts, fourteen unfinished stories, and no more ideas. *What do kids like?* She sighed. As if she knew. Mom and Dad hadn't thought much of toys or games that didn't have educational value. Their little girl didn't have time for silly stories about ducks or pigeons or whatever it was kids read. They handed Caroline her first reading flashcards at age two and never looked back, from the private schools, to the piano lessons, to the international competitions where anxious children were expected to pit their knowledge of esoteric subjects against one another.

It made her exhausted just remembering.

She glanced at her phone, the message from Dad still without her response. The only thing she dreaded writing more than this picture book.

Focus. She set pen to paper and made a list of things she thought kids liked. Dogs. Horses. Flowers? Maybe sports? Her guilty pleasure had always been spearmint green tea and a good, thick book. Not exactly exciting story fodder.

Halfway through a plot outline for a story about the remarkable life cycle of tulips—the ideas were getting worse and worse—she set down her pen and shoved her chair back. "Forget it."

The old Caroline Penn could do *anything* she set her mind to. That's what Penn's did. With enough study, enough work, she was never supposed to fail. Ever.

Until the day she sabotaged everything.

Not thinking about that right now.

Caroline stomped into the kitchen, where the stove clock read 7:45. Olivia looked over her coffee mug from the kitchen table. "You look like you're in a good mood."

Caroline plucked a mug from the cupboard. "And you're up early."

Liv shrugged. "I'm singing with the worship band this morning."

"That's new." How had she missed that? She'd been so wrapped up in her own work she hardly knew what her roommate was doing. Guilt gnawed at her. "Are you excited?"

Olivia's eyes sparkled. "It's good to be singing again."

Caroline nodded while pouring herself coffee. Liv had the voice of an angel. She was far too talented for a little town like Roseville. Of course, Mom would say the same thing about Caroline. "I can't wait to hear you." She opened the fridge. "Eggs?"

"Only if they're cheesy." Liv pulled her feet up onto the bench seat while Caroline took out the carton and a pan. "I didn't get a chance to ask you. How did it go with the illustrator last night?"

Caroline cracked an egg a little too hard, and yolk splattered the stovetop. She grabbed a paper towel. "Oh. Fine."

Liv's eyebrow rose. Caroline focused on the eggs so she didn't have to meet her roommate's gaze.

Every time she thought of her interaction with Andy Jackson, she cringed. She'd been anything but professional. Static hair, unprepared, not even sure what they were supposed to talk *about* with no manuscript yet. She'd tried to seem like she had things under control. But when she'd seen the line, his obnoxious, obsessive attention to minute details of what should have been simple caricatures, his slow, cheeky smile as he gestured to the line like they had all the time in the world—every nerve in her deadline-pressured body pinched.

So maybe she could have been a little nicer.

"When do you see him again?" Liv asked.

"Well, I need a manuscript first. Which I can't seem to produce." The whisk clacked against the sides of the bowl.

Liv made a sympathetic sound. "It's like, what, five hundred words? I'm sure you can write that late this evening if you have to and still have it in on Monday."

"Right." Caroline gave a sharp nod. "I have all day. I've got this."

"That's the spirit. I'll make us some toast."

After church, Caroline's mind spun with possibilities. The pastor had said something that stuck with her about the scribes of Jesus' time and their rigorous education. Of course, she stunk at writing children's books. She hadn't studied it.

In her room, she took just enough time to scoop Rabbit out of her cage and nestle the hamster in the breast pocket of her blouse, one of Rabbit's favorite places. She handed the little ball of fur a pumpkin seed and turned on her laptop.

She opened the search browser and typed in "how to write a children's book," absently stroking Rabbit's head as she scrolled.

Half an hour later, her pen flew. Papers scattered her desk with notes on main character profiles, plot outlines, and the word "repetition" underlined several times. And a moral. That was important.

Within an hour, she felt like she could write a book on the topic of writing a children's book. Apparently, it was a lot different than writing a novel.

A novel. She sighed. Her book would have to sit untouched for the foreseeable future.

She gathered her papers and tapped them against the desk to create a neat stack. Eight and a half pages of notes. There was no way she could fail now.

Her phone buzzed, and Rabbit squeaked. "Shh, it's okay." She looked at the caller ID. And groaned. Dad.

She hesitated. Pretending not to see the call was immature. She grabbed the phone and tapped accept.

"Hey, Dad."

"Caroline." Despite herself, his deep voice still made her sit up straighter. "Did you get my text yesterday?"

She doodled a flower on the corner of her paper. "Sorry, I was rushing off to a work event." Not technically untrue.

"Are you coming home for Easter?"

She realized she was tapping her pen and forced herself to stop. She glanced at her desk calendar. Easter was next weekend. "I have a big project going on right now."

He cleared his throat. "It would mean a lot to your mom."

Her teeth clenched. It would mean a lot to Mom to have another chance to scold her for her poor life choices, more like. "Are you still in New York?"

"For now, but we'll be in Ohio for Easter."

She leaned forward. "Ohio? Why?"

"We...wanted a change of pace."

Caroline frowned. That didn't sound like them. Dad wouldn't want to be far from Wall Street for long. And Mom would never leave her firm in someone else's hands. "For how long?"

"It's a shorter drive than to New York." He didn't answer her question. "We'd like to have you there. I can send the address."

She pressed her lips together. "Okay," she said finally. "I'll probably have to leave Sunday afternoon, though."

"That's fine!" His voice was way too eager. It made her nervous. "See you then."

"'Bye, Dad."

After hanging up, she stared at her desk. Apparently, she'd be going home next weekend. Which meant she needed to get this project going.

She'd have a solid draft by Monday, she was sure of it. She and Andy needed to get started on illustrations ASAP.

She shot him a quick text then turned back to her laptop. Time to write a story.

No, no, no, Moses' beard is all wrong. Andy frowned at the brick wall and set down his brush on a paint can lid. Gray color from the bristles spattered the tarp underneath him. He sat on the cloth, fumes causing his brain to bobble in his skull.

How long had he been working on the Sunday school classroom mural? He checked a watch on his wrist. Whoops, some gray paint had smeared on the face of the clock.

He held the watch to his eyes and squinted, using the light of the blinds in the children's classroom. 4:03 PM. He'd been at this for three hours.

With a sigh, he knuckled his eye.

Moments later, he realized he had streaked some paint on his cheekbone when the cold sensation of the liquid hit him.

I might as well take a look at my progress so far. When church had let out that Sunday afternoon, he grabbed a quick lunch at Panera and then returned at one to paint the Sunday school classroom. The children's Sunday school group had been allocated to another room, where a homeschool co-op met on weekdays, until he had finished the wall paintings.

Pastor Dan had expected him to finish with the mural by last Sunday. "I don't want anything too crazy," Pastor Dan had said eight Sundays back whilst munching on a cream cheese Danish in the fellowship hall. "Just some depictions of the Bible stories they hear during children's sermons."

But two months later, Andy had only covered a wall and a half, way behind schedule. On the back wall of the classroom, near the window with the blinds, he'd painted the story of Daniel in the lions' den, one of Pastor Dan's favorites.

Probably because they share the same name. He does like to preach on Daniel a lot.

It took Andy four weeks to work on the lions.

Their manes wouldn't cooperate with his paintbrush. When he wanted them to look orange, they appeared too amber-like. And when he hoped the hairs would spike on the lions' manes, the brush decided to make the lines of one too blurry, and therefore, ruined the entire picture.

Last week, having finally conquered the back wall, he decided to give the story of Moses a try. But the parted Red Sea proved to be a trial when the "foam" of the waves looked more like clouds.

And don't even get me started on Moses' beard… too scruffy.

He reached for his chin and realized his beard, too, could use a trim. Whiskers scratched his fingers.

His phone buzzed on the flannel board stationed next to one of the painted lions. This lion was the one whose mane had gone all blurry. He rose, and his knees cracked. "I guess it wouldn't hurt to take a break."

He moseyed over to the flannel board and picked up the phone.

Two seconds later a text message from Caroline stunned his retinas. Why, oh why, did Clark insist on giving Andy's number to her after the charity auction? Couldn't he pick up, from Caroline's crossed arms and back turned to Andy, that she wasn't too pleased with him?

Clark couldn't read a room, even if the room was covered in letters. He scanned the message and braced himself for the extra period punctuation marks people liked to throw in to show they were in a short-tempered mood.

Caroline: My first draft is due tomorrow. I'd like to meet to discuss the book. If you can make time in your busy schedule, let me know a time and place that works. A coffee place is preferable, less loud and distracting than a restaurant. Thanks.

Yikes, Clark hadn't mentioned anything about a first draft.

Then again, Caroline had the easy part—writing the words. Andy, on the other hand, had to come up with somewhere between sixteen to thirty-two illustrations. He glanced at the mural. *That could take ages.*

He placed the phone on the flannel board.

A knock on the wooden classroom door caused him to jolt. He turned and watched a woman with white hair pulled into a bun and glittering golden glasses shuffle into the room. The eyewear had golden chains that looped around her neck.

She still had her nametag on that the ushers handed out in the fellowship hall: "Maisie Williams, Church Librarian."

Although she didn't need the last part—everyone in the small congregation knew her name—Maisie thought it an important item to include on the name tag in blue Sharpie writing each week.

"I hope I'm not interrupting you." Maisie smiled and hugged a book to her chest. "Filing took me a lot longer today than I anticipated. Doesn't help that I keep getting distracted by good books."

She held up the cover. In the dim classroom lighting, he made out the title: *Follow Your Heart*. He'd have to check out that one when he had time to read.

The word *distracted* bobbled in his skull for a moment. Hadn't Caroline called him that at the auction? And in the text message?

Sure enough, the text message from his phone had blared the words "distracting" before it faded to black.

"Anyway." Maisie's glasses' chain jingled when she cleared her throat. "Thought I'd pop in to see your progress. Pastor Dan asked me to lock up, but if you'd be willing to do so for me when you finish, that would be stellar." She reached into her skirt pockets and pulled out a ring of keys. "My daughter made me a Sunday roast, so I'm afraid I need to be heading out soon."

"I don't mind locking up." He turned to the mural of Moses and his shoulders slumped. "After all, I'm nowhere near done with this thing."

Maisie set her book on top of a bookshelf nestled beside one of the walls in the classroom. The bookshelf sat underneath a bulletin board with lists of verses that the children had memorized throughout the year.

She stood in front of the mural with her thumb on her chin.

"It's simply beautiful," she said at last. "Painting this must be a full-time job with the amount of detail you've put in." She glanced at the other blank walls in the classroom. "Although, I must admit I thought you'd have made more progress by now."

His momentary, buoyed confidence plummeted. He palmed his

neck. Thank goodness by now the paint on his fingers had dried.

"To be honest, Maisie, I thought I'd be done by now too. But with so many other work responsibilities, the graphic design ads, and now the children's book, I'm a little more… distracted."

He hated the word, but it fit him best. Ever since high school, it always did.

Sorry, Mom, for how I let you down all those years ago.

Maisie brightened. "Wait a moment, did you say, 'Children's book?'"

Andy nodded and explained about the assignment from the nonprofit.

He did, however, leave out the parts about his brief argument with Caroline at the auction. Maisie had been trying to set him up with a lady from church for ages. And if she heard that his first impression with Caroline had ended in a fight, she might even be more on board with the two of them getting together.

That woman really does love to read enemies to lovers romances, doesn't she?

"Dear,"—Maisie clasped her hands—"why on earth are you working on this mural and not on that book? I'm sure Pastor Dan won't mind you taking time off. After all, you are volunteering and aren't getting paid for this. Besides,"—she tapped the bookshelf with two fingers—"this feels more important. Children need good books to read."

"I don't know." He shrugged. "I think I'm worried I'll mess it up. Illustrations in a picture book are just so"—he shuddered—"permanent."

His phone buzzed on the flannel board.

Maisie appeared to absorb his words for a moment. Then she nodded and her face lit up again. "Feeling daunted?"

"You could say that." He chuckled.

"I'll tell you someone else who was hesitant about a big task before him." She gestured to the Moses mural. "Imagine standing in front of that Red Sea. Or in front of Pharaoh telling him to let the Israelites go. No wonder he came up with a thousand excuses as to why he wasn't up for the task."

And yet, all those things still happened. The Red Sea parted, and the Israelites were freed.

Hope lit a beacon in his chest. It died moments later when another text from Caroline buzzed.

"I'll let you handle locking up." Maisie placed the ring of keys on the bookshelf. "And you better answer that." She nodded at the phone and winked. "Best not to keep a lady waiting."

Great, she's already paired the two of us.

He trudged over to the phone and saw that Caroline had sent the names of five coffee shops in town. Goodness, this woman really wanted a cup of Joe, didn't she?

Andy stared at the Moses mural and realized that maybe Moses's beard wasn't as bushy as it had been moments before. He could work with that.

And if I can work with that, maybe we can figure something out with this book after all.

"Fine, Caroline, we'll meet to talk about the book." He scooped the phone into his hands and rattled off a text. "But we're not doing coffee. If I need to get less 'distracted,' you need to let loose a little."

But how?

He stopped mid-text and exited the texting app for inspiration. The wallpaper on his phone, a picture of him and Sammy at a park, filled the screen for a moment. *Got it!*

He messaged.

Andy: I know the perfect place.

Chapter Four

"REALLY?" MR. KNOX'S MUSTACHE TWITCHED LIKE an angry caterpillar. He slapped the papers down on his desk. "Genocide?"

Caroline winced. "Well, no, the squirrels are uprooting all the sapling tree people because…" She trailed off at his look. "It wasn't my best idea. Do you like the others?"

"Let's take a look, shall we?" He whipped open the folder. "An unwary duck gets eaten by a fox."

"Like Aesop?"

He glared. Caroline couldn't meet his gaze. Her eyes darted toward the window, where water dripped from melting icicles, falling to the ground, like her hope.

Mr. Knox snorted and shuffled to another page. "A child doesn't do her homework and gets turned into a book monster."

"I…thought it was relatable." She shifted her feet. "And teaches kids not to procrastinate."

"A bird loses the power of flight and has to learn the feeding methods of woodland rodents before ultimately succumbing because of its lack of adaptive traits."

"Educational?"

"Two wayward children are lured into a house with *chicken feet* and…" He squinted at the paper. "Are eaten by an ugly old woman who rides in an iron kettle? What is *wrong* with you?"

Caroline straightened. That was her favorite. "That one is actually inspired by Slavic folklore and tales of Baba Yaga…" She wilted under his stare. "I thought maybe Eastern European legends don't get enough representation."

Mr. Knox shoved his chair back and stomped back and forth. "I asked you for a children's book. A *children's book*! How hard is that?"

Caroline pushed a wayward strand of hair behind her ear, face burning. It *should* be easy. She could write tens of thousands of words for a novel. Why was this so hard? It felt like getting rejections in college all over again—but worse, because her boss paced in front of her, red-faced. At least she couldn't see those disapproving editors.

"I'm so sorry, Mr. Knox. I'll do some more research. I—"

"Enough." He held up a hand. "No more research. Clearly it's led you to...to...this." He stabbed a finger toward the papers. "When are you talking to the illustrator? He seems like a nice guy. Probably knows something about kids."

"Later today, actually." Her voice cracked into a squeak, and she winced.

He collapsed into his chair. "Good. Have you ever *read* a picture book, Penn?"

"Not many," she admitted.

The eyes of the trophy heads stared down in judgment.

"Let me tell you what kids like." When she remained standing at attention, he pointed at her. "Write this down."

She pulled out her notepad and fumbled to poise her pen above the paper.

"Happy things. Glitter. Humor. Rhyme. Llamacorns."

"Llamacorns?" Caroline looked up.

He waved a hand. "You know. Unicorn llamas. My niece loves those things."

"Right." Caroline wrote down *llamacorns*.

Mr. Knox sighed and rubbed his forehead. "You came highly recommended, Caroline. Don't make me regret this."

"Yes, sir."

"I know you girls are swamped with the Easter campaign this week, so I'm going to go easy on you. You have until next Thursday."

Caroline glanced at the poster on the office wall, advertising their Easter outreach efforts. Something about major holidays always made people think a little more about those in need.

"I want the best story I've ever seen on my desk Thursday

morning." He nodded toward the door. "You can go."

"Yes, sir." She kept her back straight and marched out of his office into the cubicle bay.

She hoped she might make it back to her desk without anyone noticing, but no such luck. Zinnia stood with one manicured hand resting on the wall that divided their cubicles, laughing at something one of their coworkers said. Today's outfit was a study in blue. Only Zinnia could manage to look amazing in monochromes.

Zinnia waved. "Carrie! I can't wait to hear all about your story."

The coworker Zinnia had been talking to, a middle-aged woman, said goodbye and moved on.

Caroline set her papers down on her desk. "It's a work in progress, but I can't wait to share it when it's done." She offered a tight smile.

Zinnia's eyes widened. Caroline was pretty sure those were fake lashes. Zinnia leaned forward and stage-whispered, "Oh, do you not have a story yet?" She tilted back and smiled. "I'm pretty busy, but let me know if you need help. You know I'm always here."

"Thanks. I'm good for now." Caroline sat. "Do you have the Easter web copy ready?"

Zinnia wrinkled her nose and sighed. "Of course. I worked ahead this weekend. It's such an important campaign, you know?"

Breathe. "Great. Send it to me so I can look it over and get it to the web team?"

Caroline didn't look at Zinnia while booting up her desktop, but she could feel the eye roll that Zinnia never displayed in front of her. "You don't have to check me, Carrie. I already sent it to them."

Caroline spun around in her wheeled chair. "Double checking is company policy. Everyone needs a proofreader."

Zinnia shrugged and waved one delicate hand. "We're professionals, Carrie. It's just unnecessary extra work." Her red lips turned up. "But I can keep checking yours if you feel like you need it."

Caroline gritted her teeth. If she said no, she was breaking policy. But if she said yes, Zinnia would take it as a win. She swallowed her pride. "I'd like you to keep checking, please."

"Of course." Zinnia gave a brilliant smile. "Anytime, Carrie."

Zinnia ducked back into her own cubicle, and Caroline wished the day could be over already.

For the next several hours, Caroline lost herself in the mounds of work for the campaign, on top of her usual duties with their monthly newsletter, the spring edition of the magazine, the donor letters... If she concentrated on her work, she didn't have to think about Mr. Knox's raised voice or Zinnia's mocking tone.

At lunch, she grabbed her coat. She brightened her tone to fake cheer. "Hey, Zinnia. If Mr. Knox asks, let him know I went to grab lunch and meet with the illustrator."

"Have fun."

Caroline bit back a retort. From anyone else, the comment would be innocent. From Zinnia, it implied Caroline was shirking responsibilities. *Don't engage.*

Caroline's favorite diner, *The Roseville Grill*, required only a five-minute walk. She clutched her coat around her, warding off the late March chill, even though the sun peeked through the clouds, beginning to melt the snow.

Outside of the office, cold air blowing in her face, the reality of the situation hit her. She'd utterly failed. Mr. Knox hadn't just been disappointed in her ideas. He *hated* them. *"What is wrong with you?"* His words echoed in her head.

What was wrong with her? A lot of things. Like the way anytime a project, or a test, or something big really mattered, apparently she crashed and burned.

Her eyes watered from the wind. She brushed a finger under them in annoyance.

She had a degree in this. She'd gone to college for writing and graduated *summa cum laude*. A picture book was not going to stop her. She refused to let this assignment cost her her job.

I didn't make the wrong decision, Mom.

The diner bustled with activity at the lunch hour. Caroline glanced around until she spotted her roommate sitting at a corner booth. "Hey!" She wove through the crowd. "Thanks for meeting me for lunch."

Olivia grinned. "Glad our schedules matched up." Her smile faded. "Oh, no. What's going on?"

Caroline plopped down across from her. "What are you talking about?"

"Come on. I know that look." Olivia rested her chin on her fists and tilted her head, her messy bun bobbing. Liv always looked effortlessly cute, with a chunky scarf, dangling earrings, and a comfy-looking sweater, all appropriate for her job as a part-time music teacher. She always seemed comfortable in her own skin.

Caroline envied that ability.

"Well." Caroline picked up a menu to avoid making eye contact, even though she came here often enough that she knew her order by heart. "Mr. Knox didn't like any of my ideas."

"That's dumb. He wouldn't know talent if it hit him in the nose."

Caroline couldn't help smiling at her roommate's unwavering support. "They actually were pretty terrible."

"You'll write something even better. You just need time."

The waiter came to take their orders. Once he left, Liv turned to Caroline again. "So, you on a new deadline?"

"Yeah, next Thursday. Hopefully it goes better next time." Caroline's chest squeezed. "With all the layoffs, I'm not sure I can keep this job if I don't pull through."

"Hey." Olivia grabbed her hand. "You're Helping Hope's biggest asset, and Mr. ObKNOXious has to know that."

Even Liv's special name for Mr. Knox couldn't cheer her up. "I guess. You'd think he'd promote me after four years, in that case."

"It's a big company, girl." Liv took a long draw from her water glass. "You can't expect to be running it at twenty-four. Most of us just got out of college a couple years ago."

"Because graduating early did me so much good," Caroline

muttered into her glass.

"Okay, subject change. Nothing gets broody Caroline out of her funk faster than a project."

"I'm not brood—"

"You're meeting the illustrator after this, right?"

Not a fun topic either. Now she had to confront the man she'd insulted. "Yeah, I'm supposed to meet him at the office and follow him... somewhere. He said it was a surprise." She scowled. "If I get abducted by a suspicious illustrator because of this blasted project, I expect you to avenge me."

Liv belted out a laugh and crossed her heart. "I've sworn vengeance."

After their lunch, Olivia walked back toward the office with Caroline, since she had parked in the office parking lot to avoid the traffic at the *Grill*.

Olivia gestured. "Is that him?"

Caroline turned her head toward a lanky man in a blue coat leaning against an old but well-maintained Subaru Outback. *Blue coat.* Her eyes widened at the familiar garment. *You've got to be kidding me.* He was the one she showered with sludge that day she was rushing to the office. Hopefully, once he saw her car, he wouldn't recognize the vehicle. He already had enough cause to detest her.

"You didn't tell me he was young. And cute."

Caroline glanced at Olivia, who was sizing up Andy. She turned back toward the illustrator, who hadn't yet looked up from the phone in his hand.

Cute? She guessed he didn't look bad. Dark curly hair, warm brown eyes and long lashes that rested against his bronze cheeks when he blinked...

Nope. She refused to even think about such things.

He spotted them and smiled, that irritatingly slow grin again. He lifted a hand in a wave.

"I'll see you later." Olivia bumped Caroline's shoulder. "Have fun."

As Liv headed for her car, Caroline approached Andy. "So, where are we going?"

"It isn't a surprise if you know where we're going."

She put a hand on her hip. "Or you could be leading me to an empty field to murder me."

He laughed, eyes crinkling, then seemed to realize she was serious. "Oh. Here, I'll text you the address. But you said I could choose the place, right?"

It felt like a trap. "Right."

"Good." He tapped his screen, and a second later, her phone dinged.

She clicked on the address, and the map opened to "Roseville Humane Society."

"A shelter?" Caroline pinned him with a look that she usually reserved for misbehaving children in Sunday School. "I don't think they have good places to set up laptops and get to work."

He grinned. Infuriating. "I was thinking we could get some inspiration from the pups, loosen up our creative minds." She opened her mouth to respond, but he quickly added, "You said I could choose."

She took a deep breath. She wanted to shake him, impress upon him the urgency of the situation. But professionals didn't do that. "Why a shelter?" she asked instead.

"I volunteer there from time to time, and it always gets the creative juices flowing."

She bit her lip. "All right. But afterward, we should really find someplace with a table and start mapping things out."

He flipped his keys around his finger and caught them. "Deal. Let's go see some dogs."

Peaches cowered in the back corner of the kennel.

After what felt like thirty minutes, Andy had made no progress with getting the dog to move from her fuzzy brown bed. He dropped the llama squeaker toy and slumped to the concrete.

A Chihuahua in a kennel across the room yapped. It had been doing so for the past half hour. He grinned at it and then at Caroline, who was sitting on a chair a volunteer had brought her. "Guess that dog over there doesn't have trouble opening up."

He squinted at the nameplate on the Chihuahua's cage, written on a whiteboard in green marker. "Goliath." Someone at the pet shelter had a sense of humor. But certainly not that volunteer who gave them a tour of the place half an hour prior.

When the worker talked, it sounded like someone had sucked all the life out of her voice.

Caroline didn't appear to hear what he'd said. Instead, she glued her gaze onto Peaches. Wrinkles had formed on her forehead, like she was thinking hard.

At last, she spoke. "Maybe we're going about it the wrong way. With some dogs,"—she gestured at Goliath who pounced on a tangled braid of rope—"they have no problem getting along with strangers, but with others..." Her glance swiveled to Peaches, who had set her chin down on a small navy pillow. "You have to take your time."

Caroline rose from her seat and crouched as she approached Peaches. Her voice skyrocketed an octave and she cocked her head to the side.

"You're a sweetheart, aren't you?"

Peaches' orange-red tail wiggled a little on the bed. Caroline squatted to grab the llama toy. Andy tried his best to avoid smelling her perfume, but the woman must've put on an extra douse today from her lack of sleep the other night. Didn't smell bad at all.

Like peaches, in fact. It reminded him of his mother's peach cobbler.

Sadness filled his chest, and his stomach growled.

Man, he missed his mother, but could he bring himself to face her alone after everything that happened at school? Sure, they saw each other a few times a year at family gatherings, but when had he last spent time with *just* her, over a bowl of peach cobbler and French vanilla ice cream?

"Now,"—Caroline placed the llama squeaker toy next to Peaches' chin—"if you don't want to play with this, that's okay. Take whatever time you need." She motioned at Andy. "We know that we're both strangers. And sometimes it takes time to get used to someone new."

Peaches' brown eyes darted from the toy to Caroline. Caroline backed to her seat and sat again.

Two seconds passed before the dog opened her jaws and clamped down on the toy. It squeaked.

Andy and Caroline clapped, and both said something along the lines of, "Good job!" "Atta girl!" "We are so proud of you!" They'd spoken at the same time, and it was difficult to differentiate who declared what.

With this newfound praise, Peaches' tail whacked against the concrete wall of her kennel.

She lifted herself onto her short, stubby legs and carried the toy to Caroline. When Caroline grasped it, they played tug o' war back and forth until Peaches pulled the toy away, tail going as fast as a turbine.

Then she brought the toy to Andy. His heart warmed. *She has chosen me.* They wrestled the llama back and forth until Peaches yanked it away, dropped it on her bed, and returned to him.

He scritched her foxlike ears. "I guess you're right, Caroline. Peaches just needed a little more time with us."

Peaches panted with her tongue dangling out of her mouth on one side. After a few moments, she padded over to Caroline to get a fair share of pets. Caroline giggled and patted Peaches on the head, between the ears.

"You're really good with her." Andy watched the dog's tail flick. "Do you have any dogs at home?"

Caroline's features darkened.

She dropped her hand, and Peaches licked her fingers. "I wish, but I work so much at the office that I wouldn't have time to take it for walks." She pressed her lips together. "I do have a dwarf hamster named Rabbit, though."

He grinned and viewed Goliath across the room. The mini dog spattered water onto the floor from his water bowl. "Are you sure you didn't name that Chihuahua? You seem to have a thing for weird names for pets."

With a scoff and a twitch of her lips, Caroline rolled her eyes. "Rabbit is a very clever name for a dwarf hamster, I'll have you know. It's completely original. All of the other dwarf hamsters would be jealous."

I could be hallucinating, but I think she's smiling.

Mirages aside, she did have a nice grin. It brightened all of her features, her rosy cheeks, high cheekbones, brilliant eyes.

"Well." Andy leaned forward to try and pet Peaches. His arms didn't quite reach her back. "Maybe you should write the children's book on Rabbit. I could even illustrate some bunny ears onto it."

She thought about it for a moment. Then shook her head.

"Clark won't go for it. He yelled at me today for all the terrible first drafts I submitted to him. I have a feeling that if I send him a book about a dwarf hamster, he'll lose all faith in me."

Andy deflated. *I didn't know her boss yelled at her.*

Sure, Clark had come off as rather bombastic on their phone call and at the charity auction. But something told him that Caroline had taken most of the heat from him in terms of this project.

Maybe she had a reason to be so terse at the auction.

Did her whole job rest on this one task? Would she get demoted or get a pay cut if she didn't deliver a quick product? Dizziness swarmed into his skull. That was a lot of pressure for himself and Caroline.

"It does seem ridiculous that he wanted a first draft by today." Andy fiddled with the aglet on his shoelaces. One of the knots had gotten loose. "I know a woman at my church who writes picture books, and it takes her months to come up with a good idea."

A worker in a red shirt dropped a treat into Goliath's cage.

Goliath demolished the crumbly brown bone in two seconds. Peaches, observing all of this, waddled to the front of her kennel and waited as the worker made her way down the line. "I am happy you brought up the picture book." Caroline's voice drew his attention away from the worker. "I think I'm already hitting a case of writer's block. That's why I texted you. I thought you might have some ideas on what it should be about."

"Oh boy." He rubbed his palm against his neck. Did it suddenly get hot in here? The building had blasted the heaters when they got in, making everything smell like dry dog food. "I don't suppose we could do one on the dogs here at the shelter?"

The color red, from the worker's t-shirt, appeared at the front of the cage. The employee dropped a treat onto the floor. While Peaches chewed on it, the worker guide pursed her purple lipsticked lips.

"Not to interrupt your conversation," she hoisted her hand, the one not carrying the bucket of treats, on her hips, "but my niece probably has a million picture books on dogs and pet shelters. It's a saturated market."

Thanks for your help, random lady. He'd been volunteering here for a while but had never seen her before. She must've been a new hire. By the look of her young face, most likely a high schooler who had service hours she needed to fulfill for school credit.

The teenager tossed dark brown curls over her shoulder and disappeared.

Caroline frowned. "It was a good thought. I like the idea of doing a book on something that matters and not on 'llamacorns.'"

"Llama-what?"

"Don't ask." She huffed and banded her arms around her knees. Then she fisted her hands, placed them on her temples, and groaned. "Why can't I just think of a simple idea? I thought children's books were supposed to be easy to write."

Peaches had finished her treat and started to lick the concrete to ensure she hadn't missed any crumbs. When she completed her sweep of the floor, she returned to Caroline. Caroline unfolded herself from her crumpled-up stance and stroked the dog's head.

A few cages down, a dog barked. The yap echoed off the concrete floors and walls.

"I'm sure we'll think of something." Andy held out his hands and Peaches waddled to him. He scratched her underneath the collar, and Peaches let out a satisfied grunt. *Dogs don't get pet in this spot enough.* "Worst case, we got this shy dog to warm up to some strangers."

He thought about it for a moment, while Peaches scratched her side with her back leg.

"Maybe books are like Peaches. You have to take your time with them if you want to do it right."

Chapter Five

CAROLINE'S FINGER HOVERED OVER THE MOUSE pad. She didn't want to click the email. She would rather be back at the shelter, playing fetch with Peaches in the yard where they had taken her for a walk once she warmed up, Caroline laughing as Andy ruffled the dog's ears.

Where did that train of thought come from?

She clicked.

The message took a second to load. She could hear Zinnia typing on the other side of the cubicle wall, somewhere a phone ringing, two coworkers conversing in hushed tones. She really shouldn't be checking her personal email at work. But Andy had said he would pass along her info to some lady at his church for picture book recommendations, and she'd given him this address without thinking.

Nothing from Andy or the church lady—not surprising, as she wouldn't expect both him and the woman to have gotten around to it already at ten in the morning—but this email had been sitting at the top of her inbox, "RE: Thriller Submission - Caroline Penn."

Several months ago, she had worked up the nerve to polish her novel, do some edits, and send the manuscript on another round of submissions, this time to secular, general market publishers and literary agents. If it was too dark for the Christian publishers, maybe the others would give her book a shot. So far, this was the first to respond.

The email popped up. She leaned forward, then sank back into her chair with a sigh. A form rejection. She hit "delete."

"How did it go with the illustrator yesterday?"

Caroline looked up.

Zinnia's red nails tapped on the divider. "Oh, sorry, Carrie, were you busy? I just figured since you were scrolling through your own emails you were bored."

Caroline bit her lip. How long had Zinnia been watching? Had she seen the rejection email? "Things are going well with the illustrator, thanks."

Her phone buzzed on her desk, and she glanced at it. A Facebook notification—Andy Jackson had sent a friend request. *A little forward, Andy.*

"Do I get a peek into what you're writing?"

Caroline attempted a lighthearted smile. "I wouldn't want to ruin the surprise."

Zinnia's eyes narrowed, but she flashed white teeth. "Ha, of course not." She wiggled her fingers. "I'll leave you to it."

Caroline picked up her phone. Should she accept the friend request? Or maybe wait. She didn't want to look too eager.

Too eager for what? Connecting on another potential brainstorming platform?

She hit "Accept."

She turned back to her computer and began proofing the files for the May magazine. A few minutes later, a message flashed across her phone screen. She picked up the phone and glanced at it.

Andy Jackson: The shelter does profiles on a different dog each week, and look who they chose this time.

He'd included a link to a Facebook page, which she tapped.

A smile spread across her face. Pictures of Peaches—upside down, right side up, tail blurry from wagging, tongue out—were accompanied by a blurb:

Hiya, my name is Peaches! I love belly rubs, lots of treats, and my stuffed llama. I may look a little silly and take some time to warm up to strangers, but once I know you, I'll be your best friend forever.

Caroline grinned. She tapped out a message to Andy.

Caroline: Why wouldn't they feature the cutest dog at the shelter? I'm sure she'll find a home in no time.

Her heart squeezed a little at that. She wondered if she could find out who adopted Peaches. Maybe she could befriend them and visit her in her new home.

Nice, Caroline. Cozying up to people with the ulterior motive of seeing their dog.

It was too bad neither she nor Olivia worked from home. Otherwise, she'd adopt Peaches herself in a heartbeat.

On a whim, she sent Andy a picture of Rabbit gnawing on a pumpkin seed.

Caroline: This is my hamster that I mentioned yesterday, by the way.

It didn't take him long to respond.

Andy: Cute. Even smaller than I expected. Like a fluffy baseball with a twitchy nose. Doesn't look anything like a rabbit, though.

Caroline snorted and set down her phone. She was halfway through proofing another page when her phone buzzed again.

Andy: This is my sloth that masquerades as a golden retriever.

He sent a picture of a big, floppy golden snoozing with its tongue hanging out.

Caroline bit back a laugh.

Caroline: I won't tell anyone his secret. What's his name?
Andy: Sammy.

She couldn't help herself.

Caroline: Sammy? That's not very original. And you made fun of Rabbit.
Andy: It's after Samuel Peploe, the Scottish painter.

The dots appeared and disappeared, as if he was considering whether or not to type his next words.

Andy: The texture of Sammy's fur reminded me of Peploe's strong colors. He was one of my favorite early 20th century artists in school. Sammy's coat looks like bold strokes with a thick brush.

Caroline blinked. She had assumed Andy hadn't had much of an education—but why was that? Because he was laid back? She felt a twinge of guilt at the assumption.

Caroline: Okay, you win at names. I just thought a hamster named Rabbit would be funny. Sammy is adorable.

I should really get back to work.
Instead, another message appeared.

Andy: Maybe I can bring him with me for one of our planning sessions sometime.

She should say no. They'd gotten hardly any work done yesterday because they were too distracted with Peaches. Another dog was not going to help.

She looked back at the picture. *I must stroke those absurdly silky-looking ears. And that fluffy, fluffy belly needs a good rub.*

Caroline: I'd like that.

That evening, Caroline unlocked the door to her apartment humming. The smell of something sizzling on the stove wafted through the entryway.

"What's cooking, Liv?"

Olivia popped her head around the corner while Caroline hung up her coat. "I thought tonight we could both use some stir fry." She raised her eyebrows. "But you look like you're in a good mood. I thought you said you got a rejection today?"

Caroline shrugged. "That's to be expected. Stephen King's first novel was rejected thirty-nine times, you know."

Liv's eyebrows rose even higher as Caroline strode into the kitchen and inhaled deeply.

Caroline closed her eyes for a moment. How long had it been since she'd sat down to an actual warm meal? She opened her eyes to wash her hands and help Olivia.

"Sooo." Liv tossed the veggies and meat with a spatula. "I didn't get a chance to ask you last night since I got home late."

"Were you working at the gas station?" Caroline pulled plates from the cupboard.

"Yeah. Picked up some extra shifts since the Smith kids moved out of town and don't need a teacher anymore. Anyway—"

"They moved?" Caroline paused. "Didn't you tutor three of them?"

"Yes." Liv gave her a longsuffering look. "Now are you going to let me finish a sentence or not?"

That would be a hit for Liv. Three kids was a quarter of her roster. But Caroline let it go. "Sorry."

"I was *going* to ask you how it went with the illustrator."

"Oh." Caroline fiddled with her earring. "It was...unexpected. We went to the animal shelter."

Liv turned off the burner. "Are you writing a book about dogs?"

"No, probably not."

Liv pursed her lips. "So it wasn't for research. You don't seem upset about that."

"I'm not," Caroline admitted. Why wasn't she? It had been a total waste. Then it occurred to her. "I think I'm in love."

Olivia's mouth dropped open. "Excuse me? You've known the guy, what, three days?"

"No!" Caroline sputtered. "Not with the guy." She stumbled over her words. "I meant with a *dog* I met. Her name is Peaches."

Olivia's expression morphed from shock to amusement as she threw back her head and laughed.

Then Liv's expression softened. "I know how much you want one, but we can't."

"Trust me, I know." Caroline sighed. "Besides, I do have Rabbit." Liv turned back to the stove. "But if you did fall madly in love with the guy, I wouldn't be surprised either."

Caroline froze with the silverware drawer half open. "What's that supposed to mean?"

Liv smirked. "Oh, I don't know. Tall, handsome, nice hair, *and* he's a fellow creative."

"You always notice the hair." Caroline rolled her eyes. She plucked two forks from the drawer. "You know how I feel about relationships."

"Okay, Miss Independent." Liv grabbed a plate. "But one day this whole prove-you-can-do-it-on-your-own thing is going to get old. What are you going to do once you *do* prove yourself? When will you know if you've made it?"

Caroline scowled. She loved her roommate and Liv's honest, direct wisdom, but sometimes she didn't want to hear it. Especially when Liv might be right. "I'll know when I get there."

Her phone buzzed, and she pulled it out. As her eyes skimmed the message, she felt the blood drain from her face. She clutched the counter with her free hand.

"Liv. This isn't good."

Andy flicked his wrist. The ball swished through the basketball hoop.

"Dude!" Elijah clapped Andy on the back. Then, with the same hand, Elijah flipped his long hair out of his face. "That's gotta be your tenth point this quarter. You're on fire today."

They both turned to the blank scoreboard hoisted near some mesh net dividers in the rec center.

Through the transparent dividers that separated the courts and the track, a woman in a neon jumpsuit ran past.

"Actually," Elijah said, "I think that was your twelfth point, Andy. Way to go, dude."

They never kept score with their scrimmages with some friends from church. That would require someone knowing how to operate the ancient scoreboard table that sat between their court and a court next to them where the fourth-grade girls league played at the same time.

Which led his dark-eyed roommate to make up the points half the time. Actually, Andy probably shot four baskets in a row, making a total of eight points this quarter. But nobody really cared about the final score, at least, not the decided results Elijah claimed their team had.

On the plastic seats where they'd thrown their bags and towels, someone's phone timer went off. The quarter had ended.

Andy daubed the sweat from his upper lip on the back of his hand and panted on his way to his crumpled maroon towel. He bent down to pick it up, tossed it on his shoulder, and crouched again to take a sip of his Gatorade.

A mixture of orange and salty electrolytes swathed his tongue.

The sound of basketballs drumming the court next to them, and the shriek of girls laughing and chasing each other around, echoed in the huge rec center room.

Elijah took a long breath after gulping down half a bottle. Probably the last of the cherry Gatorade. "What gives with the winning streak, man? You're lucky to score two points total during these scrimmages."

Andy sat and put his drink on the floor. His basketball shoes, tattered at blue toes, squeaked against the slick flooring. He swiped his forehead with the towel and dropped the cloth on the ground.

Nearby a guy with large biceps and basketball goggles hunched over with his hands on his knees. His breaths came out ragged and wheezy.

Another teammate with red hair passed an inhaler to him. "Hey, guys, let's take an extra-long break, so Mr. Hollywood here can get his breath again. Movie stars, am I right?"

"Mr. Hollywood," or Ryan Torino, rolled his eyes. "Ha-*wheeze*-ha. Fun-*wheeze*-ny." He put the inhaler to his mouth and sucked in a puff of medicine.

They'd let Ryan on the team recently and heard all about his indie film projects, mostly in national parks that bordered their town. Andy had considered telling Clark to audition for some of them, as the man had a certain amount of pizzazz and diva-dom that came as a requisite to movie stars.

Then again... Ryan isn't shooting horror *movies.*

Elijah placed his water bottle on the ground and tucked his hair behind his ears. He leaned over and scooped up a pink scrunchie and wound his hair into a topknot bun.

Andy chuckled. "Dude, you need a haircut."

"And you need to answer my question about the points. Did they lower the hoops to make it easier for you to shoot? Did you put stilts in your shoes to make yourself taller?" He thumbed his chin, mock-thinking. Then he snapped his fingers. "It's a girl, isn't it?"

His roommate shook his shoulders.

"It's Maisie from church, that older librarian, isn't it? That woman is smooooth talking."

Andy rose and gave a playful shove to Elijah's shoulder. "No. I don't know, man. Maybe I'm just having a good day."

Elijah considered this for a moment.

"Nah, the only man worse at basketball than you is Ryan. And at least he's going to be famous someday, so we can give him a free pass." He grinned. "So, tell me about her."

"Listen, the only other girl I've been talking to is that author. And that's strictly professional."

Between the gaps of the mesh court dividers, he saw a glass window that led to classrooms on the other side of the wall. Inside a brightly lit one, a Zumba class danced to some inaudible beat.

"Riiiiiiight." Elijah winked.

"I'm serious, dude, she's not into me." Something about saying this brought a pang to his chest. Did he *want* her to be into him?

Memories from the kennel flicked across his vision in the harsh white lights of the gym. She had done well with Peaches. He shook his head to erase the memories like a picture on an etch-a-sketch.

"Well, if she's not into you, maybe she'll be into this hot stuff." Elijah pointed at himself. "Do you have a picture of her?"

Andy bristled. Then he relaxed.

Chill out, man. It's not like she's dating you. No need to get jealous.

"She accepted my friend request on Facebook today."

He bent down to pick up his bag that smelled like socks and sweat. Yikes, he needed to wash this thing soon. Then he pulled out his phone and clicked onto his Facebook app. He typed her name into the browser, and when her profile appeared, he showed her photo to Elijah.

Elijah let out a low whistle.

"Not my type, but she is beautiful." He paused. "Are you *sure* you don't want to ask her on a date? Maybe have Easter dinner with the fam and her. It's never too late to introduce her to your mom, you know." He winked again. Sweat from his forehead got into his eye, and he winced and swiped it off.

Light died in Andy's chest.

"I don't think I'm seeing the family for Easter. It would just be my mom this year, since the rest of the family is on some trip to New York for the holidays, and—" He broke off and shoved his phone into his bag.

"You don't want to see your mom?"

He sighed. "I don't think she wants to see me. We barely talk when the whole family is there—" With another exhale, he zipped up his bag and glanced sideways. Ryan still stooped on a chair, catching his breath.

Might as well get some practice baskets in.

After he checked to make sure he'd tightened his laces—they felt somewhat loose last quarter—he jogged onto the court and picked up a ball. He dribbled it to the free throw line. Then he aimed at the basket, flicked his wrist, and … missed.

Huh, maybe I need to get closer to the basket.

While he retrieved the ball, thuds sounded behind him. He turned and watched Elijah shoot a basketball from the three-point line, the farthest place away from the basket. The ball swished. *Three points for Elijah.*

"If it helps," Elijah loped forward to rebound his ball, "I probably won't be with the fam for Easter either. Gonna be applying for jobs."

Andy froze and dropped his ball. It bounced a few times at his feet before rolling into the mesh divider.

"Did you get fired?"

Elijah shook his head and dribbled his ball to the three-point line again. Joggers behind Andy panted as they passed. He heard the muffled sound of a rock band coming from one of their headphones.

"But,"—Elijah clasped his ball—"they've been talking about layoffs coming around Easter time, or soon after. I don't love the sales job at the insurance company, but at least I have a consistent paycheck rolling in."

Andy's heart pounded inside his chest.

With Andy's sporadic jobs, Elijah's paycheck ensured they could cover the expenses for the month. He already owed Elijah for a few missed rent bills.

On the sidelines, Ryan lifted himself from his seat and stooped to grab his water bottle. They'd start the next quarter soon. Already their redhead teammate had grabbed his phone to begin the timer.

"Well,"—Andy grimaced—"maybe you can be like Ryan and pursue getting a job as a musician. Do what you love."

Elijah nodded. "Yeah. For sure." Neither the nod nor the "sure" sounded or looked sure. He scrunched up his face and aimed for the basket.

This time, Elijah missed.

Chapter Six

CAROLINE SKIMMED THE TEXT over and over.

Dad: Too loud here to call, just have a second to text. Ambulance with your mom. Maybe heart attack, not sure. Pray hard, will call soon.

Olivia wrapped an arm around her shoulders. "Hey. What's going on?"

Caroline couldn't speak. She held up the phone so Liv could see the screen.

Liv covered her mouth. "Oh, girl." She folded Caroline into a hug.

Thoughts wouldn't form. It didn't make sense. Her last conversation with Mom had ended in yelling and tears. Her tears, not Mom's. Mom would never cry. She had a steel rod for a spine.

"She drinks kale for breakfast." Caroline stared at the wall. "She runs two miles every morning. She's the healthiest person I know."

Olivia squeezed her shoulders. "We don't know what it is yet. Maybe a really bad flu?"

Mom scoffed at the flu. Flu shot, vitamins, essential oils—Mom didn't let sickness come near her. Or Caroline. To this day, Caroline had a hard time resisting the urge to sanitize everything.

"Heart attack." Caroline's voice echoed in her ears, like someone speaking from a distance. "She'll be fine, though. People survive."

"Exactly." Liv pulled out her phone. "Do you mind if I text my prayer group and ask for prayer?"

Caroline nodded numbly. She should probably have thought of that herself.

Please, God. Let her be okay. She bit her lip. *We still have so much to talk about.*

Olivia kept one arm around Caroline's shoulders while pecking out a message with one hand. Caroline knew she should probably leave Dad alone to focus, but she couldn't help it.

Caroline: Praying. How is she?

No response.

Liv moved to the counter and scooped stir fry onto a plate. She pushed the dish into Caroline's hands. "Hey. You still need to eat. It will keep you occupied while you wait for news."

The two of them sat at the table. Olivia said a blessing over their food, and Caroline mechanically speared broccoli with her fork. She chewed, tasting nothing.

"Should I book a flight?" The words burst out too loud. "I think they're still in New York. Maybe. Or they might be in Ohio now. I don't even know."

Liv tapped Caroline's phone sitting on the table. "I know it's hard, but once your dad responds, you'll be able to act. Right now we can just pray and try not to panic."

Unwarranted annoyance surged in Caroline's chest. Action was the only way she knew how to respond. She needed to do something, fix something. What had Mom always said? *If you have a problem, don't whine about it. Resolve it.* But how could Mom, or Caroline, fix something like this?

"I'm a horrible daughter," Caroline blurted.

Liv gave her a stern look. "Girl—"

Caroline's phone buzzed, and she snatched it up.

Dad: Mom is okay, conscious. Still not sure what happened, doctors running tests.

Caroline's fingers flew.

Caroline: Are you guys still in NYC?

"What did he say?" Liv asked.

"They don't know what happened, but she's doing okay." Caroline's eyes remained glued to the screen, waiting for the three little dots to appear indicating her dad was typing.

Dad: Yes. We planned to head to Ohio on Friday.

Caroline hesitated. She had a deadline. Mr. Knox was already upset with her. Could she afford to leave right now? If Mom was okay...

Caroline: Keep me updated.

She sighed and rested her head in her hand. A good daughter would be flying home right away, not thinking about angry bosses and how expensive last-minute tickets could be. Her non-profit salary didn't exactly leave her rolling in money. And if Mr. Knox decided he was done with Caroline's inability to produce quality product—and her decision to leave in the middle of the work week during their busy Easter drive—she and Liv weren't in a great place to survive while Caroline found another job. Especially not after an expensive plane ticket.

"I can't afford it, Liv. I can't go."

Olivia shifted, hesitating. "Your dad would buy you a—"

"Don't say it." Caroline scowled.

Liv put her hands up. "Okay. Just saying, you have options."

Caroline refused to accept anything from her parents. That would give Mom proof. Proof that Caroline threw her future away on a stupid dream.

Caroline sighed. "We'll see."

Details trickled in all evening. Mom had collapsed in her office. Thankfully, Dad had just stepped off the elevator to see her, so he called an ambulance. Heart attack and stroke were ruled out. However, high blood pressure, depleted adrenaline, low immune system, and elevated cortisol all showed up on tests. The doctors came up with a simple, yet dizzying explanation.

Burnout.

Caroline leaned against the doorway to her room, facing Liv. Her roommate had changed into rabbit patterned pajamas, but remained awake despite the late hour, ready for updates. Caroline hadn't been able to convince her to go to bed.

Caroline barked out a mirthless laugh. "Apparently you actually can work yourself sick."

Olivia crossed her arms, hugging her chest. "What are you going to do?"

"I'll feel out Mr. Knox tomorrow." Caroline tapped a finger against the doorframe. "If he's in a good mood, I'll ask him for Thursday off."

Olivia raised an eyebrow. "Just Thursday? You're going to fly there and back in one day?"

Caroline winced. "I can make it work."

"No." Liv shook her head. "It's silly to come back for one day. Ask for Thursday and Friday. Then you can spend Easter with them."

"I'll see what happens. If he's in a terrible mood, I'll ask him on Thursday about taking Friday."

Olivia sighed. "Okay. But someday I'm marching into that office and giving Mr. ObKNOXious a talking to."

When she walked into the office the next morning, Caroline hoped she'd done her makeup well enough to hide the dark circles under her eyes. She'd hardly slept. She wore blue, because she'd heard blue was supposed to be a calming color. Maybe it would make Mr. Knox see her in a more favorable light.

Quiet hovered over the office in the early morning sunlight. She'd come in extra early, hoping she could accomplish three days' worth of projects in one day. Not even Zinnia sat in her cubicle, ready to deliver scathing comments with a saccharine smile.

Her phone buzzed.

Dad: Mom is out of the hospital. Ohio is going to have to wait. We'd still love to see you here.

Caroline set down her bag and flopped into her chair.

Caroline: I'll be there.

While proofing articles and typing ad copy, Caroline thought of ways she could ingratiate herself to Mr. Knox. By the time he arrived, long after the rest of the office, she had played at least twenty different variations of the conversation through her head.

She waited for him to brew his coffee, shuffle through the memos on his desk, and settle in. Once it looked like he had started in on his usual late-morning game of solitaire, she mustered up the courage to stand. Taking a deep breath, she smoothed her skirt and straightened her blouse.

"Off to discuss the book?" Zinnia asked.

The last thing Caroline needed was fake sympathy from Zinnia for telling the truth. "Yes." She turned and walked away before her coworker could say anything else.

She knocked on Mr. Knox's open office door. He glanced up. "Come in," he boomed. "Do you have an early idea for that book for me?"

Caroline suppressed a wince. "I don't think it's quite ready." Inspiration struck. "I'm heading down to the Hope Club this evening to screen the ideas with the kids. I was thinking it would be good to have a test group."

His eyebrows rose. "Excellent idea! Take the illustrator with you."

"Thank you." Her hands clasped behind her back. "I was also hoping I could ask you something. I'm almost finished with all of the assignments for this week, and I should have the rest finished by the end of the day. And of course I would have my phone on me, and I can bring my laptop. I can even still proofread for Zinnia if necessary, and—"

"Good grief, spit it out." Mr. Knox waved a hand.

She took a deep breath. "My mother is in the hospital. I was hoping I could take…" Liv's voice echoed in her head. *Ask for Thursday* and *Friday.* "Thursday and Friday off, to go see her."

He leaned back in his chair. "My condolences." Judging by his expression, his condolences weren't considerable. "You're almost ready on that book? Do you think this will affect your timeline?"

"No, sir. I expect to still get it in on time."

His head bobbed. "I'm a sympathetic man. Take the days off and leave your laptop at home. Zinnia can pick up anything you don't finish."

She did wince this time. Zinnia would never let her hear the end of that. "Thank you, sir."

As she exited the office, she let out a breath. It worked.

It looked like it was time to call Andy and let him know they were testing out nonexistent ideas at the boys' and girls' club.

"Is visiting charities going to be our thing?" Andy and Caroline paused in the hallway of the children's center as their tour guide spoke with a kid. Something about a lost frisbee.

Andy's cheeks warmed. "I mean, I didn't mean *our* thing. There's not an us, obviously." He laughed and then pretended he had a cough.

Wow, smooth, man.

What about Caroline made him so tongue-tied?

He'd been on plenty of blind dates, after all, most of which Maisie had set up. Had tons of practice talking to women. All of them were very nice girls, but so many of them lacked ambition, possessed no drive. Once, when he asked a girl named Hadassah, blind date number three with long hair that went to her hips, what she wanted to do, she scrunched her shoulders and said, "Haven't given it much thought. I'd love to have lots of kids, though. At least six."

Now that he thought of it, he'd gotten tongue-tied that night too. When he said goodbye to Hadassah he'd meant to say, "Have a lovely night," but it came out as, "Have night lovely... yeah, umm, goodbye."

Not that he didn't want any kids. He rather liked the idea of a son named after his second favorite artist, Vincent ...van Gogh, but he'd hoped he wouldn't have to explore that path for a few years.

Besides, an ambitious woman could spur him to want to work harder, to stay on task. Like his almost-teacher Ms. Austen almost had. That woman had gumption.

If only his guidance counselor, during his sophomore year of high school, hadn't switched his class at the last minute. Would he have turned out differently?

Caroline's hair fell in front of her face like a pair of wispy curtains. "It's not a charity, exactly. More like a club for troubled boys and girls. It's run by Helping Hope."

The last word snagged in her throat. She swallowed and hunched her neck. Did something happen to her? Dark circles under her eyes and gray tint to her skin hinted at a lack of sleep.

"Anyway." Caroline cleared her throat and then fiddled with a bracelet on her wrist. "Since I can't seem to give Clark any good ideas, I figure we'd come here and ask kids what they want to read."

With a huff and brushing off a piece of lint on her skirt, the tour guide gave a weak smile. Her lipstick had smudged on her cheek.

"Sometimes we have a problem with kids taking items and not giving them back. When they don't know where their next meal is coming from, they can hoard items. But for the most part, they're absolutely wonderful. I can't wait for you to meet them."

At last, in the dim lighting of the hallway, Andy spotted a name tag underneath the lapel of the woman's suit jacket.

"Linda."

With a gesture of her hand, Linda motioned for them to move into a kitchen. Workers in plastic hair nets waved and then stuffed brown paper bags with chip bags, apples, juice boxes, and plastic-wrapped sandwiches.

Each of the brown bags had a different name of a child. Andy spotted a cursive "Wyatt" on the last sack on the counter.

"We supply each kid with a bag to take home every time they come to the Club," Linda explained and leaned against a large silver refrigerator door. "One less meal to worry about."

A pit drilled into Andy's stomach. He knew what that was like.

When his college classmates asked where he'd gone to school and he told them the name of the private institution, they thought he had plenty of money. In truth, the academy, by declaration of the state, took on a number of children from low-income homes to increase the diverse economic representation of the school. Showing that kids of all financial backgrounds could receive a quality education.

The teachers, who lived off of the tuition that parents paid, didn't like that arrangement.

His mother had still received food stamps, made crock pot recipes stretch for two weeks, and little did his friends know that when they gave him snacks they didn't want in the cafeteria that they'd fed him for the weekend.

"Now," Linda grunted as she shoved herself off the fridge, "would you like to meet some of the kids?"

She backpedaled to a pair of double doors that led in and out of the kitchen. Through the round windows, Andy spotted a group of kids sitting in a circle.

"This is our six-to eight-year-old group." Linda rested her hands on her rotund tummy. "We usually have them play a game before they leave. Helps to exercise some of their energy before we send them to their homes."

One child, a girl with countless braids, bobbled back and forth like a rocking horse. An instructor called out something indiscernible, and the kids raised their hands, some giggling. Rocking horse girl stopped see-sawing for a moment to raise her arm.

Linda swung open the door. Shrieks and giggles pricked Andy's ears at first.

Hadassah would probably have wanted to adopt all these kids.

After waving to the children, Linda placed a finger on her lips. A few seconds later, the kids hushed, with the exception of a few who decided this was a good time to sing a catchy song to themselves.

"Hi, kids!"

Andy jolted at Linda's voice shooting up two octaves from its gruff timber.

"I have brought two special friends with me today. Caroline," she said the word slowly, "and Andy. They're both writing a children's book."

An "ooo" sounded from the crowd. One boy with a buzz cut raised his hand.

"Yes, Trevor?" Linda's eyebrows disappeared into her graying bangs.

"Is it going to be about unicorns?"

Caroline's lips twitched into a smile. "Maybe! That's why we need your help. To figure out what you would want to read."

"I hate unicorns," Trevor declared and stuck out his tongue.

"Then it won't be about those. I'm assuming no llamacorns either?"

Trevor blew a raspberry. Caroline's shoulders relaxed. It could've been Andy's imagination, but she'd sounded relieved.

Another girl, the one in braids, raised her hand.

"Yes, Philipa."

"I need to go to the bathroom."

Linda blanched and glanced at the monitor, a lanky man with a wrinkled forehead, who shrugged and held up his clipboard as if to say, "I can't move from this spot, lady." Linda nodded and then turned to Caroline and Andy.

"I'll take her to the restroom. Are you two okay with leading them through a round of Corgi, Corgi, Chihuahua?"

Both Andy and Caroline cocked their heads at the same time. Linda squinted at them and then her face relaxed moments later when realization hit her.

"It's their version of Duck, Duck, Goose. Kids like corgis, I suppose."

Huh, maybe we should write a book on the dogs at the shelter. The worker there did say puppy books saturated the market, though. And they needed a good idea so Caroline wouldn't get yelled at again by Clark.

Linda didn't wait for their reply. She bustled over to Philipa, held out her hand, and the two of them headed toward the sideways doors that led into the hallway.

Andy and Caroline shared a glance before they padded across the scratchy-sounding carpet toward the circle. Kids scooted to the side to make room for them. When Caroline went to sit, a kid with freckles held up a hand. "No, you gotta be our Corgi."

Caroline, apparently flustered, stood from her half-squat position. "Oh, all right, umm," she tapped the bald head of the child, "Corgi—"

Andy supplanted her spot and grinned at the kid. "Do you like to read?"

"Corgi—"

The kid shrugged and then picked his nose. "I like if it has lots of pictures."

This kid is talking my language. "Oh yeah? Do you like ones with pictures of dragons and superheroes?"

After a moment's thought, the kid shook his head. "Too many dragon books. My teacher Mr. Ervin made us read one about a dragon who kept all the gold to himself."

"Corgi—"

The kid's features darkened, and he clawed at the scratchy texture of the black carpet. "It was sad."

Okay, so he wants a happy book. Let's hope Caroline didn't think of any ideas that ended in tragedy.

"No dragons, no llamacorns, no superheroes. It sounds like you want a book with ordinary people." When he spotted the kid's scrunched nose, he added, "Ordinary people who do really cool things.

Like firefighters and doctors."

"Corgi—"

"Hmm." The kid nodded. "That does sound better than a dragon who dies from eating too much gold."

Yeesh, who wrote that children's book? That sounds like nightmare fuel.

"But," he sniffed, "what if I can't be a doctor? Grandma says I cost a lot. And you gotta pay a lot for school. At least, that's what she says."

Stones formed in Andy's chest, so heavy he thought he'd fall over. He'd had the same thoughts as a kid when he read picture books about doctors and people living in large houses. His teachers in his poorer school district made sure, from a very early age, to make it clear that he and his classmates would never experience the same luxuries of character they read about.

"Corgi—" Caroline, halfway across the circle, tapped the head of a giggling girl who wore a pink unicorn t-shirt.

"So." Andy caught his breath and remembered to inhale. The rocks inside his ribcage started to dissolve. "Are you saying you'd like to see someone in a book who's like you?"

"Chihuahua!" Caroline bopped the pom-pom ponytail of a girl, and the girl bounced up and shrieked as she chased Caroline around the circle.

After staring at the floor, the kid's eyes lit up. "Yeah!"

The girl with the pom-pom hair tagged Caroline when they were five feet away from Andy. Caroline sat in the circle, and when she locked eyes with Andy, she cocked her head.

"What?"

He grinned. "I think I have some ideas."

Chapter Seven

CAROLINE TOOK A DEEP BREATH, SHIFTING her grip on her duffel bag. She hadn't stood in front of this door in six years. The last time she'd seen the dark wood, she'd been slamming the door behind her.

She lifted her fist and knocked.

The door opened a few seconds later, revealing a broad-shouldered man with clean-cut salt and pepper hair. He wore a relaxed polo, a deviation from his usual dress shirt or suit and tie, but he still maintained a commanding presence.

He broke into a smile. "Caroline."

Her throat tightened. "Hi, Dad."

He hesitated, then stepped forward and wrapped his arms around her.

She hugged him back, breathing in the familiar scent of his cologne. The fragrance took her back to childhood, to her excitement when he would get home from business trips and swing her through the air.

Though she dreaded talking to Mom, hugging Dad felt like coming home.

He stepped back and reached for her bag. "I'll grab that."

"Thanks. How's Mom?"

He didn't answer right away, stepping aside to let her in, then closing the door after her.

Caroline's gaze roved the foyer, all modern art and glittering glass and marble. Cold, sterile. Nothing like the saggy chairs and worn carpets of her apartment with Liv, lacking the pictures and dorky cross stitch that hung on the walls of her home with her friend. She internally cringed to think of what Mom would have to say about her Roseville dwelling.

"She's resting. She'll be happy to see you, though."

I doubt it.

He swung her bag. "Come on, we can set this in your old room, then we'll go see your mom."

Caroline followed her father into their home. Her sneakers squeaked on the tile, and she regretted wearing them, no matter how much more comfortable they were than heels to wear on the plane. She inhaled, still a bit groggy from the early morning flight. The scent of lemongrass still filled the air, six years later. *Lemongrass.* "Is Carmela still around?"

"The cleaning lady? She retired." Dad entered a hall past the kitchen filled with stainless steel appliances. "There's another lady, Denise, who comes by on Thursdays."

"Oh." Caroline felt a pang of sadness. She had never actually told Carmela goodbye. The older woman cooked and cleaned for them two days a week, and often babysat Caroline when Mom and Dad were both busy. If two scents defined Caroline's childhood, they were the smell of Carmela's lemongrass cleaning solution and the aroma of the cookies Carmela would sometimes bake. Carmela believed little girls needed chocolate chip cookies and not just kale.

Dad pushed open the door. "Here we are."

Caroline stepped into her old room.

She felt like she had entered a time capsule. A college banner hung on one wall next to a stylized rendition of the periodic table. Her bed was still spread with a poofy sky blue comforter tucked in at the corners, while a matching white dresser and armoire complemented the bedspread. From the shag rug on the floor to the saucer chair in the corner, it was a step back in time to teenage Caroline.

But everything looked a bit too perfect. The rug appeared too chic, the saucer chair too sturdy to be the normal teen purchase from Walmart. Instead of posters and pictures plastered to the walls, only a few decorations hung tastefully. Caroline had tried to build a space like a normal girl, but Mom couldn't abide clutter. Mom would choke if she saw the bookshelves cramming every inch of wall space in Caroline's current room.

And the "filthy rodent" Caroline kept as a pet. She smiled at that. "You didn't convert it into an office or something?" Caroline asked as Dad set her bag on the bed.

He shrugged. "We don't need another home office." He scratched the back of his neck, an uncharacteristic nervous gesture. "I have to tell you something. I didn't tell your mom you were coming."

Caroline's eyes widened. "You didn't?"

He avoided eye contact. "She had so much going on yesterday getting released from the hospital...I didn't want to add anything else to think about."

Something else to think about. Because Mom had a nervous breakdown. Mom was upset, and fragile, and Caroline had to be the very last person on Earth who Mom would be glad to see. If Mom had known that Caroline was coming, it might have hindered her recovery as she stewed about seeing her wayward daughter.

Caroline remembered slamming that front door, backpack slung over her shoulder. At eighteen, she was old enough to leave. Old enough to choose her own path, one that didn't include schmoozing politics or slick attorneys or spending her days worrying and scheming about the stock market. Stories had been her escape, a way to transcend the pressure to be perfect, a way to be somewhere else, someone else, if only for a little while. So she set out to write her own.

"You don't want the embarrassment of a stupid daughter?" she had screamed. "Then you don't have to have one at all!"

After she had bombed the SAT—three times—and ACT—two times—her prospects had gone down the toilet as far as her mother was concerned. Caroline was the private school prodigy who destroyed her chance for an Ivy.

But a smaller school took her, and her GPA earned her enough scholarships to graduate in two years with minimal debt. After those five failed tests, Caroline had worked harder than ever to prove leaving and pursuing her own dreams wasn't the stupid choice. That it hadn't been a mistake to turn down her parents' money for a school of their choosing in a career that they would consider acceptable.

She'd learned what Mom valued. And it wasn't her daughter.

Caroline forced a smile. "I guess we'll surprise her."

She followed Dad across the hall. Her heart raced faster and faster. She rehearsed what she might say. *Hi, Mom, how are you? It's good to see you.* Was that too casual? Too normal? *Hi, Mom, look, I'm not living under a bridge. Yeah, I even have a full-time job. I'm writing a book, too.* She winced. Best not to mention the book. Not with how it was progressing at the moment.

Dad knocked on the door. "Kristy?" He cracked it open.

"Mike, did anyone call my cell?"

Caroline's heart pounded in her throat at Mom's familiar, sharp voice.

Dad frowned. "The doctors said no technology right now. You're resting." He glanced back at Caroline. "Someone is here to see you."

"They came to our home?" A sigh. "Give me a moment to make myself presentable."

He looked into the room, then back at Caroline. "She's right here, and she doesn't care what you look like."

In the oppressive silence, Caroline heard slow footsteps on the other side of the door. Dad stepped back, and the door swung all the way open.

Even in her loungewear, Kristy Penn usually cut an impressive figure. Her straight shoulders and the way she held her head high commanded respect no matter what she wore. Sharp cheekbones and toned muscles spoke to extreme fitness.

But that wasn't the case anymore. Mom's shoulders sagged. Dark circles under her eyes and thin limbs spoke of exhaustion. Her honey-colored hair hung loose and dull rather than in her usual bun. She looked like she had one foot in the grave.

All eloquence left Caroline. "Hey, Mom."

Kristy's eyes widened. She looked her daughter up and down.

Caroline waited, trying not to fidget. *Say something.* Her mom's last words to her rang through her head. *"If you want to throw away your life, don't let me stop you."*

Surely, six years later, things would be better. Time healed all wounds, right?

Kristy Penn's mouth set. Her eyes hardened. "What are you doing here?"

Dad winced.

Caroline struggled for words. "You were sick. I came to see you."

"And now you've seen me." Kristy held her arms out. "What do you think? Come to gloat?"

"What?" Caroline realized she was bunching the hem of her shirt in her hand and forced herself to stop. "No. I was concerned about you. I wanted to see you."

"I'll live." Kristy looked at Dad. "Did you know she was coming?"

He cleared his throat. "Yes."

"Ah." Her sharp gaze returned to Caroline. "Thank you for letting me know."

"Kristy…" he began.

Maybe the floor would open up and swallow Caroline. Maybe she would wake up and this would all be a bad dream.

"This changes nothing, Caroline," Mom said. "A minor health setback." Her face reddened. "I don't need your pity. I don't need—" She broke off, leaning against the doorway as the color drained from her face and her limbs quaked.

Dad stepped forward and took her arm. "We should get you back to bed."

Caroline stayed rooted to the spot as Dad led Mom away.

Kristy looked back over her shoulder. "You didn't need to come."

Now, Caroline wondered why she did.

A bedroom door in Andy's apartment creaked.

He glanced up from his computer and watched Elijah stumble into the main room area. Elijah rubbed a fist in his eye and yawned. Then he scratched his back and tottered toward the kitchen.

Andy glimpsed the clock in the kitchen. 10:02 A.M.

"Don't you have to work?" He checked his computer calendar. Sure enough, it was a Thursday. With all the craziness of this week, he'd lost track of which day they'd entered.

"Some places let off for Maundy Thursday."

Light from the fridge illuminated the dark circles under Elijah's eyes. Andy had spotted him late last night scrolling through LinkedIn job listings and saving them. In case.

Once Elijah procured the milk from the top shelf, he twisted off the lid, gave the contents a sniff—when had they last gone grocery shopping?—shrugged, and reached into a cabinet for a box of granola. He dumped both into a blue bowl that had a chip on the top of the pottery. Bang, went the silverware drawer, where Elijah selected a spoon with the least amount of food residue. They needed to get the apartment repairman on their dishwasher soon, since it didn't clean the silverware properly.

Elijah dug the spoon into the bowl and shoveled granola into his mouth.

A sudden, icy, realization hit Andy. "Your boss didn't let you go, right?"

The spoon dangled from Elijah's lips.

Milk dribbled down his chin. He shook his head and plopped himself on a recliner in the family room. "The head of our department made his rounds yesterday. I think I'm safe for now." He managed to catch Andy's squint. "Was looking for listings last night in case. They say the best time to interview is when you still have a job."

Andy's shoulders relaxed.

Wouldn't know these things, working freelance. Since paid time off and holidays didn't exist for Andy's line of work, he'd have to intentionally take a pay cut if he wanted to enjoy a day off.

But he always refused to do freelance work on Christmas and Easter.

Facing his screen again, he pulled open a Word document that listed a series of ideas he had for the book. While the sound of Elijah crunching on granola filled the silence, he scanned through the items:

- A story about the importance of a club for kids from troubled homes?
- Profiles on some of the kids from the club?
- Teaching children how to play the game of Corgi, Corgi, Chihuahua?
- A story on the kids at the club adopting Peaches as their mascot?

Why did every idea end in a question mark?

Probably because whenever he did a group project in school, he'd shrink into his desk seat and watch a loud girl slap her palms together and say, "Okay, folks, here's what we're going to do for this assignment." He'd accept the tasks allotted to him, do them right before the deadline, and stay silent as the girl spoke for the majority of their group's presentation.

Even now, he'd watch his inbox, receive a work task, complete it, and turn it in to the assigner. No agency, no initiation on his part involved.

His teeth peeled off some skin on his lip. *I wish Caroline would answer her phone. She'd have an idea of what we should do next.*

He'd texted her about having some concepts for the book and hoping to meet again to discuss them. Besides, a get-together with Caroline gave them more reasons to meet with Peaches again or at the children's club. But he'd messaged her right after their time at the club, and she hadn't replied. Odd, he thought, considering she usually returned texts within minutes.

By now, Elijah had devoured the contents in his bowl and washed out the rest of the leftover milk in the sink. His roommate shoved the dish into the dishwasher, slammed the door to the machine shut, and ambled to his bedroom.

Andy leaned forward and planted his chin on his fist.

Caroline could be busy at work today. Most places, unlike Elijah's office, kept workers until Good Friday. And knowing Clark, the greasy Scrooge man probably didn't let Caroline take off anything more than Easter Sunday.

It was possible she couldn't answer the texts because she got overwhelmed by work tasks.

Even he tried to ignore his inbox today. Any time he saw the sheer list of bolded unread emails, his temples pounded.

Elijah emerged from his room with a bass guitar and a few sheets of paper scrunched in his non-guitar-holding hand.

"Hope you don't mind." The grogginess still hadn't left Elijah's voice. "A local church apparently is missing a bassist for Easter. Pneumonia. So a friend in the band asked me to fill in."

"Not at all." Andy stared at the blinker on his Word document. How it faded in and out of the white. "I like to listen to music while I work."

"Thanks, man." Elijah grabbed a music stand nestled behind the TV and placed the paper on it. "They're really in a pinch. I hear that their worship leader may be switching churches soon. So the bassist going down for the count was the last thing they needed, especially on Easter Sunday."

Elijah shoved a pick between his teeth as he marked the paper with a red pen. He paused and pulled the pick out of his mouth.

"Speaking of Easter, do you have any plans?"

Weights dropped on Andy's shoulders. He eyed his phone that sat on a small table near the family room couch. His mom had texted him this morning, asking the same question. But he couldn't bring himself to answer.

"Not yet." Andy forced a lemon-fed smile. "You?"

"Parents are out of town this weekend. Maisie invited us to her house for a potluck, though. Something tells me Hadassah will be there." Elijah winked. "You know Maisie and her inexplicable potluck matchmaking sessions. She knows she can get us with those scalloped potatoes."

Andy belted out a laugh. "Yeah, I'd say no because of Hadassah… but those potatoes are pretty good."

He glanced at the Word document one more time and then slammed his computer shut.

"Lij—"

Elijah's head snapped up at hearing his nickname.

"—you don't think it would be unprofessional to go to Caroline's workplace and bounce some ideas off her? Maybe I can even suggest them to Clark, so if they're bad, he won't yell at her. I'll get the heat instead."

A mischievous sparkle twinkled in Elijah's eyes.

"Ohhhhh." He grinned. "I see why you don't want to go to Maisie's potluck. Prince Charming is going to save the Princess from her evil boss."

Not a bad idea for a children's book. Andy rolled his eyes. "Whatever, bro. But seriously. You don't think I'd be crossing any lines?"

Elijah sashayed his shoulders. "I think the fair maiden would deem the gesture lovely."

Okay, you know what, I'm going to do it. Only because I don't want to see Elijah move his shoulders and wink like that ever again.

The sooner he left the apartment, the quicker he could purge that image from his memory.

He shoved his computer into a messenger bag, ran fingers through his tangled curls, did the sniff test on his shirt—not too bad, and *oh, good, I remembered cologne today*—and headed out the door.

On the drive over, he listened to some singles Elijah had uploaded onto Spotify. Not too bad, but the music could've used a little less throbbing bass. He arrived at the building and parallel parked. Last time, when he'd gone to pick up Caroline, he noticed employee parking out back and a few guest parking spots. But he figured he'd let someone else take those if they had an important meeting with Clark today. After he fished in his jeans pockets for loose quarters to pay the parking meter, he entered a revolving door and asked the woman up front for directions to the Helping Hope office floor.

With a glare at his wrinkled flannel, she gestured at the elevator and muttered, "Fourth floor."

"Thanks." His shoes squeaked on the linoleum flooring, and he stepped onto an elevator that dinged open. He punched the number four and listened to jazz music on the way up.

Once he stepped off the elevator, he spotted a placard for "Helping Hope" dead ahead.

After adjusting his bag, which had begun to slip off his shoulder, he marched toward the entrance and skidded to a halt when he saw no one sat at the front desk. Maybe the receptionist had left for a brief break.

"Can I help you?"

A woman leaned against a cubicle. She had the most severe and skinny eyebrows he'd ever seen. Like she'd drawn them on with pencil lead. A thin suit jacket banded around her tiny waist, the two lapels connected by a red button, which matched the rest of the suit.

"Hi." He fiddled with this bag strap. "I was wondering if Caroline Penn or Clark Knox were in office today? I have some ideas I want to discuss."

She pursed her lips and then replaced the expression with a smile. "You must be the illustrator. Caroline likes to scroll through Facebook during work hours. She was on your profile a lot the other day."

Wait, she was scanning my profile? Of course, he *had* sent her a friend request.

The woman extended a hand with the scariest scarlet fingernails he'd ever witnessed. "Name's Zinnia. Carrie and I are practically besties here."

He thought Caroline was best friends with her roommate. She

talked about an Olivia a lot, not a Zinnia.

He shook her hand. Wow, the woman had a strong grip. His fingers relaxed, and he released.

"Any idea where your bestie or her boss went?"

Zinnia's face sagged. "Oh, I'm so sorry. Clark's out for lunch. The man can eat for hours. And I guess he said something about Carrie being out for a family emergency. I'm afraid they won't get here for a while."

His blood iced. Family emergency? No wonder she hadn't responded to his texts.

"But she's been giving me all of the deets about your picture book. Any ideas you need to bounce off her,"—she spread-eagled her arms—"consider me to be a substitute Caroline." She paused and cleared her throat. "Of course, until she gets back. No one could replace sweet Carrie."

He bobbled back and forth on his heels, not realizing how long he'd been standing in the same spot. His feet ached from a lack of movement.

What should he do? She never mentioned a Zinnia. *But Caroline and I aren't exactly close. And she doesn't* owe *me every detail of her life.*

What he wouldn't give, in this moment, for a boss to tell him what to do next.

For now, he'd have to settle with what he often did while he awaited tasks to pour into his inbox—absolutely nothing.

"Thanks for the offer, Zinnia." He forced his bag strap onto his shoulder. "But I think I'm going to hold off until Caroline gets back. Something tells me it'll be worth the wait."

With that, he marched out of the office. The weight on his shoulders somehow lifted.

Chapter Eight

MOM DIDN'T SPEAK TWO WORDS TO Caroline for the rest of her visit. Caroline stood staring up at the Statue of Liberty. The sun shone over Lady Liberty's crown, making Caroline squint, but she still huddled into her coat in the chilly breeze coming off the water.

Her flight didn't leave until Sunday afternoon. She knew she would lose her mind spending another moment in the silent tension of her childhood home, so she left for the day. Dad would understand.

Her heart warmed. Dad. Maybe he'd been ineffectual in her arguments with Mom, but despite Mom's prickliness, Caroline had watched him steadfastly care for her mother the past couple of days. He had cancelled all trips for the next week, dedicated to being there for his wife.

If only he had been around more often during Caroline's childhood. Maybe he could have been a buffer between her and Mom.

She pulled on her gloves before stuffing her hands in her pockets again. If Mom would just speak to her...

She strolled along the wide sidewalk, past tourists taking pictures and tour guides speaking in a multitude of languages. It had been odd riding the ferry alone to the island, watching families chatter, kids giggle. They reminded her of happier days.

She remembered the first time Dad took her to the Statue. She must have been six or seven, and they had moved to New York only a year or two before from Washington, D.C., where her mom had been a junior partner in a legal firm and her dad had spent his time as a lobbyist.

"It's a messier city than D.C.," Dad had said, "but I like it. You see real people walking down the streets. Not just suits, but wannabe musicians on the street corners with their guitars, and future Broadway actors, and aspiring writers...New York City is about hope, Caroline."

About dreams. Not just about power and laws."

Caroline didn't remember much about D.C. But she did recall Dad's words about New York. She knew the honking horns and chaos and bustle. She hadn't been old enough to understand his words about hope and dreams then. But she did now.

She leaned against the chilly railing and looked up at the green statue, torch held high. "Lady Liberty is all about hope," Dad had told her. "Back in the day, they called America the land of opportunity. You could be anything you wanted to be in America, they said. People came from all over the world. They still do." He had frowned. "It isn't just about the money or the fame, Carrie-girl. It's about finding what you were meant to do, who you were meant to be." He squeezed her little hand. "Remember that."

Now, she wondered how much he had taken his own words to heart. Mom wasn't a fan of spontaneous outings. She had scolded him when they got home, told him Caroline had homework to do. But she hadn't seemed too annoyed. Mom was happier then. Less severe. Maybe the hopeful atmosphere of NYC hadn't been lost on her yet.

Caroline gripped the railing. She had chased liberty her own way, in a small Michigan town. But had she succeeded? Working for Helping Hope and Mr. Knox?

Not even close.

After this picture book. After she proved herself to Mr. Knox. Maybe she could move on. Finally get a job at a big publisher, be a mover and shaker in the industry. A person like that wouldn't have to cower to Mom or Mr. Knox or anyone. She just had to come up with a worthy idea.

She glanced at the time on her phone--3:45 P.M., ten minutes before the last ferry left. She headed toward the dock. Tomorrow was Easter Sunday, and she had an awkward evening and morning to spend with her father before flying home Sunday afternoon.

The next morning, Caroline sang along to the music as she stood next to Dad. Mom had stayed home—she didn't really leave the bedroom—but according to Dad, she'd said they should go to church without her.

Sunlight streamed through stained glass, dappling the crowd with color. Little girls in pastel Easter dresses and elderly ladies with fancy hats filled the pews like more colorful panes of glass. A choir swayed while the choirmaster enthusiastically directed. Caroline didn't know anyone here, but she could feel their Easter morning excitement.

"It's good to be in a church again," Dad murmured.

Caroline's eyes cut to the side. She lowered her voice. "You haven't been going?" That didn't sound like him. He had always made it a point to find a local church in which to spend Sunday morning no matter where he traveled.

He sighed. "It's been a while."

After service, they went out for an unconventional Easter lunch of hamburgers and French fries. It took Caroline back to their occasional father/daughter "don't tell Mom" outings.

Dad set down his burger. "I want to apologize."

Caroline paused with a French fry halfway to her mouth. "Why?"

"I should have been there." He kept his eyes down, swirling a fry in ketchup. "I wasn't there while you were growing up. I don't know what I was thinking—I guess that there was plenty of time—but one day I came home and you weren't a little girl anymore." He looked up. "Your mom and I...we both wanted the best for you. But we weren't the best at showing it."

Caroline swallowed. "I know you did, Dad. You don't need to apologize." He was an ambitious man chasing dreams of success, but he had always made time for her when he was home.

Mom, on the other hand...Caroline had always felt more like a status symbol than a child. *Look, everyone. See my genius child? I'm a successful woman in every way. Now let me be your attorney.*

"But I do." He leaned forward. "I was so focused on building the perfect life for us that I forgot to spend time with the people I thought I was doing it all for."

He sat back and sighed. "Your mom and I were going to go to Ohio for Easter to take a bit of time away. There was an old cabin there I used to visit as a kid." At Caroline's raised brow, he chuckled. "Not a rustic cabin like you're thinking. Your mom wouldn't go for that. More like a lodge." He sobered. "I could see her health deteriorating. I thought maybe a vacation could help. I guess I waited too long, though."

Caroline reached across the table and put her hand over his. "We'll figure this out. We're all going to be okay."

He smiled and squeezed her hand. "It's good to have you here, Carrie-girl."

When they returned home, laughing and talking, Caroline pulled up short as they entered the kitchen.

Mom set down a box of granola. Caroline noticed her hand trembling a bit. "You're home.". Mom's voice was flat.

"I have to leave soon to catch my flight."

She nodded. And that was that.

The next morning, Caroline pressed the button in the elevator, blinking tired eyes. She'd hardly slept, Mom's thin, trembling hands flashing behind her eyelids.

Zinnia's broad smile greeted her the moment she stepped into the office. "Carrie! You poor dear, how are you?"

She forced a smile in return. "I'm fine, thanks."

Zinnia sighed, tucking an imaginary piece of blonde hair behind her ear. "You were gone for so long, I was wondering if I would have a new coworker soon."

Two days. Caroline set down her bag in her cubicle more forcefully than necessary. *I was gone for two days, Zinnia.*

"I think that illustrator was confused too. He came in to talk to *me* about the book." She pursed her lips and shook her head. "The poor man was telling me how he doesn't really have anything to work with yet. It's a shame."

Caroline suppressed a scowl. Now Andy was complaining about her to Zinnia? Would he gripe to Mr. Knox next?

Zinnia glanced at Caroline, gauging her reaction, then looked off into the distance, her lips twitching in a mischievous smile. "He's not what I expected. He's not half bad looking. A little rumpled, but maybe that's an artist thing." She leaned forward. "I think he might have been interested in me. I usually go for more sophisticated men, but..." She looked at her nails and shrugged. "I might make an exception."

"Sounds like you two would be good for each other," Caroline ground out, booting up her computer.

"Yeah." Zinnia leaned against the cubicle wall so dramatically Caroline wondered if it would collapse. "I heard Mr. Knox saying something about giving the picture book job to me if you couldn't get him a good idea by Thursday. He wouldn't want to put too much stress on you. Not when you're going to be out all the time like that."

Caroline's blood simmered. She turned fully to Zinnia and flashed a brilliant smile. Or was she baring her teeth? She hoped Zinnia interpreted it as the former. "Thanks, Zinnia. But I have a killer idea." She swiveled back toward her computer. "I think you'll really like it — but it's a surprise."

To everyone including me.

Andy squinted at the jar of mayonnaise in their apartment kitchen lighting.

One or two bulbs had gone out in the lighting fixture above them. Yet one more thing to ask the maintenance man to check on. The apartment only seemed to hire one guy, "Phil," who had a slow waddle walk and a molasses coated voice. Phil would spend hours discussing gross finds he'd excavated from u-bends in apartment kitchen sinks.

Much as they needed him to repair a number of issues, Andy didn't think he could stomach one more story about "Phil's Treasure Hunts."

"You think we should use the whole jar of mayonnaise?" Elijah squirted mustard into a bowl. Yellow splatters from the condiment decorated the kitchen counter. To the side of the stove, a sheet full of hard-boiled eggs awaited a deviled filling.

"Are you sure you know what you're doing, Lij?"

Elijah had insisted on making the recipe for deviled eggs from memory. Even though, to the best of Andy's recollection, the two of them had never created the dish together, let alone for the potluck at Maisie's house.

Maisie, who had a surprise visit from extended family on Good Friday, decided to bump the potluck to Monday evening. This gave Elijah and Andy approximately two hours to rush and pull together a dish, since they'd forgotten to grab supplies until Elijah returned home from work.

After he squeezed an extra squirt of mustard into the bowl, the bottle wheezing, Elijah opened the topmost cabinet near the microwave. He grasped a bottle of paprika.

"How hard can they be? Besides, I figured it beats bringing store-bought food to these potlucks. Hadassah makes me feel guilty when she makes homemade peanut butter bars." He pressed both fingers together and did a chef's kiss. "Those are a masterpiece."

Then he proceeded to dump enough paprika into the bowl to turn the mustard reddish brown. Once he capped the paprika, he squinted at the bowl, then at Andy.

"Do you think it needs more?"

"I think"—Andy set down the mayonnaise on the counter and padded toward the family room bookshelf—"we need to check Mom's cookbook. Because that looks nothing like what she makes for my family on Easter."

The last part of the phrase caught in his throat.

Andy swallowed the words and perused the top shelf with his index finger until he landed on a maroon leather-bound book. He nudged it out of the bookcase and flipped to the deviled eggs recipe.

"Speaking of your mom." Elijah dug a large spoon into the mayonnaise. "Is she sad you didn't do Easter with her? I know you said it would've been awkward, just the two of you."

Pressing his thumb into the book to preserve the page, Andy watched as Elijah plopped a large spoonful of a white glop into the bowl. "I'm sure she was fine on her own. She has lots of friends at her church. They probably did something together."

"I still can't believe you can't face her, years later." Elijah stirred the mixture until a freakish orange color showed from the bowl he'd tucked into his arms. "I mean, the incident happened a decade ago."

"Can't face her" wasn't completely true. They'd spoken. But ever since the incident, their conversations came out strained. Forced. Especially since he'd gone away for college and moved out of the house right after graduation.

Andy slumped into the family room chair.

Memories reeled.

Now he was back in Walton Academy with a binder in a shaky hand. He checked his class listings again on the paper he'd printed out at the library. They couldn't afford a printer at home.

After his interview with the academy, the guidance counselor made a last-minute change to his schedule, two weeks before school year began. They gave him a different English teacher so he could have a study hall at the end of the day.

A heavy breath flooded out of his nostrils. "It's okay, Andy," he told himself and ran a nervous hand through his curls. "You were an A-student at your last school. That's why they transferred you here. Because you have promise."

He side-stepped a group of girls huddled around a locker.

One, in a flower crown, laughed so loud the noise pricked his ears. Even though he knew she wasn't giggling about him, he couldn't help but think that they'd all caught onto him.

Onto the fact that his mother dug into the freezer that morning and found a frozen sandwich, who knew how old, so that he'd come to school with something to eat for lunch.

And about how the school, as part of a government initiative, needed more kids from poorer districts like Harrison Heights High.

They knew, they had to.

He had poor written all over him, from the tattered jeans to the hoodie with a hole in the left elbow.

He adjusted the straps on his backpack that had slid down his shoulders.

No. You worked hard to get here. You got five hours of sleep a night to study for tests at Harrison, and you practiced for days for your interview. Your mom hired tutors with money she didn't have to get you into this place.

If anyone deserved a spot here, he'd earned it.

When he reached the end of a narrow hallway, he stopped at a green door. On it, a sign read, "Procrastination on your part does not constitute an emergency on mine." He gulped and scanned the number placard on the top of the door and then looked at the schedule he held in his shaky fingertips.

Yep, he'd come to the right classroom.

Gushes of air flew in and out of his nose. Behind him, a student jostled into his shoulder to enter the classroom.

All right, Andy, you can do this. First class of the day.

Home room really didn't count. That involved him sitting in a corner of a large band room and waiting for the instructor to call his name. He practiced the word "here" over and over in his head so his voice wouldn't crack or draw attention to himself.

He stepped inside the classroom and found the teacher had placed name placards on the desks in alphabetical order by last name. When he found his nameplate, in scarlet cardstock, he sat.

Posters from various local productions of stage plays covered the walls, along with velvet curtains. A white board next to his desk listed the assignments due for the week. Already the teacher, Ms. Buren, had filled each day with textbook readings and various papers, all scrawled in red Expo marker ink.

His mouth had gone dry. *This school goes heavy on the homework assignments.*

The bell rang. A woman in a red dress and heels to match stationed herself at the front of the classroom. Glasses glittered on her long, slender nose.

"Good morning, class." Each word had a period after it. Short. Terse. "This summer, I sent each student an assigned paper. You were to write on your favorite literary classic and what it means to you and turn it in to me prior to the start of the term. I have graded your papers."

How could he forget?

He'd spent hours on his essay on *A Portrait of Dorian Gray*.

"I graded each of your papers out of a score of one hundred points. The class scored an average of ninety-five."

Ninety-five points, not bad.

By the private school's strict grading standards, that constituted an A minus. As long as he maintained a B-average, the school said they'd keep him there, on his full ride scholarship.

"I would also like to remind the class, as I detailed in your summer homework packets, that although we have many homework assignments, papers of this nature are a significant portion of your grade. We will only do two large papers per semester." Ms. Buren bent to pick up the papers on the desk, if he could use the word "bent." The woman had the pin-straight spine of a ruler. "Fail one of these assignments and your grade will suffer most severely."

Her heels pounded the linoleum as she weaved through the rows.

When she reached Andy's desk, he tried his best interview smile on her, the kind where someone squinted their eyes and split their cheeks with a wide grin. She returned it with a glower.

He knew that look. Some kids in his homeroom had gifted him the same expression when they noticed the holes in his hoodie. The "oh, you're poor" look.

Then Ms. Burn slapped the paper on the desk.

Scarlet ink covered the page. She'd crossed out entire sentences with her red pen. On top of the paper—his heart sank—read his score. Fifty-six out of one hundred.

His eyelids reduced to slits to prevent the mist from his eyes spilling onto his cheeks. She'd docked five points per being verb used, another five points for every split infinitive, and ten points for one instance when he used the word "causation" instead of "correlation."

When he glanced sideways at another classmate's paper, who had gotten a ninety-eight, he only saw one comment. Two points taken off for a being verb.

Wait, did she give me a lower score because she knows my family doesn't have money? He had emailed her, after the guidance counselor made him switch classes, to ask about any summer assignments. He made sure to explain he was one of the transfers as part of the new school's initiative, hoping and praying she'd give him some slack for any lost time he'd have to make up on summer homework.

She'd replied with an email with the homework packet and a curt, "Attached."

Now, as he stared at the paper, he knew that she knew about his financial situation. Every red pen mark declared, "You don't deserve to be here."

"Eee-yuck." Elijah pulled Andy out of the long memory and grimaced after trying a spoonful of his orangey mixture. Andy'd almost forgotten about the eggs, being so drawn into the past.

"This is definitely not the right recipe. Got your mom's, Andy?"

Andy brandished the cookbook.

Elijah thrust the spoon into the sink. "Last time I'll ask, dude, but are you *positive* you don't want to call your mom and explain why you couldn't do Easter?"

"I can't face her, man." Andy placed the book on the kitchen counter, trying his best to avoid putting the cover on a mustard splatter. "Ms. Buren's class dragged my GPA down, and they expelled me. Mom gave up everything to get me in that school. "After that…" He glanced at his fingers and then rolled them into a fist. "I haven't turned an assignment in on time since."

Chapter Nine

CAROLINE LEANED AGAINST THE WALL IN the hallway and squeezed her eyes shut, trying to muster a cheerful demeanor to walk into the office.

It was Tuesday morning. In forty-eight hours, she needed to have a manuscript on Mr. Knox's desk. That elusive idea still hadn't come to her.

Dreams from last night still haunted her thoughts. Mom's emaciated hand reached for her, fist curling until one accusing finger pointed at Caroline. "You did this to me. You left me to waste away."

Caroline shuddered. And for what? She'd deserted her mother to fail in a nobody job in a nowhere town. *Mom was right. I did throw my life away.*

A second rejection that morning hadn't helped. This literary agent had been harsher than usual.

Ms. Penn,
   This is a pass. We encourage you to work on your craft.

And that was it. What did that even mean? Her writing was so bad he couldn't even form words?

I just wanted to do something that gave me life. To write the books that used to help me escape. But now I need to escape more than ever.

Her own mother wouldn't speak to her. *You're doing fantastic, Caroline. Just fantastic.*

"I don't usually nap in the hallway, but to each their own."

Caroline opened her eyes, taking in the white-haired lady standing in front of her. "Miss Evie. I haven't seen you around in a while." She glanced at her watch. "And so early."

Miss Evie leaned on her cane. "I came from coffee with my prayer sister. I thought I'd check in on Helping Hope. Make sure my rapscallion son isn't causing too much trouble for you."

Caroline bit her lip. *If only you knew.* "Things are fine."

Miss Evie raised an eyebrow. "I know what that kind of 'fine' means. Especially paired with someone hiding outside the office."

"Well." No sense in lying to Miss Evie. "I'm having trouble with the picture book."

She nodded. "Not perfect? Not just right to be in churches and schools and homes around the nation and beyond? Not the message that thousands of children need to hear?"

Caroline blinked. She'd hardly thought about what the kids needed to hear. She'd been too busy trying to figure out how to please her boss. "Mr. Knox wants something fun and lighthearted." She ticked them off on her fingers. "Glitter, humor, rhyme, llamacorns."

"Pish. Clark doesn't know what he wants. Well. He knows he doesn't want Baba Yaga." She winked.

Caroline's face heated.

"You want my advice?" Miss Evie tapped her own chest. "Listen to what the Lord is telling you, in here. Don't worry what my son will think. Figure out what book you're supposed to write, and everything else will fall into place."

Caroline nodded and took a deep breath. How had she forgotten the readers? The kids were what mattered.

The kids. When she was a child, books transported her to worlds where she could be a pirate, a princess, anything. Caroline the frizzy-haired nerd from an NYC private school could immerse herself in a world of danger, excitement, and meaning beyond homework and competitions and rules. Books reminded her that her life could be more.

The start of an idea began niggling at her brain. Nothing solid, nothing she could put on paper. Just an idea—hope.

"Thanks, Miss Evie. You're right. I'll think about the kids."

Miss Evie patted her shoulder. "I know you'll come up with something wonderful. It's why I suggested you to Clark."

Caroline straightened her shoulders and marched into the office.

She had beaten Zinnia—thank goodness—so she had time to settle in and write.

She pulled up a blank document and started brainstorming. What sort of things gave kids hope?

Once Zinnia arrived, Caroline had moved on to proofing ad copy. She would let her thoughts percolate for a while.

Caroline waited for a sarcastic remark from Zinnia in greeting, but for once, her coworker gave her a wave and got to work. Maybe she needed new fodder for antagonizing Caroline. She would have plenty of ammo soon if Caroline couldn't deliver in two days.

She hesitated. Andy seemed to help her think. It would be good to get his perspective, and from what she'd seen at the boys and girls club, he was great with kids. But she wasn't happy with him for talking about her to Zinnia.

What right did she have to be mad? He'd only told Zinnia the truth. He *didn't* have anything to work on yet, thanks to her.

She picked up her phone.

Caroline: Hi, Andy. I'm sorry I fell off the grid this weekend. I had a family emergency. How are things going?

She hit send, then winced. *How are things going?* What was that supposed to mean? *How are things going with you doing my job and coming up with an idea for me because I'm incompetent?*

She set down the phone and returned to the proofing, trying not to listen too hard for the buzz. Did Andy think she was a loser?

So what if he does? He isn't my boss.

The phone buzzed and she snatched it up.

Andy: I'm sorry to hear that. Are you okay?

She bit her lip. She wasn't looking for sympathy.

Caroline: I'm fine. It turned out not to be that big of a deal.

Not technically a lie. It wasn't a heart attack, after all. Just her mother working herself near to death and refusing to speak to her daughter. She continued typing.

Caroline: I've been thinking about the picture book. Do you have any thoughts?

The response took a moment.

Andy: I'm glad to hear it turned out okay. I had some ideas at the boys and girls club, but nothing solid. What about you?
Caroline: I don't have anything concrete either, but I've been thinking about a word. Hope. I know it isn't much to go off of, but at least it's something.

She sent the message, then it hit her. *Hope.* Helping Hope. The organization was all about helping others. Maybe her inspiration would come from one of their many programs.

She and Andy had already visited the boys and girls club. Maybe they should try a different one.

Andy: I like that. Definitely a starting point.

Caroline struggled to form her inspiration into words.

Caroline: I'm thinking about visiting another one of Helping Hope's programs. It might give us inspiration. This organization is all about hope, but to be honest, I don't get out of the office and into the field very often. I may need to witness more of it firsthand.

She glanced toward Zinnia's cubicle. Thankfully, her coworker hadn't peeked over the divider and noticed Caroline texting.

Andy: I was at a potluck last night and a lady from church, Maisie, mentioned Soup and Smiles needs more help. It isn't a Helping Hope program, but you can join me this evening if you want.

She hadn't wanted to drag Andy along on more of her inspiration missions, but if he would be there anyway…

She imagined Andy's wide smile as he ladled soup into bowls. He seemed to have an easy way with kids and animals—she wondered if that care extended to everyone in need. Her heart warmed at the thought of him at a potluck with a little old lady from his church.

The man may have no sense of urgency, but he might actually make up for it with personality. Maybe.

Caroline: Perfect. What time?

Somehow Caroline even made a plastic hair net look beautiful, Andy thought.

She ducked into a white apron with the words "Soup and Smiles" written on the front in cursive. Then she tied the apron strings twice around her slender waist and moved to the kitchen counter to snap on a pair of blue gloves.

Andy washed his hands in a silver sink and put on his soup kitchen regalia when he finished toweling off the cold water.

A man in a Soup and Smiles t-shirt with a large smile on his face to match waited for both of them at the front. To their left, by a silver-hued table, a variety of volunteers ladled soup into bowls. In the corner of the kitchen, an older woman stirred a large pot with a tall wooden spoon.

The man, name tagged as "Joseph," rubbed his gloved hands together when they both joined him near the two swinging doors that led in and out of the kitchen.

Through the door windows, Andy spied empty tables covered in checkered tablecloths and lined with an array of white plastic seats. Maisie had mentioned the guests who received meals at the soup kitchen didn't arrive until a half hour after the volunteers got to work setting up the placemats.

"Did Maisie send ya?" Joseph's dark brown eyes glittered in the butterscotch kitchen lights.

Andy nodded. "Sorry I didn't hear about it sooner. I know you had a huge rush at Easter."

Cold air spilled from a frosty window near the stoves. Although it wasn't open, a crack showed on the corner of the pane.

Even though they were in the season of spring, Michigan couldn't decide if it wanted to give up the wintry weather quite yet. Soon they'd experience a tumult of rain showers and air that held the constant scent of precipitation.

He thought about a flower garden, situated a mile away from Soup and Smiles, that he liked to visit during the late April months. Vibrant tulips and marigolds lined the spiraling pathways there. They often served as inspirations for colors in the subject of Andy's paintings.

Oh, man, when did I last paint the mural at church? I better get on that sometime soon.

Joseph waved a hand, as if wafting away the scent of aromatic herbs that had filled the kitchen. "No worries at all. We love it whenever we have new volunteers." He gestured to a stack of pastel yellow placemats. "We have these left over from Easter, but I don't think our guests will mind. I'll have you both put one in front of every seat, and when you finish, we'll get you the plastic cutlery to place in each spot."

Andy scooped the heap of placements into his hands. They strode out of the kitchen and a blast of heat warmed his neck and ears. Caroline marched to the table in the farthest corner of the room, near a wall decorated with paper Easter eggs.

He clapped the placemats on the center of the table, and they began setting one by each seat.

"So." Caroline wiped her forehead with the back of her glove. "You had ideas for the picture book?"

His lips twitched. "You don't let the grass grow under your feet, do you?"

She smirked. "When you have a boss like Clark, you don't have time for grass to grow." She hunched over and exhaled heavily to imitate him. Clark did like to breathe out of his mouth. Then she jabbed her pointer finger in the air. "The grass is taking too long. Zinnia, get me some plastic grass. They won't know the difference if they don't look too closely.'"

She unrolled her spine. White lights danced on her hair net cap.

"Fair." Andy positioned a placemat with a bent corner in front of a seat. "What do you think about doing a picture book that talks about the kids from the club?"

Yellow surrounded each spot on the table. In the time it took him to set up table linens in front of two chairs, Caroline had covered the rest of the spaces. She grabbed the placemats and bustled to the next table. This one was stationed under a dangling paper bunny decoration.

"I like the idea." She kept her eyes glued on the chairs. "And I do want a story about hope. But Clark seems to be all about silly stories, so I feel like that may be too serious for him."

Andy's eyebrows drew together.

Nothing serious, huh? Well, that nixes most of my ideas. Good thing I didn't run into Clark at the office the day I went.

"Really? I thought you all were a nonprofit. Profiles on the kids seem to be well within the company mission."

"You'd think, but he's obsessed with llamacorns." Her face and shoulders relaxed. She locked eyes with him. "Honestly, I think the 'llamacorn' stuffed animals he buys for his niece are actually for himself."

Andy's cheeks and abdomen hurt from trying to stifle the laugh. Images of Clark on a couch, surrounded by a flood of various plushies, flitted across his vision.

"Thanks for that visual. I can't decide which is worse. Clark with a unicorn stuffed animal or my maintenance guy's stories of his treasure hunts in people's u-bends."

Her glove flew to her mouth to stifle a giggle. She'd dropped the placements onto the table, and they butterflied all over the checkerboard.

They both reached forward at the same time to re-stack them and accidentally grazed hands.

He yanked his arms back, as though he'd touched a soup burner from the kitchen. Electricity pounded in his fingertips. Pink faded from Caroline's cheeks a moment later.

"Anyway." She tapped the placements against the table to straighten them. "Is that the only idea you had?"

"Well, nixing all the serious ones, I thought maybe we could do one on the game of Corgi, Corgi, Chihuahua. That seems silly enough."

She nodded. Twinkles from her eyes disappeared.

"I suppose." She meandered to the next table, steps slower this time, as though she'd lost her energy. "But our names are going on the cover. And that doesn't really scream, 'I'm passionate about writing.'" She shrugged. "I mean, it feels like one of those picture books that any mom could pick up in the store and say, 'That's so mindless. Even *I* could write that.'"

Andy reached for a placemat on the center of the table. This one managed to have a grease stain on the center of it.

"Do you mean our names are going to be on it?" The thought of the permanence of his moniker on a cover sent a shudder down his spine.

Caroline bobbled her chin, and her shoulders dropped when she sighed. "I know it's a work assignment, but I like to throw one hundred percent of myself into what I do. If I'm not passionate about the subject, I could compromise the integrity of the project."

She clasped her hands. Everything in his fingers itched to hold them.

Whoa, dude, slow down. She's a professional work colleague.

Where are these thoughts coming from?

Her fingers unweaved. "Anyway, I talked with someone this morning who put things in perspective. Maybe we shouldn't jump the gun on this project. If the book is going to the bookshelves in churches and charities, we should do this right. And that might mean waiting a little longer to come up with the perfect idea."

Silence filled the checkerboard space in between them.

Then Andy reached for another placemat.

"I think that's the best idea we've had so far about this book. Not picking an idea. Until we find the right one."

Chapter Ten

"YOU HAD ON A HAIR NET." Caroline covered her mouth with her hand, trying to suppress giggles. "How did you still get soup in your hair?"

Andy rolled his eyes upward, as if he would be able to see the top of his head, and ran his fingers through his hair. He isolated the lock dabbed with red sauce, presumably tomato soup. The cold outside air blasted them as they stepped out of the building into the darkening evening after two hours of serving soup.

"I think it jumped," Andy said, pulling a wrinkled tissue out of his pocket to aid in his quest.

"It jumped." Caroline raised an eyebrow.

"Yeah. That second pot. Didn't you see the label? 'Jumping soup.' Maybe we should do a book about that."

She snorted, but her grin didn't fade. She stepped down from the curb into the parking lot.

Her foot missed and she stumbled. Andy's hand gripped her elbow, steadying her. Her face heated. He let go quickly, but the imprint of his strong fingers seared onto her skin through her sleeve.

She cleared her throat at the embarrassing cliché. *I promise I didn't do that on purpose, Andy.* Obviously. Because he was only a work partner. "Thanks."

"So, did this evening help you find any inspiration?" Andy stuffed his hands in his pockets and didn't make eye contact.

"No." She shook her head, reaching into her purse for her keys. Then she paused. "But it did help me find something." She looked up toward the dark sky and smiled. "Perspective."

She pulled out her keys and stopped at the blue hatchback. "This is my car. Thanks for walking me."

He made eye contact again and offered her his slow smile. It was a bit lopsided, she noticed. His grin reminded her briefly of Peaches' tongue lolling out the side of her mouth. "If you ever want to volunteer again," he said, "let me know, and I'll tell Maisie."

"Only if they're serving jumping soup." She grinned.

He laughed. "Maybe it will get you next time."

As she pulled away from the parking lot, she glanced back at Soup and Smiles. The unassuming building had been filled with warmth and laughter. Young and old from all over the town sat together, sharing a meal, offering grateful smiles to the servers. "God bless you, my dear," a gap-toothed old woman told her, smiling so wide her eyes were hidden by wrinkles.

Caroline didn't know what the book would be about, but she knew what she felt in that soup kitchen—love and hope. Hope based not on a pipe dream, but on the belief that with each day, God would provide.

Maybe hope didn't have to be about fame, fortune, or big dreams. Maybe the greatest hope could be found in everyday lives.

I feel like I'm onto something. If only she knew what.

Caroline entered the apartment humming and hung up her coat. Olivia sat at the kitchen table in a messy bun and pajama pants. Music theory books, hymnals, and collections of Brahms, Debussy, and Schumann scattered the surface before her while she tapped a pencil to her lips. She hardly looked up.

"The Romantic era?" Caroline asked, crossing the room to flip through Brahms.

Liv blinked, returning from music land. "Yeah. Sometimes I forget you were classically trained too." She gestured to the books. "The youngest Etmann girl, Claire, has a recital coming up, and I think her interpretive style works really well with Romantic era composers, so I'm trying to find a few pieces for her to choose from."

Pages rustled. Liv opened the Debussy and pushed up her reading glasses. "Maybe 'Reverie'? Of course, Debussy is really more Impressionist, as much as he liked to insist he was Romantic. I *love* Debussy's 'Snow Is Dancing,' but it may be too hard for Claire. It takes a very special touch…" Her eyes drifted back to Caroline, and she tilted her head. "What's that face?"

Caroline chuckled. "You're so cute when you go into music-nerd mode."

Liv stuck out her tongue. "And where have you been all evening?"

"At the soup kitchen." Caroline opened the cupboard and reached for a glass.

Liv pulled her legs up onto the chair and crossed her arms around her knees. "You're wearing a dopey smile."

"What?" Caroline focused on sobering her expression. She *did* have a wide grin. Where did that come from?

"Ah." Liv nodded sagely. "Andy was at the soup kitchen too, wasn't he?"

Caroline's cheeks warmed. She stuck the glass under the faucet. "Yes, but I don't see how that's relevant."

Liv snorted and pulled a pink sticky note from the stack. She flipped through Debussy and marked a few pages. "If you say so." She pursed her lips. "I was thinking about 'Clair de Lune,' but—"

"Overdone," Caroline agreed.

Liv snapped her fingers. "Read my mind. Now tell me about Andy."

"Liv!" Caroline sighed. "I thought we moved on."

Her roommate smirked and took off her reading glasses, folding them. "While you're reading your weird speculative space thrillers—"

"I don't read *space thrillers*—"

"—*I* read romance novels like a normal person, and I sense romantic tension. Now spill."

Caroline rolled her eyes. "I'm just happy to be doing something worthwhile. And I might have some ideas for the book."

Liv squinted at her. "No more Russian fairy tales, right?"

Caroline flicked water at her. Liv shrieked and threw up her arms, cackling.

"Hope," Caroline said. "Something about everyday hope."

Liv picked up her pencil again and pointed it at Caroline. "Now *that* is the best idea I've heard so far."

The next morning in the office, Caroline leaned forward, scanning a PDF proof for a poster for the Hope Club on her screen. The graphic designer had done a good job, but a couple of letters had been deleted from the copy at some point. Caroline marked the errors and emailed it back.

The *Hope* Club. The word was everywhere. Andy suggested doing a book about the kids at the club last night. Caroline had brushed it off—a story about underprivileged kids didn't seem up Mr. Knox's lighthearted alley—but maybe the story didn't have to be about what they were.

Perhaps it could be about what they could become.

She grabbed her phone and her coat. As she headed for the door, Zinnia looked up and frowned. Bright pink lipstick today. "Lunch break already?"

"No, making a work call outside so I don't bother anyone." She pulled on her coat while walking.

Zinnia raised a brow. "There are office phones."

"Multitasking." Caroline didn't have to try very hard to dredge up a smile. She finally had an idea that could work. "I need some fresh air anyway."

In truth, she didn't need Zinnia listening and realizing that, less than twenty-four hours before the deadline, Caroline still didn't have a manuscript, much less an actual idea.

She couldn't wait until she made it outside. She pulled out her phone and hit the call button beneath Andy's contact info while stepping into the empty elevator.

The phone rang for only a moment before he answered. "Hello?"

"Hey, Andy. Are you busy at the moment?"

"Working on a couple freelance things, but nothing pressing."

"Fantastic." She stepped to the side as the elevator stopped at the second floor. An older gentleman in a suit gave her a dirty look while getting on. She lowered her voice. "You know how you suggested we do something with the kids at the club?" The man gave her an even dirtier look, and she clarified, "The children at the boys and girls club run by Helping Hope?"

"Sure, but I thought that was too depressing for Mr. Llamacorn."

The elevator doors opened, and Caroline let the man step out first. "Right. I thought so at first. But I think I was looking at it the wrong way." She stepped into the lobby. "Sometimes, the 'hope' you find in books seems unattainable. Not everyone is going to be a superhero or a president or a famous scientist or…" She swallowed. "Or a bestselling author. But that doesn't mean we shouldn't celebrate the everyday hope. So what *do* these kids want? And how do they get there?"

The front doors opened, and a chilly breeze sent strands of hair tickling her cheeks. Outside, the sun sparkled on puddles of melted snow.

The line remained silent for a moment. Then Andy said quietly, "These kids want hope that their messy families can still work. That their lives are valid too. That even if things aren't perfect, they can still be good."

Caroline halted in the middle of the sidewalk. *Even if things aren't perfect, they can still be good.* Nothing at Soup and Smiles was perfect. Cheap plastic tablecloths, homelessness, unskilled soup servers—yet smiles and love and *hope.* "They don't need another person telling them to reach for the moon. They don't need to feel like their life hasn't begun until they get there. They need hope that meaning and love and happiness can be found right where they are."

Pedestrians wove around her, some giving her annoyed glances for blocking the sidewalk, but she didn't care. *Right where they are.* What if someone had given her that affirmation as a child?

Andy's voice came out hushed. "That's it. I think we have our idea."

Andy stared at his phone for a solid two minutes after Caroline hung up. Shakiness pounded in his fingertips and arms, and they, by now, had reduced to the wobble of Jell-O.

We finally had an idea. The idea.

His cheeks hurt, and he realized a moment later that his large grin from the phone call hadn't disappeared.

Across the room, Sammy stared out the window and whimpered. His tail flicked back and forth. Around noon every day, the squirrels liked to circle the trees like corkscrews outside their apartment complex.

Andy stared at his shaking arm. *I need to get some exercise to get rid of these jitters.*

It felt as though someone had funneled a gallon of coffee into his bloodstream.

He clapped his palms on his knees, and Sammy darted his head in Andy's direction, cocking his neck.

"You wanna go outside?"

Sammy jumped to his feet, and his front legs bounded up and down, nails clicking against the floor.

Andy's eyelids squinched and nose scrunched. "I'll take that as a yes."

He heaved himself from the family room chair and set his laptop on the center table. Then he grabbed Sammy's harness and leash from a basket situated near the dog's kennel and stuffed his jeans pockets with plastic bags in case Sammy's breakfast needed to make a quick escape.

Right as he opened the door, Elijah stood on the other side with his keys in hand.

"Did work let out early?" Andy had to tug the leash to keep Sammy from barreling straight into his roommate.

"Left my lunch in the fridge."

That would explain the Tupperware containers filled with goodies Maisie had foisted onto them at the potluck that Andy spotted in the fridge earlier. They still hadn't made a dent in the honey and brown sugar glazed ham. She'd sent them home with nine meals' worth of the melt-in-your-mouth meat.

Andy, by Tuesday, had his fill of the dish and asked Elijah to take the rest with him to work to share with his office buddies.

Elijah angled sideways to skirt past Andy. Once his roommate slipped inside the apartment, Andy and Sammy bounded down the stairs from the second floor of the apartment and out the doors. Sammy, predictable as always, tore toward the large tree.

Littered with squirrels, the large trunk towered past their apartment window.

While Sammy had his paws on the tree trunk, the door to the apartment complex swung open. Elijah held up a brown greasy bag, panting. Had he sprinted down the stairs? Maybe he was running late on his lunch break.

If so, Elijah didn't indicate, because he strolled over to the tree with his free hand in his suit pants pockets. A long, thin black tie dangled off his neck.

"You look happy, Andy."

A light breeze kicked at Andy's bare ankles. He'd never been able to find pants long enough to cover his legs at the stores, without them being too large around the waist. Weak sunshine lit his cheeks, and a bird's song interrupted the skid of tire wheels from the street ahead.

"It's a beautiful day."

Elijah smirked. "Uh-huh. I know that smile. You get that way any time you get off a call with Ca-ro-line."

Sammy interrupted the "line" part of the word when he growled at a squirrel that had crawled too close to the base of the tree. Its bushy tail disappeared behind a branch.

"What did you two talk about today?" A grease spot on Elijah's bag had formed the shape of a corgi. Or at least, the ears were two very prominent triangles.

Oh, Elijah. The dude liked to have long conversations, forgetting about work duties entirely. Who knew how much longer he had on his lunch break?

Andy tugged at the leash to try and coax Sammy to test the grass that surrounded the tree. "We finally figured out *the* idea, and she asked me to do a couple concept sketches for our presentation." His voice broke on a nervous laugh. "I guess that means I need to get started on illustrations, huh?"

With a nod, Elijah set his bag on the grass. Okay, so they weren't going anywhere any time soon.

"That would explain why you can't stop shaking. Since, you know, you actually have to work now."

Andy held back an eye roll and settled on glancing at a nest of robins on the crook of a tree branch.

"Hmm." Elijah rubbed his chin. "That still doesn't explain the smiling. You never smile when faced with working on a task."

"Maybe I think this task is meaningful."

"Nope." He flicked a piece of hair that had fallen in front of his nose. "Even with projects like the mural at church, you still get nervous."

The dog tugged on the harness.

Sammy had found a patch of dandelions nearby that he found fascinating and had dug his snout into the clump.

Moments later, Elijah snapped his fingers, his face brightening. "It's Caroline. You want to ask her out."

Shock jolted Andy's skin.

"As-ask her ou—? Are you crazy? We're professional work colleagues."

"Call me crazy, but you definitely don't smile that way when you're talking to Clark-o."

Andy's features sagged.

Ah man, Elijah had called his bluff.

"What's the worst that could happen, dude, if you asked her to coffee?"

Sammy's leash pulled him a few feet. No wonder. Sammy had found a cluster of pigeons near a gutter in the street. "I don't know. If she says no, wouldn't it be weird between us?"

"Never know until you try." Elijah stooped to retrieve his brown bag. Then he punched a finger at Andy. "Make sure to *call* her. Don't do it over text. Women hate that."

With these final words of encouragement, Elijah bounded toward the apartment complex parking lot. A yellow rusty car beeped a moment later when he clicked his keys.

Apparently done with his fascination with the pigeons, Sammy returned, tail a-wag.

"I don't suppose you want to call her for me?"

Sammy's tongue sprawled out of the side of his mouth.

Andy sighed.

"Might as well give it a try. Otherwise, Elijah'll never let us hear the end of it."

Worse, Elijah might enroll the help of Maisie and set the two of them up on a blind date. He did notice how Elijah and Maisie had talked conspiratorially over the scalloped potatoes dish at the potluck. They had pointed fingers in Andy's direction, and he heard the word "Caroline" from his position by the veggie dip.

Sammy and Andy returned to the apartment and Andy's finger shook as he dug into his pockets for his keys. He failed to plug the keys into the hole in the knob for the first ten seconds, fist trembling this way and that.

Once inside, he unleashed Sammy and crumpled into his favorite family room chair. Then he stared at his phone for a few moments.

Electricity pulsed in his fingertips, the same way it had when he and Caroline brushed hands at the soup kitchen.

He scooped the phone and his finger hovered over Caroline's number. Then he threw a prayer heavenward while he clicked the green call button. He pressed the phone to his ear. The dial tone battered his eardrums.

Please don't pick up. Don't pick up. Don't pick—

"Hello?"

"Oh, hi, Caroline!" His voice had gone squeaky. He cleared his throat. "Is this a bad time?"

Please say it's a bad time.

"Well, Clark needs me to get some tasks done, but he's left for his usual two-hour lunch break. What's up?"

He puffed out a long breath through his nostrils. "I'm so excited about the book."

There was a pause. "Umm, yeah, me too. Are you calling about that?"

"No, I,"—he winced—"I—umm, you know how we've had lots of fun at the soup kitchen, the dog kennel, and the kids club?"

"Yes?"

"Well, I was." He tugged the collar of his shirt, which had crept up his neck. "Was wondering if you'd want to meet someplace that isn't charity related. Like coffee, just the two of us."

His heart thundered so much in his ribcage that he couldn't hear anything else for a few seconds. Didn't help that Caroline's line had gone silent.

Then her voice crashed through the receiver. "Are you asking me on a date?"

Oh, boy. Did his tongue feel swollen? "I mean, I don't want there to be any pressure. Just a get-to-know-you thing, you know? It's fine if you say no. No worries."

There were worries. Lots of 'em.

An indistinct ring of an office phone sounded through the receiver for a few seconds. Someone in a cubicle nearby must've picked up a call. Did Zinnia or one of her other coworkers overhear his miserable attempt to ask a girl on a date?

"I'd be fine with coffee," Caroline said at last. Then her voice turned teasing. "*Only* if you promise to get me those sketches early. Clark is in a weird mood lately. Better to appease the beast and get him everything before our due date." She whispered the last part, almost like she didn't want someone to hear. Not Clark, of course, who'd already left for his long lunch break.

Silence for ten heartbeats.

"How does tomorrow night sound, Andy? At 6:30 P.M.? I can send directions to a coffee place in the area that Olivia highly recommends." His shoulders relaxed. They'd jutted up five inches during the duration of the call. "Tomor—yeah. Sounds great. Okay, 'bye!"

Without giving her a chance to reconsider, he clicked the off button and slumped into the chair. Had the weather been any hotter, he may have melted.

Chapter Eleven

A DATE.

As Caroline drove home that evening, she clutched her fingers around the steering wheel, trying to calm her too-fast heart rate.

"Are you asking me on a date?" Why had she said that? What if he'd said no? How awkward would that have been?

But he *was* asking her. And in a rare moment of confidence, she'd even picked the place and time.

A moment of control freak, more like. Had he thought that was weird? Did he regret the invitation? Did he actually, specifically ask, or had she assumed? And what if he was going on the date to be nice, and it would make their work relationship awkward?

She turned the corner onto the street leading home.

Are we even allowed to date within the workplace? That had to be some sort of taboo, right? You couldn't have professionals getting personally involved. *Maybe I should have said no.*

She burst into the apartment. "Liv! I'm having emotions."

Olivia poked her head out of her room. "Caroline Penn is having emotions! This is a groundbreaking moment. Sit at the table and allow me to brew my special emotion tea."

Caroline threw off her coat and plopped down at the table.

Liv slid a mug of water into the microwave. Then she bounced over to the table, skipped the chair altogether, and perched on the edge of the tabletop. "Tell me," she commanded. "What has caused this earth-shattering occurrence?"

Caroline took a deep breath and leaned forward. "I think I'm going on a date." She buried her face in her hands. "But I've never been on a date before."

"I knew it!" Liv crowed. "It's with Andy, isn't it?"

Caroline nodded, too embarrassed to pull her hands away from her face.

"Tell me more. What happened? Where are you going?"

Caroline recounted the conversation, then ended with, "It *is* a date, right? Or did I totally misread that?"

Liv gave a sharp laugh. "Of course it's a date. But it seems like a very chill date. Nothing to get worried over."

"Easy for you to say." Caroline played with the hem of her sleeve. "You've been on a date before."

"Come on. You've been on at least *one* date before in your twenty-four rotations around the sun."

"Not one." She wasn't allowed to date in high school, she was too busy in college, and here in Roseville, eligible bachelors didn't often stroll into Helping Hope's office. And she didn't really go anywhere else besides Sunday morning service.

Huh. That might be a problem. Did she even have any friends besides Liv?

Caroline winced. Nope. Only coworkers. Even she and Liv were only friends because they had been random-draw roommates in college. Liv left after a semester to head home to be with her father during health issues, but she and Caroline kept in touch—mostly thanks to Liv's extroversion—and once Caroline graduated and ended up in Roseville, Liv offered to be roommates again. All interactions initiated by Liv.

"I'm hopeless. Maybe I should cancel. This is a bad idea."

Liv rolled her eyes and grabbed Caroline's hand. "Girl. Pre-date jitters are normal. It's going to be fine. You two can sip coffee, chat like normal human beings, and have fun."

"Chat about *what*?"

"Just be yourself." Her eyes twinkled. "Though maybe you should limit the nerding out about Byzantine history to no more than fifteen minutes."

Caroline shoved her, but she couldn't hide her smile. "Okay, fine." She sobered. "You don't think this is a terrible idea?"

Liv mirrored Caroline's serious tone. "Caroline. You have no idea how long I've been praying that some man would walk into your life, push past all the prickliness, realize what a treasure you are, and stick it out to care for you no matter how hard you try to push him away."

"I don't need a man to take care of me," Caroline protested. "I can do just fine on my own."

"I know that. You're a force of nature, and you could take on the whole world by yourself. But you shouldn't have to." Liv half-smiled. "At some point, you're going to need to accept that you're worthy of love whether you're at the top of the New York Times bestseller list or scrubbing toilets. We all need breaks sometimes, and you need someone to remind you of that. Someone who you can trust to help you."

Caroline's eyes stung. Now she *really* had emotions. "Okay, I'll go." She pointed a finger at Liv. "But if it ends up being weird and he bails on this project, I'm enlisting you to do the illustrations."

Liv held her hands up and laughed. "Then I better pray this date goes really well—for both of our sakes."

The next morning, Caroline donned her favorite blazer/slacks combo. She held the printed pages in front of her, Times New Roman, double-spaced. Mr. Knox was a stickler about hard copies.

She checked herself up and down in the mirror, made sure every hair was in place, and looked back at her packet. It held a ten-page proposal, detailing the need, the plan, the marketability, and audience potential and statistics, with the final few pages dedicated to sample text and variations on the theme. The front read, "Book Proposal: Imperfect Hope."

The only thing missing was Andy's sketches. But he had time. He'd get them to her, and she could print them off at work.

"Okay. You've got this."

She placed the pages in a folder, then slid it into her bag. She pulled on her black heels—what Mom called "power heels"—and headed for the door.

By the time she got to the office, her hands trembled. She decided to pretend that was from the coffee.

Despite the early hour, Zinnia had still somehow managed to beat her to the office. "Today's the day, huh, Carrie?" Her lips, magenta today, turned up. "I can't wait to hear about your book. I imagine it's polished to a shine after all this time."

"I hope so." Mr. Knox wasn't in yet, so Caroline sat down to get some work done before he arrived.

Seconds seemed to move like hours. Her fingers itched in an irrational urge to text Andy. He still had at least an hour. She needed to focus.

Finally, she couldn't stand it.

Caroline: Hey, Andy. Do you have any of the sketches we talked about?

The response took so long she had to start on ad copy to avoid losing her mind.

Andy: Sorry, they're not ready yet.

She gritted her teeth. Not ready yet? She fought the urge to scream. Did he have no concept of time?

Near ten, her office phone rang. She jumped and grabbed it. "Helping Hope, Caroline speaking."

"Caroline!" She held the phone away from her ear as Mr. Knox's voice reverberated through the speaker. "I'm running late, but we have some donors who want the ol' tour. I need you to meet them."

If she had to paste on a chipper smile for donors, she may not be able to contain that scream from earlier. She took a deep breath through her nose. "Of course."

"Good. They should be here any minute. Go down to the lobby, tell them I sent ya. Just keep them occupied for five minutes."

Caroline set the phone in its cradle and sighed. Then she pushed back her chair. "Hey, Zinnia, I'll be back. Donors want the tour."

The look Zinnia gave her was almost genuinely sympathetic. "Good luck."

From the lobby, Caroline could see the rain pouring down, battering the front glass. Thank goodness it hadn't started yet this morning. On the other hand, it now would mean cranky, wet donors.

A well-dressed older couple pushed through the front doors, shaking out their umbrellas. *That must be them.* Caroline started forward. "Hi, there, I'm from Helping Ho—"

At that moment, her foot hit a puddle and slipped. Before she could catch herself, her legs flew out from under her and she landed hard on her hip and elbow. Her breath left her in a sharp gasp.

"Oh my!" The woman hurried forward, dripping umbrella in hand, followed by her husband. "Are you all right?"

"I'm fine. Sorry." She tried to scramble to her feet before they could reach her but slipped again. A lock of hair fell over her eye, and she pushed the wayward strands back, wincing at her throbbing hip and elbow. "My apologies. I didn't see that puddle." But now she could feel it, a wet spot on the seat of her pants.

"No need to apologize." The man gave an easy smile and offered her a hand. "We just want to be sure you're okay."

Cheeks burning, Caroline accepted his hand. Standing, she brushed off her pants. "I'm so sorry. You must be the potential donors, right?"

The two looked at each other, then at her. "We're here to see the chiropractor," the woman said.

Caroline wished for the floor to swallow her. "Oh. So sorry. I took you for the wrong people. Please have a nice day."

As the couple passed her, Caroline's gaze drifted to the doorway. She froze.

Mr. Knox stood inside the doors, eyebrows arching nearly to his receding hairline.

"Good morning, Mr. Knox." Her voice squeaked, and she cleared her throat. "I don't think the donors have arrived yet."

"And a good thing too." He strode closer. "Are you all right, Penn?"

"Fine, thank you." *Please let this be a dream.*

"Turns out the donors are running late as well. They're saying after lunch now. Why don't we both head up?"

Caroline trailed Mr. Knox to the elevator, acutely aware of her damp pants, the hair falling from her bun, and her bumbling performance.

He pushed the button and they stepped in. "Do you have that book proposal ready for me?"

"Yes, sir."

"Excellent. Meet me in my office." He glanced at her. "Unless you need a moment after..."

"I'm fine." She pasted on a brilliant smile. "I'll grab the proposal and meet you there."

The doors opened and she practically bolted for her desk, burning with shame. Her eyes stung almost as much as her bruises, holding back tears. This was *the* day, and she'd begun her presentation by falling in a puddle. The picture of competence.

She took a few seconds to smooth her hair, straighten her blazer, and check her proposal. *Lord help me.* Then she marched into his office, where Mr. Knox sat behind his desk, hands folded, waiting.

The stuffed heads stared down in judgment as Caroline began her pitch. "Mr. Knox, I would like to ask you what the name 'Helping Hope' means to—"

"I don't need a speech, Penn." Mr. Knox waved his arm. "Just hand me the proposal."

So much for that hour of practicing. "Of course." She thrust the folder toward him.

He flipped through the packet, wetting his finger occasionally to turn a page. Even as her heart raced, Caroline's nose wrinkled. She hated when people felt the need to smear their saliva on the page.

He grunted a few times, paper rustling.

Caroline could hear her heartbeat in her ears. What did he think? Why wasn't he commenting?

In far less time than it could possibly have taken him to read the entirety, he lowered the proposal and looked at her. "This isn't what I was expecting."

"Is...that a good thing?"

He tossed the packet onto his desk with a *splack*. "Let me get this straight. You want to write a children's book with no talking animals, no scientists, no superheroes, no rhyme. Just normal kids?"

"That's right." Her chest tightened. "Kids that children can relate to."

He shook his head. "I know you've been under a lot of pressure. Maybe I should give this project to Zinnia."

"No!" She clenched her arms at her sides and lowered her voice. "I can do it. Is there something you don't like? I can fix it."

"It's more of finding something I *do* like." He leaned back and heaved a dramatic sigh. "What were you thinking, Penn? More depressing stories?"

"That's the thing. They aren't depressing. They're about hope in the everyday, in the little things."

He waved her off. "What did I say, Penn? I said rhyme, I said glitter, I said humor. Not..." He gestured at the packet. "This!"

She blinked rapidly, holding back tears. "Maybe if you spent a bit more time with it, sir..."

The phone on his desk rang. He glanced at the caller ID. "We'll talk more later. It's the donors."

Caroline drifted out of his office in a daze. *He hated it.* She'd failed.

She plopped down at her desk, snatching a tissue to hold under her eyes, just in case. She couldn't let her mascara smudge.

She had to get Mr. Knox the perfect manuscript by tomorrow. If he didn't like this one, she would give him a different one. They had to convince him to give them one more shot.

She grabbed her phone.

Caroline: Mr. Knox is going to need some convincing. How are the sketches going?

Another long delay. She opened her email and began responding to one before her phone screen lit up.

Andy: I haven't started on them yet, but I will soon!

She stared at the screen. They weren't just "not ready yet"? He hadn't even *started*?

She restrained herself from the multitude of scathing responses she wanted to send.

Caroline: I'm going to have to cancel tonight. A lot of things came up, and I need to do stuff for the book for Mr. Knox.

For some reason, sending that text hurt most of all.

Andy's phone's glow faded into the shadows by the flannel board in the church room.

With a groan, a heater above him kicked on and blew burnt-smelling air on his neck. He sighed and put the phone on the floor, next to a black trash bag. Because he wanted to get more of the mural done before the date with Caroline, he picked out an outfit to change into after he added the finishing touches to the Moses painting and got started on the next wall—Jonah.

Man, he hadn't intended to do two water-themed paintings in a row. First the Red Sea, and next, a big fish to swallow Jonah.

White smears of paint feathered his jeans. He unwrapped the knot he'd put on the trash bag and pulled out his clothes he'd meant to wear for his coffee date.

A nice black t-shirt glowed in the lights from the blinds behind the flannel board. Someone must've turned their headlights on in the parking lot, since it was raining outside, and too dark for sunshine. He dug out the other item, a nice pair of pants, and he set the two to the side. It took him nearly ten minutes to put together the outfit. Something that said casual, but not, "Yes, I love wrinkles."

That, of course, nixed most of the items in his closet.

Now that didn't matter, because Caroline already had cancelled their date before he even had a chance to iron anything.

Not that their iron worked properly.

Once Elijah tried to experiment by using it on crayons and a white t-shirt, a weird trend that had been going around social media. Long story short, orange crayon now caked the metal soleplate.

Andy put the clothes into the bag, tied the plastic into a knot again, and sat on a chair in the classroom. Paint fumes prodded his headache with pokers.

He buried his face in his hands.

A knock alerted him moments later. He glanced up and spotted Maisie at the door, with her usual book folded into her arms.

She placed the book with yellow fabric binding on the bookshelf and pulled up a small seat for herself. Meant for a kindergarten-aged child, the chair disappeared under Maisie's homemade green fabric dress.

"Need a break from this room?" She waved under her nose to fumigate the scent. "It's a wonder you don't get a migraine from staring at these walls for hours."

"No, thanks, Maisie." He frowned. "What are you doing here? I thought you only worked on Sundays in the church library."

She scrunched her shoulders. "Our secretary has been out of the office. Allergies or some sort of spring bug. I'm filling in with some of her duties this week. Besides,"—she gestured at the book on the shelf and winked—"gives me plenty of time to catch up on books I left behind at church."

The corner of his lip tugged up his cheek.

Then the hollow sadness that filled his chest caused his mouth to droop.

"If it's not the paint fumes, what's getting you down?"

He studied his shoes.

Globs of blue paint formed drops on his tattered sneakers. Good thing he'd brought a change of shoes for the date too... well, it was a good thing, until about two minutes ago.

"I, um." His toe poked through a hole in the sole. "I asked a girl on a date. We were going to go today, but—" He trailed off and stared out the window. Raindrops spattered the pane. Above, a shield of gray clouds blanketed the skies.

"She got cold feet?"

Maisie's green dress covered her footwear, but he recalled that she wore almost the same pair every Sunday—mud-colored walking shoes. Now that he thought of it, she did wear the same ones with a floral dress at the potluck.

Maisie steepled her hands on her stomach and leaned into the small chair.

"Did I ever tell you about how Bill and I met?"

Bill, Maisie's late husband, had passed away five years before due to a heart attack. As a former CEO of the town's most successful insurance company, the very same one in which Elijah worked, this shocked nearly everyone in the congregation that a successful and healthy man, in his early sixties, could pass at such a young age

Andy leaned forward and shook his head.

Maisie pursed her lips. "Well, I'd been working at a diner, and this city slicker decided to come in every day, sit in the same seat, and always ordered extra ketchup packets. Don't ask me why. He had a weird condiment hoarding problem."

A chuckle tickled Andy's throat.

At the potluck, Maisie had an entire bowl full of ketchup packets from various restaurants. Perhaps she'd kept up the tradition or wanted to rid her drawers of the excess tomato sauce.

"He was a bit of a shy sort, even though you could tell he had important business. Always wore suits. Well, one day, he got enough courage, and he asked me to the movies."

She grinned. "And I said no."

This jolted Andy. His seat squeaked beneath his weight as he rocked back.

"Wait, why? Did you think he was ugly or something?"

From what Andy could recall from Bill, before Andy had left for college in another part of the state and his mom moved to Tennessee, away from the church, Bill had brilliant blue eyes and white hair that could've once been blond. The man competed in marathons and half marathons with regularity, so he had defined leg and arm muscles, and a well-built frame.

If Bill maintained similar exercise habits in his youth, no doubt he would've sported an excellent physique.

"No, no." Maisie waved at the air, as though brushing away the mere suggestion. "I'd been going steady with a few boys who hadn't treated me right before he came along. I wasn't ready to go to the movies with a man I barely knew. Besides, his ketchup stealing habits would give anyone the willies."

Raindrops thundered on the roof of the church now.

Andy's face scrunched up. "I'm confused. You two obviously got married. But you told him no. What happened?"

She leaned into the chair and stared at the ceiling. Twinkles danced in her pupils.

"He kept coming to the diner each day. Didn't ask me on a date again. But he and I got to be good friends. After we went on some group dates with friends, I realized he wasn't so bad. So I finally took him up on his offer for the movies."

Maisie fiddled with her empty ring finger.

"And the rest is history."

With a groan, she lifted herself onto her feet and swiveled to Andy's latest creation. She hiked up her dress a few inches to avoid tainting the fabric with the wet streaks of paint left on the tarp below.

Once she had a good long look at the wall, she turned around.

"Sometimes, when people are healing, you have to give them time. Humans try to fix each other, when in reality, that's not our job." She stepped off the tarp and held a cross necklace strung around her neck in her fingertips. "Maybe you need to let her heal, and then she'll get over her cold feet."

Caroline hadn't told him much about her past, but he'd gotten the sense that she had a strained relationship with her parents.

Even if she hadn't gone on a series of bad dates with less-than-pleasant men, family problems could cause enough of a rift in a person that could take years to mend.

"I don't know if it's cold feet per se." Andy pressed together his hands and leaned forward. "But she is overwhelmed with work and family stuff."

Maisie arched a brow. "Hmm. Work, you said?"

"I guess her boss is getting on her about the picture book we're supposed to be writing. So it was a"—he gestured at the window—"rain check. Not a cancellation."

At least Caroline hadn't outright said she *never* wanted to go on a date with him. He admired Bill, in that moment, for his persistence and patience with Maisie. How he wished Bill had still been around to give him pointers on how to maintain distance until the right time.

Maisie shook her head. "Tsk, tsk, poor dear. From what I've heard from Elijah at the potluck, she might be working herself to death. That's what happened to Bill. Got too invested in insurance and forgot altogether how to rest."

The ceaseless drumming of the raindrops on the roof slowed. Now, he could see the parking lot through a haze of water sheets.

Maisie moved to the door. She paused when she reached the frame.

"I think what's best is that you work to help Caroline finish that book as soon as possible. She won't even consider the possibility of a date unless that burden is off her mind."

She signaled at the Moses painting.

"That can wait. Remember, 'For unto whomsoever much is given, of him shall much be required.' You've been given an important task with this book. Make sure to finish the job."

With that, she grabbed her yellow book and disappeared into the hallway. Andy blew out a long breath and stared at the array of picture books on the bookshelf.

No pressure.

Was this how Caroline felt, all the time? Enormous demands coming from all sides?

Well, no wonder she'd turned him down. If everyone had expected so much out of her her whole life, she wouldn't have time for anything else, not even herself.

Chapter Twelve

"No sketches," Caroline muttered, slamming on the brakes when the car in front of her slowed. "Andy has no sketches, Mr. Knox hates my idea but has no better ones, and I have no good prospects if I get fired from this one."

She shouldn't be upset with Andy, considering she'd given him an intense and maybe unreasonable deadline. Or Mr. Knox, who only had the best interest of the company in mind.

The only person she could be upset with was herself.

But she *was* upset with Andy. On their phone call yesterday, she'd asked him to get a rough sketch or two—no color, only concept art—to her for her meeting with Mr. Knox. And he hadn't followed through. Maybe if he had seen artwork, Mr. Knox would have been more open to the idea.

The afternoon hadn't gone much better than the morning. Mr. Knox was too busy with donors to talk much, but he had given her brief instructions. "No time today, but tomorrow I need something more to convince me this idea has what we need."

She didn't know what that special something could be, so she was headed to the source of their inspiration—the boys and girls club.

She'd sent a few quick texts to Andy throughout the day. They weren't particularly polite.

Caroline: Knox isn't happy.
Andy: What happened? Anything I can do?

There already was, and you didn't do it.

Caroline: I need those sketches. By tomorrow.

She might have felt bad on a different day. A day when Mr. Knox hadn't hated her idea, and she hadn't gotten the email that arrived in her inbox two hours before she left work.

Dear Caroline,

You probably don't remember me, but I'm a friend of your mom's. We worked together as clerks back in the day before we moved on to different firms, and we still see each other in court frequently and catch up. I was so sorry to hear about her illness. I wondered how you were doing, and it surprised me to find you in Michigan. I imagine you might want to be nearer to your mother. One of my associates needs a secretary, and I would be happy to recommend you.

I can't offer you a position on my team right away, but secretarial work at a firm would be helpful for law school applications, and I would be happy to write a recommendation letter. I know you might not want to work directly under your mom—I certainly wouldn't have wanted that as a young woman—but don't let that keep you from following her into law. Tom is a good associate, and he'll be happy to help you learn the ropes over the years until you can become a full associate yourself. It's not too late to start again, and your current degree should help to recommend you to a good program in a way that will cancel out any high school test scores.

Let me know what you think. I know you're a brilliant young woman, so I have no qualms about making this offer.

Sincerely,

Darlene Winters

The signoff was familiar—the owner of a prominent corporate law firm, a woman who had come over for dinner a few times.

Her cheeks burned in embarrassment. Now Mom's friends thought she was a degenerate daughter too? Great.

She pulled into the parking lot, killed the engine, and pressed her forehead to the steering wheel.

Her blood boiled thinking over the email. *"High school test scores."* Mom told her friends about that? How did that conversation go? "Can you believe my daughter? How was I cursed with this child? Should I disown her, do you think?" Caroline pictured a crowd of women in power suits nodding sympathetically and calling for Mom's delinquent daughter to be tossed out.

She drew in a deep breath. No, Mom would be too ashamed to share that information with many people. Darlene was one of Mom's best friends, or as close to a friend as Mom tended to get. Caroline winced. Apparently, she'd inherited Mom's lack of friendship skills. In any case, just because Darlene knew didn't mean everyone did.

Caroline sat up and clenched her teeth. Not that it mattered. What did she care what the New York legal scene thought of her? As long as they didn't talk with the publishers, who cared?

Despite the shame, a small part of her felt relief at the offer. If things continued spiraling this way, she might need a new job soon. If she could ever admit defeat and swallow her pride enough to take the opportunity.

She shoved open the car door, stepped out, then slammed it behind her. She hadn't bothered to change out of her heels and blazer, but the rain had stopped, leaving only a few puddles in the darkening evening. The kids wouldn't care what she wore, right?

Click, click, click. Her heels echoed on linoleum as she entered, but the distant sounds of shouts and laughter mostly drowned it out.

Their tour guide from last week, Linda, sat in a folding chair behind a rickety plastic table, signup sheets spread across the surface in front of her. Linda smiled and waved. "Caroline, right? Here to see the kids?"

"I'd love to. Anything you need help with?"

"Actually." Linda clapped her hands together. "I'm so glad you asked. One of our usual tutors couldn't come today. You're a well-educated woman. Think you could try your hand at some sixth-grade

English?"

Homework help. The tension began leaving her shoulders. That was something she could do, certainly better than the child wrangling she'd been expecting. "Absolutely."

She signed in, and Linda led her to a quieter room where students and tutors sat in pairs. Linda showed Caroline to a low table near the corner, where a boy of about twelve with a mop of light brown curls and freckles dotting his nose slouched while staring at an unopened book.

"Hi, Wyatt." Linda's jolly voice rang loud in the quiet room. "Maya couldn't come today but look who I found. This is Caroline from Helping Hope's headquarters. She's an author."

Caroline cringed. *Not quite.* She smiled and waved. "Hi, Wyatt. Nice to meet you."

"Hi," he mumbled.

"I'll leave you to it." Linda headed for the door.

Caroline pulled out a chair beside Wyatt. "What are we working on today?"

"It doesn't matter." Wyatt fiddled with the pages of *Explorations in American Literature*. "There's no point. I have a test tomorrow, but I'm going to fail it like I always do."

Her eyes widened. "You don't have to think that way. We can work on it. Maybe you won't pass this time, but if you keep trying, eventually you will."

He shrugged. "That's what people have been saying all year."

"Then maybe there's something to it." She gestured to the book. "So why don't you tell me what you're working on?"

"Mark Twain right now."

Caroline glanced at his open backpack sitting next to the table and glimpsed *Tom Sawyer, Huckleberry Finn, A Connecticut Yankee*, and a few other titles. "Did you read all of those?"

"Yeah." He leaned down, grabbed the stack, and dumped them on the table with a thump.

Caroline gasped, reaching for a title. "They're having you read

Joan of Arc?"

He gave her a suspicious look. "You don't like it?"

"I love it." She admired the glossy cover, a newer edition, and in surprisingly good condition to be in the hands of a sixth-grade boy. "But they never assign it in schools. Twain considered it his best work, and we completely overlook it because it isn't funny. He prepped for twelve years to write this book." She set it down. "I'm glad to see it getting some appreciation."

"Oh." Wyatt scratched his neck. "They didn't actually assign it. I wanted to read it because it looked good."

The boy picked up a four-hundred-something-page classic because it "looked good"? Yet he was failing his tests? Something didn't add up. "And was it good?"

"It was." His eyes sparkled. "Especially during the trial, when they were asking her questions, and I didn't know how she could answer them, but she annihilated them."

Caroline grinned. "There are so many good lines."

He leaned forward. "I liked it better than *Tom Sawyer*, but that was my second favorite because it's funny."

"Me too." Caroline nodded toward the books. "It seems like you have a pretty good grasp on the books. Why the worries about the test?"

His face closed off again. He looked at his hands in his lap. "They put me in the advanced class. Everyone is older than me. Every time, I think I've got it, but then they pass out the tests, and my brain stops working." He looked up, scowling. "They shouldn't have put me in all of these classes. I'm not good enough to be in them. I keep failing."

Caroline bit her lip. "I'm going to take a wild guess that all of your classes used to be super easy. You didn't have to try or study at all to get A's. Am I right?"

He nodded.

"Then they moved you up. And it was a lot of pressure, right? You wanted to make sure they didn't make a mistake. You wanted to prove you really *are* smart."

His eyes widened. "Yeah. How did you know?"

"I've been there." She studied the boy. His eyes shone with excitement moments ago discussing a favorite book, but they were dark again now. Stressed, haunted. Her reaction to the increase in pressure as a kid had been to work harder and harder. But she'd seen other kids react like Wyatt. They shut down, unable to function at all. Then, she'd thought they just weren't smart.

Now she knew better. Brilliant kids could buckle under the pressure and freeze. Might even be more likely to do so.

Her mind flashed to Andy. Why *hadn't* he completed the sketches? He seemed to care a lot about the project. But she remembered the long line at the caricature booth at the charity event, how he obsessed over the perfect details.

Maybe some things didn't end with childhood.

"Listen." Caroline leaned on the table. "At the end of the day, it doesn't matter how you score. Tests don't tell you how smart you are, how valuable you are, how much you're loved. School is about learning. Did you learn a lot about Mark Twain?"

"Yeah, I guess."

"You even read extra on your own." She tapped *Joan of Arc*. "I think you're doing great."

"Really?"

"Really. I think we simply need to figure out a way that we can let your teachers know that you're learning as well. That's what the tests are for—to make sure you're understanding the information." She took a deep breath, gaining confidence. "I don't think the problem is studying more. I think it's about being able to show what you've learned. Why don't we talk about what concerns you about the tests and figure out a way to attack it?"

As she watched Wyatt's eyes fill with hope, she didn't know how things would turn out with Mr. Knox, or the book, or her mother, or even her life. All she knew was that she was glad her path led her to the Hope Club tonight.

Andy sipped his drink.

Matcha coated his tongue and filled his mouth with a weird green taste. He should've known better than to trust Elijah's drink recommendations at their local coffee shop She Brews.

Next to the squishy blue couch upon which he perched, wood decor covered a wall. Cursive Bible verses and quotes like "Stressed and Blessed" etched in white calligraphy filled his line of vision.

Up front, at a wooden counter, a group of teenage girls ordered bubble tea with flavored boba poppers. String lights hung around the squat shop like upside down blooming flowers.

He stared at his laptop and the email that had come in an hour before from the local Parks and Recreation Events Coordinator.

Dear Mr. Andy Jackson,

First, I want to apologize for the late notice on this. Our graphic designer for this specific event had dropped out at the last minute. But I happened upon your business card at a local coffee shop and enjoyed perusing your portfolio on your website.

An invisible fish hook tugged at one corner of Andy's lips.

Elijah had taken the business cards Andy ordered from Vistaprint, when they ran a special in November, and put them all over town. His roommate claimed it would, "Boom business."

Business did not, in fact, boom, but every once in a while, the occasional email trickled in from someone who wanted him to create something for them. Often they wanted a "free" design, so those leads didn't get him any true customers. But sometimes the emails promised an actual payment.

He continued re-reading. To make sure he'd done the assignment correctly.

We have a father-daughter dance coming up next Saturday (the Saturday after next) at the local fitness center. I've included all the specifics in the PDF file including the rush-fee we noticed on your website for any projects that need to be completed quickly.

We ask that you have the project to us by the end of the work day on Friday, 5 P.M.

When Andy had clicked on the PDF to see the memo, his eyes bulged. That would pay for a few missed cell phone bills. He couldn't remember the last time he'd sent in a check for those.

After he received the email, he closed his Illustrator app he'd been using to sketch proofs for the picture book. He hadn't done too shabby a job, he thought, spending hours in the shop creating the bare bones of the pictures that would go with some of Caroline's sample text she sent.

Besides, she hadn't given him *everything* yet. Surely, he couldn't be expected to turn in a project to her when he didn't have the words to go with the illustrations.

Once more, he pressed his cup to his lips and winced at the verdant flavor.

He looked at the graphic he'd created for the Parks and Rec coordinator. A pastel blue silhouette of a father twirled a pink profile of a young girl. In bold block letters, "Father Daughter Dance" announced itself on the top of the graphic.

"Looking good, Andy," a voice called this over his shoulder.

Andy whipped his neck to the right and found one of their basketball players, Griffith, behind him.

Griffith, a short man with striking amber eyes and a stocky build, situated himself in a neon green chair, near a fake fireplace. Andy didn't know much about the player apart from the fact he frequented She Brews to work on writing his stage play productions, which were performed at the local community theater.

After he placed a cup of something with wisps rising on a nearby table, Griffith turned and gestured at the graphic Andy was about to attach to the email.

"That for the picture book?" Griffith had a problem with what he called "projecting." He used his stage voice for every occasion. This provided a particular trial during basketball scrimmages when he'd shriek about fouls or penalties on the other players.

And his timbre also caused every neck in the coffee house to angle in their direction. Instrumental music from a Christian radio station filled the silence for a few moments.

Then the din of conversation resumed. The girls with bubble tea, now stationed at a circle of chairs, giggled when the flavored boba popped on their tongues.

"Side job." Andy took a note from Caroline's texts and tried to keep the conversation short. Maybe then Griffith would get the hint to leave him alone.

Andy had, after all, come to the coffee shop for a change of venue that evening. With his neighbors constantly pounding the ceiling with their footsteps—he could've sworn they were playing a game of basketball up there based on the loud stomps he and Elijah heard—he figured a calmer atmosphere would serve him better.

That had worked out well until about two seconds ago.

Griffith didn't seem to catch the hint and leaned closer over the back of his chair.

"My dad didn't have any daughters, but I remember doing a lot of stuff with him like the Cub Scouts Pinewood Derby." He held up three fingers, to symbolize a Cub Scouts honor. "I remember how he'd cheer on the wooden cars we built as they went down the race track. We never won, since Norbert Tinkler always cheated and put too many weights on the front of his car, but I felt loved in those moments, you know?"

Three fingers went up from Andy, the Boy Scout salute. He'd also participated in Cub Scouts in his earlier years, but never once had his father appeared.

He remembered how one year he'd painted his car just how he'd recalled Dad's vehicle the day he left, never to return–scarlet with a rusty fender.

Everything in Andy hoped that if he somehow won the derby or got first place in something that all the newspapers would declare his name. Maybe the paper would get as far as wherever Dad had traveled, and he would come to congratulate him.

It never worked.

And eventually, Andy had to give up Cub Scouts because he didn't sell enough popcorn, their troop's fundraiser. No one in his neighborhood could afford the skyrocketed prices of caramel and cheese corn mixes.

A light died in his chest and he glanced at the graphic again. This time, everything screamed "wrong" about it—the font choice, the color palette, the alignment of the text.

"You okay, dude?"

Griffith's loud voice pulled him away from the screen. A bell tinkled as a couple in brightly colored outfits entered the shop.

"Fine, yeah. Just realized I have a lot to do." Andy forced a smile.

Miracles did happen, because Griffith appeared to get the hint. He nodded and scooped up his drink in one hand. "The director for my next show just came in. Probably should talk some details over with her." He clapped a beefy hand on Andy's shoulder. Throbs of pain pulsed in his shoulder blade. "See you next Tuesday at basketball."

With that, Griffith bounded off his chair and droplets of coffee spilled down his cup.

Andy exhaled and glimpsed the graphic once more. Nowhere near perfect. He'd have to spend hours more on this. Why couldn't they have picked a graphic designer who didn't have a deadbeat dad for this assignment?

He minimized the tab for the graphic and his leg banged the coffee table in front of him when he saw a new email pop into his inbox... from his mother.

His teeth ripped off some skin from his bottom lip and his mouse hovered over the email for a moment. Tightness seized his chest when he clicked it.

Hi, Andy,

I hope this email finds you well. You haven't been great about answering text messages, so I thought I would try you here.

Although I would never want to cause you any distress, I must say that I was very sad not to see you at Easter this past year. I'd debated about sending this message. But Pastor Moses at my church says we should go directly to those who have caused us any hurt instead of talking about it with others.

All to say, I know you'd mentioned being busy with work. This did catch me by surprise, however, because you've made it to all the Easter gatherings in the past. I couldn't help but think you avoided this one because it would be the two of us, without any extended family present.

I know it's a lot to ask you to drive all this way, but even if you can't visit any time soon, I'd love to have a phone call, to talk about what's caused this rift between us.

Forgive me for being dramatic, but after your father left, any time someone stops communicating with me, I cannot help but assume the worst.

Let me know what you think.

Love you, always,

Mom

Itchiness covered his eyeballs. He shut his eyelids to prevent any tears from sneaking out.

I'm so sorry, Mom. I didn't mean to become like Dad.

Guilt bubbled in his abdomen until his stomach seared. He grimaced and opened his eyes.

"You've done everything for me," he whispered, "and I couldn't return the favor."

With a sigh, he clicked shut his laptop.

Maisie was right about me holding off on going on a date with Caroline. If I'm anything like my dad, I'll leave nothing but destruction in my wake.

Chapter Thirteen

CAROLINE TAPPED THE STEERING WHEEL IN time to the rhythm, humming along to an upbeat worship song. Her headlights swept over the roads, finally snow-free after the rain earlier that day turned the last of it to puddles.

She recalled Wyatt's hug before she left and smiled. She'd have to go back to see him again—ask how the test went. Though she didn't expect perfect results overnight, hopefully he would be able to answer at least a few questions without freezing up, and next time even more.

Her phone buzzed in her purse. At a stoplight, she pulled out the device and glanced at the screen.

Clark Knox: Srry got busy. Idea might work. Bring illustrator tmrw.

Caroline stared at the text until someone honked behind her. She dropped the phone and lurched forward, the light now green.

The text didn't give much detail, but maybe he wasn't completely upset. She and Andy had a chance tomorrow to convince him. If Andy had any sketches.

As soon as she pulled into the apartment complex's parking lot, she tapped out a message to Andy.

Caroline: Mr. Knox wants both of us to come in tomorrow. Would you be able to?

The answer was swift.

Andy: Sure. What time?

She glanced at the clock on her dashboard. She always arrived extra early, but it wasn't fair to do that to Andy. His artist lifestyle probably led to a different sleep schedule than hers.

Caroline: Is 8:30 too early?

She got out of the car and shut the door behind her. The phone buzzed again.

Andy: Works for me.
Caroline: Good, I'll see you at the Helping Hope office.

She took a deep breath, formulating her request politely. If he suffered from too much pressure, like Wyatt, maybe he needed a bit more understanding from her. *Not everyone deals with stress by creating ten-page proposals complete with statistics to go with their children's book manuscript.* Had she gone overboard?
Maybe a little.

Caroline: I know I gave you a tight deadline on the sketches. Do you think you'll have time to do a couple before then?

Inside the building, her phone buzzed again. She paused in the hall to check her phone, wrinkling her nose at the stench of someone on the floor cooking what smelled like week-old cabbage.

Andy: I have a few, but they're pretty rough. Not final at all. But hopefully enough to give Clark an idea.

Caroline's eyebrows rose. He must have been working hard today if he had nothing this morning and more than one now. And knowing Andy and his perfectionistic tendencies, his "pretty rough" would be what someone else would call "nearly done."

She hesitated. Artists and creatives could hold unfinished projects close to the heart—she should know. But her curiosity won out.

Caroline: That will be great. Can I see one of them?

She dug her keys out of her purse and shoved the right one into the lock of her apartment door, giving the handle the special jerk that allowed the bolt to slide.

The door opened, and the cabbage smell from the hall hit her full in the face. She dropped her phone in her purse and clapped a hand over her nose, illustrations forgotten. *What is that?*

"Caroline?" Liv's voice carried from the kitchen.

Caroline tossed her purse on the entry table and slung her coat over the rack, burying her nose back in her sleeve. "Liv? Are you...cooking something?"

She stepped into their kitchen to see Liv with spatula in hand, squinting in consternation at a green slimy mass in a pan. "Does this look right to you?"

"Depends. What are you trying to make?" *Poison?*

"It's this Irish-Korean fusion cabbage dish I saw on Pinterest. I bought a head of cabbage and cooked it a couple weeks ago so I could use it later for the actual recipe, but I forgot about it." She poked at the mass. "It was a little squishy, but I figured it would get floppy when I cooked it again anyway."

Caroline tried to cover her mouth, but the giggles escaped anyway. "So I was half right. Someone is cooking *two*-week-old cabbage."

Liv snorted. "Maybe not my best idea, but it was worth a shot. What do you mean you were half right?"

"I could smell it out in the hall." She burst into laughter. "It's *awful.*"

Liv dissolved in giggles. "Oh, no, I stunk up the entire floor?" A slimy bubble popped in the pan, and she clutched her middle, laughing harder. "I think I may have created a monstrosity."

"You made *Flubber*."

They cackled until tears welled in Liv's eyes and Caroline had to gasp for breath.

Liv grabbed the pan. "This is going straight into the trash."

"No!" Caroline blocked her path in horror. "There's no way you're putting that in the trash. The entire apartment will smell for days—well, even more than it already will."

"Then what am I supposed to do with it?" Liv spun toward her.

Caroline squeaked and ducked back from a splash of glop that sloshed over the edge of the pan. "Not throw it on *me*."

Liv broke down in snort laughs. "My cooking literally stinks."

Caroline groaned. "That was just bad. Maybe put it down the garbage disposal?"

Her roommate dumped the pan into the sink and turned on the water. Then she flipped the switch for the garbage disposal and began shoving cabbage down the drain with the spatula.

The water seemed to bring out the smell even more strongly. Caroline made a choking noise.

Then the garbage disposal gurgled, ground, and began shaking the entire sink. "What in the…" Liv leaned over to take a closer look.

The sink spluttered, throwing up green gunk. The slime splatted against Liv's face. She screamed. Caroline gasped.

"Papertowelpapertowelpapertowel!" Liv screeched.

Caroline ripped a handful off the roll and shoved them at Liv.

Liv shrieked and laughed simultaneously, swiping goop from her face.

Once the gunk was all finally shoved down the disposal and Liv had scrubbed her face, Caroline called for delivery pizza.

They collapsed into the chairs at the table, breathing hard from giggling. "Still love cooking?" Caroline asked.

"Of course." Liv waved a hand. "A minor setback." She pointed a finger at Caroline. "You don't have to be *good* at something to love it, you know. As long as you realize you're going to epically fail every once in a while and that's okay."

Caroline blinked. "That was...pretty deep, Liv."

"Eh." Liv shrugged, adjusting her bun that had mostly fallen out during the fiasco. "More importantly, how was your date?"

Caroline's smile fell. Right. Liv thought she had been with Andy. "Well. I didn't actually go on a date."

Liv sat up. "What? Why not?"

Caroline recounted her day of disasters—Andy's lack of sketches, her fall, Mr. Knox's disappointment. "So, instead, I went to the Hope Club to hang out with some of the kids."

"I'm glad you saw the kiddos, but girl, I thought you liked this guy. And I was sure he liked you, a lot." Liv frowned. "Why do you think he didn't get the sketches to you?"

Caroline puffed out a breath. "I did give him a tight deadline. And after working with one of the kids at the Hope Club, I'm wondering if Andy kind of...froze up. He's a perfectionist. I might have been too hard on him." She raised an eyebrow at Liv's smirk. "What?"

"I don't know, I just sense some anger simmering down and being replaced by a 'gonna give the guy another chance.'" A knock sounded on the door, and Liv stood. "I'll get it."

While Liv went to get the pizza, Caroline looked down at her cell. A notification still hovered over her text message app. *Andy.* She'd asked to see his sketches, then forgotten all about it during the cabbage debacle.

She opened the message and tapped on the images. Her breath caught.

Liv strutted in balancing a pizza box like a butler. "Our dinner, madam."

Caroline barely looked up as Liv slid the box onto the table. "They're gorgeous," she breathed.

"The pizza?"

"No." Caroline turned her phone around. "These illustrations. I just realized I haven't seen Andy's artwork before. Nothing besides the caricatures."

Liv's eyes widened. Caroline saw her gaze flick over the color swatches, the graceful lines, a style somewhere between impressionism and realism. "He's good."

"It fits the book perfectly." Caroline turned the phone back around. "It's about real kids, real people, but still full of hope, that little bit of whimsy."

"This book is going to be gorgeous."

"Now that he has sketches and I have the manuscript, we can plot out what drawings will go with what text, how we'll do the page breaks, what the kids will look like…" Caroline tore her gaze away from the phone and looked back up at Liv. "You know, I think it was worth the wait."

Liv plopped down in a chair and smirked. "Knox can't possibly say no."

Caroline grinned back. "I'm looking forward to that meeting tomorrow."

Andy bumped his leg against the conference table when he heard a knock at the door. He and Caroline swiveled around in their rolling chairs and found Clark at the door. The man's greasy face shone in the lights, eyes the size of basketballs.

Okay, maybe golf balls, but Andy prayed he'd never see that much white in the man's eyeballs ever again.

Clark waved a phone and then slicked his palm across his scalp.

"Hope I'm not interrupting. My sister sent some wonderful pictures of my niece." He motioned to the whiteboard full of Caroline's green Expo scrawlings. "Figured it may help with the inspiration for your book."

Outside the large, open glass windows to the conference room, Caroline's coworkers scuttled in and out of cubicles. One, with a coffee cup in hand, spilled some on her thumb, yelped, and tried to suction off the liquid from her finger.

Eyebrows raised, Caroline cleared her throat. "Oh, umm, not at all. We'd love to see the pictures."

A bounce in his step sent Clark bounding their way. Caroline and Andy were seated two chairs apart, to, as Maisie would say, "keep the Holy Spirit between them." Not that it really mattered in that fishbowl of a conference room anyway. A different person in a different suit ambled past every minute.

Besides, Caroline had turned him down for the previous date. She probably *wanted* to keep things professional between them.

When Clark reached the space between their seats, he swiped through a number of photos. His niece, in a tutu and wearing a unicorn hat on her head, grinned at the camera as she clung to monkey bars in a park. A gap between her teeth showed.

Caroline's features softened and she clutched a hand to her heart. "She's adorable."

Clark beamed and shoved the phone into his black slacks' pockets. "Her name's Irina. My sister and her husband adopted her from Russia." He rested his back against the whiteboard, and an Expo marker clattered to the gray carpet.

Neither Caroline nor Andy moved to pick it up. That would involve fishing around Clark's sleek black shoes.

"Irina's part of the reason why I started Helping Hope." Clark folded his arms and stared at a fluorescent light on the ceiling. "Although she got to live in a wonderful home, so many kids don't."

Outside the conference room, Zinnia halted with a water cup in hand. She leaned against the side of a cubicle and waved at them. Then she pressed the paper cup to her lips. Andy thought he recalled a water cooler that bubbled near the conference room.

Zinnia squinted at something, perhaps the whiteboard.

A number of people had done that earlier. Confused as to why two people had taken up the conference room, he guessed.

Then Zinnia smiled once more, drained the glass, and disappeared from sight.

"Anyway." With a grunt, Clark shoved himself from the wall and almost crashed into a swivel chair in front of him. He composed himself and marched toward the door. "I figured you two could use a lot of inspiration." His heels skidded on the carpet when he halted at the entrance. "There's a lot riding on this, Miss Penn. Irina wants a signed copy of the book. Make sure it's worth keeping on her shelf."

Clark and his blazing red tie disappeared from the room.

Phone rings and a peal of muffled laughter sounded from outside the door.

Caroline exhaled, tucked a flyaway strand behind her ear, and shoved her chair back.

"You know..." She massaged her left shoulder. Andy hadn't realized his had gone tight too when Clark had entered. He couldn't imagine the chiropractic bills Caroline had accrued in this position due to stress. "I haven't seen Clark like that before."

"Greasy and having unrealistic expectations for all his workers?"

She clapped a hand to her mouth to stifle a laugh and eyed the door. For once, no one was stationed in front of the windows. Then two workers in ties came into view and stopped to chat about something. Andy caught spare bits of words like "football game" and "Sunday."

"No." She stood and grabbed an eraser from the silver tray on the whiteboard. "He doesn't mention too many details about personal life."

The board squeaked when she moved the eraser in circles.

Andy rose and got to work on the other side of the board.

After a minute or so, they'd removed the green markings from the board. The dizzying smell of Expo marker clogged his nose.

"Thanks." Caroline capped the green marker they'd used, placed the drawing utensil on the silver marker-holder, and slumped into her seat. "I should bring you to work more often. Anyone outside of Helping Hope doesn't believe me when I talk about how," she leaned in and whispered, "crazy Clark can be sometimes."

Andy snorted and returned to his seat. "I've worked with some interesting graphic design clients, but I think Clark tops the list for most eccentric. Although there was that one time a lady tried to pay me for a job by giving me all the coupons she'd been collecting for months."

He regaled her with the tale of "coupon lady."

Much as he loved a three for the price of two deal on ground beef, he had to explain to a disgruntled woman, who wore a large purple coat with embroidered peacock designs, that his website had clearly stated cash, check, or PayPal in terms of payment.

Caroline grinned. "She sounds perfect for Clark. When can we set them up?"

"Ha, well if I had enough money for a lawyer, I'd be suing her socks off, because she never did pay me for the job."

She pressed her fingers to her lips, eyes widening. "Oh, no! That's terrible."

He shrugged. "You get used to it in the freelance world. People feel like paying is optional. Doesn't help that I'd spent hours on that project, trying to make sure to get everything just right. The perfectionist in me always adds another few hours, or even days, to a project."

Shoot, speaking of, he hadn't made any more headway on that graphic design project for the father-daughter dance. He needed to finish that to pay for the cell phone bill this month. Too bad he'd spent all of last night on sketch ideas for the book.

Caroline gripped her left elbow with her right hand and swirled her chair to face the lacquered table. Papers scattered the center of the wood, most from Caroline's copious notes she took on book ideas, and one legal pad left behind from one of her coworkers from a previous meeting held there.

Next to the papers sat a brown bag filled with bagels Miss Evie had brought them from Panera for their planning session. He rather liked the woman and thought she and Maisie would get along well and become good friends if they chanced a meeting at a potluck.

Cinnamon still swirled on his tongue from one of the sweeter and crumblier pastries from the bag.

"Speaking of perfectionism." Caroline didn't lift her eyes. "I went to the Club the other day to talk with the kids."

What did that have to do with perfectionism? He scooted his chair closer to the table until the edge punched his stomach. "How was it?"

"Good. There was a kid there that reminded me a lot of you." She inhaled, exhaled. "And reminded me that everyone has different ways they work best." She met his eyes. Like a deep blue of the sky at dusk. He could drown in their beauty forever. Then she pulled her gaze away. "I'm sorry I expected you to be another me."

Warmth crawled up his cheeks when he realized how long he'd continued to stare at her after she'd broken eye contact. He glanced at his hands that were steepled on the table.

"To be honest, Caroline, it's good that you're giving me that extra push. My roommate Elijah sometimes tries to do it, but I need someone to keep me on task. I get too distracted."

She also put her hands on the table. He ignored the itches in his fingertips to hold them.

"I'm also sorry for blowing off coffee. Sometimes, when Clark gives me a bunch of deadlines, I freeze and go into shutdown mode. Liv, my roommate, can tell you plenty of times I've cancelled plans last minute because of work tasks."

He knew that icy feeling that filled his chest when he saw an email come in with last-minute corrections from a client. How often had he, too, skipped out on basketball or other commitments because he had to meet a quick deadline?

Her thumbs whirled around each other. "How about we try to schedule coffee again? It might be good to meet with you to talk about something other than work."

Warmth filled his ribcage, but ice replaced it seconds later. Would he hurt any chances he had, like Dad did? He tossed up a quick prayer. Peace settled into his chest a moment later.

His lips twitched, but he tried to force them downward. *Play it cool, dude. If you show how excited you are, you might scare her off.*

"Sure." Despite himself, his voice still quavered. "That sounds great."

Chapter Fourteen

CAROLINE PACED, CLUTCHING RABBIT TO HER chest. The hamster nuzzled her hand, hoping for more treats. Caroline pulled a carrot stick out of her pocket and held it for her pet to gnaw, thoughts spinning.

A date. A date. I asked him on a date.

Her outfit didn't feel right. Usually for big events, she knew how to dress. Business formal, business casual, cocktail, anything.

She didn't know how to dress for a coffee date.

Mom had prepared her to succeed in business and society. She'd raised Caroline to conquer the world. And men were just a distraction. Hence, Kristy Penn had married later in life, to a man who had his own career to worry about.

Caroline scowled. She didn't want to think about Mom right now.

She settled on fitted jeans, a cream long-sleeved shirt offset by a lightweight brown infinity scarf, and short, flat matching brown boots. It was something Liv would wear—though Liv would add more jewelry—and Liv was the most stylish person Caroline knew.

She decided to forgo her usual tight bun, but now she worried about a static fiasco like at the fundraiser.

Too late now. She put Rabbit back in her hamster palace and headed for the door.

Mr. Knox had kicked everyone out of the office early for the weekend, an unusual display of magnanimity, so Caroline had gone home to change, see Rabbit, and eat something a bit more substantial than she was likely to find at a coffee place. She didn't think they would serve chicken and kale salad.

That's because no self-respecting, God-fearing human should eat kale, Liv would say.

The planning session in the conference room had gone well. Really well. Andy had wonderful ideas for illustrations to go with her prose. And his artwork...

It hit some soft, nostalgic part of her soul.

There's no need to be anxious. It's just Andy. Andy the dog-loving, mural-painting, slow-smiling man who turned planning sessions into volunteering. She had no reason to be nervous because of him.

Then why these absurd butterflies?

The bell over the door jingled fifteen minutes later as Caroline stepped into the coffee shop, nervously clutching the handles of the handbag on her shoulder. Her eyes darted over the calligraphy wall, the wooden counter, the fake fireplace, and the assortment of chairs, tables, and couches. Instrumental worship music floated from the speakers while a low hum of conversation from scattered customers buzzed underneath. Quiet, but not too quiet. Homey.

She spotted Andy at a table near the fake fireplace and her heart picked up speed. He seemed distracted watching the flickering projection of a fire, giving her a moment to compose herself. He'd put on something more casual since their office meeting as well, a nice green shirt and jeans. Good. She fit the dress code of a coffee date, it seemed.

She couldn't quite bring herself to move her feet forward, so instead she noticed how the Edison bulbs hanging from the ceiling cast a glow over his cheekbones, the way his hair was getting slightly too long and brushing the top of his ear. For a moment, she thought about how she would describe him in her novel. She pictured him in scale armor, spear in hand. No, that didn't quite fit. He would probably be an archer. Corselet, greaves, arrows at his right and a sword on his left hip. Maybe her protagonist needed a love interest.

She blinked. *What am I thinking? I am not writing Andy into my novel.*

No history of the Eastern Roman Empire. Expunge Constantine and Justinian from your mind. Be normal.

Andy looked up from the fire, and their gazes met. His eyes

widened for a moment, glancing at her outfit, then he raised a hand in greeting. She forced her feet forward, and he stood to meet her.

"Hey." His fingers fiddled with the back of his chair. Was he nervous too? "Long time no see."

She snorted at his lame joke. "It might surprise you, but I didn't bring any notes or proposals this time."

His shoulders relaxed a bit. *He's definitely nervous too.* Somehow that made her feel better. He squinted at her in mock suspicion. "Are you sure you're not hiding a notepad in your purse?"

"Well, I do always carry one just in case."

He laughed. "Want to get something to drink? I recommend anything but the matcha."

They went to the counter to order drinks, then headed back to the table. Caroline sat, cupping the warm mug in her hands and appreciating the design on the top of her latte. She would probably regret the caffeine this late in the day later, but at least tomorrow was Saturday.

"Okay, I have to know," she blurted. "What got you into art? How did you settle on your style? I know it's *kind of* work related, but..."

He grinned. "Art isn't work. Well, it is, but it's a passion first. It's probably the same thing with your writing."

"True." She went into publishing and editing because she wanted to be surrounded by words all the time. "Tell me all about it, then."

His gaze unfocused, as if he was looking into the distance. "I was young. It was cathartic, I guess. I would come home after school or sit at the kitchen table after chores and pull out a beat-up sketchbook and draw for an hour or two to unwind. I could draw anything I wanted— the world like I thought it should be."

He took a sip of coffee, head tilted in thought. "Originally, I did it for my mom. I wanted to make her happy and give her pretty things that would make her smile after my dad left. That's when it started, I think." He looked down, flushing. "I guess that was too much information."

Caroline bit her lip. He began drawing for his mom. *That couldn't be more wholesome and adorable.* "Not at all. Thank you for sharing."

He cleared his throat. "Anyway. I went to school for art, kind of developed all sorts of different styles there. You have to if you want to make a job out of it—graphic design, digital art, everything. But I always liked impressionism. It looks senseless up close, but when you lean back, it makes something beautiful. I thought it would fit this project. Something not quite perfect, but still good."

"All those little pieces. Like mosaics." She giggled. "Whoops. Are we talking about work again?"

"Nope, our passions." He grinned. "Exactly like mosaics. I can't tell you how long I've spent looking at Byzantine mosaics. All those tiny pieces adding up to the whole..."

Byzantine? No way. Caroline leaned forward. "Do you have a favorite?"

"Christ Pantocrantor, in the Hagia Sophia," he answered immediately. "I love the detail, even in what looks at first like a plain background. I can pull it up on my phone if you want."

"No need. I'm very familiar with Byzantine art. I'm... I'm kind of writing a novel set in the early Byzantine era right now."

His eyes widened. "You're kidding. Your turn. What's your favorite mosaic?"

Conversation ebbed and flowed around them in a warm tide, but Caroline didn't think anyone could be as delighted in their exchange as she felt in this moment.

"You're going to think I'm basic, but it's the one of Justinian in the Basilica of San Vitale. I'm an early Byzantine gal."

"Not my favorite, but I can see what you like about it. I prefer late Byzantine."

"We'll have to agree to disagree." She smirked.

He leaned back, shaking his head, and smiled. "Who would have thought? What about you? What got you into writing?"

"Nothing as noble as cheering up my mom." She grimaced. "Actually, my mom was the opposite of cheered. She thought I was wasting my time. Books were always my escape from school pressure and competitions and transcript building... I guess when you read long enough, you start wanting to write stories of your own."

"So you're writing a Byzantine novel. What's it about?" He held up a finger. "And I don't mean that sort of vague 'it's historical with some battles and stuff.' I've had writer friends—I know how it goes." He leaned forward. "I want the exciting version, full details."

Her heart swelled. No one ever cared about her stories. Even Liv only politely tolerated her rants about plot and characters and conflict. "You're really ready for this?"

"I'm all ears."

I should go on dates more often. All the time. She met his warm brown eyes, grinned, and launched into her story.

Andy's heart soared like a balloon in his ribcage.

As he entered the doors of his apartment complex, he thought that if someone had filled him with any more helium, he might lift away.

Caroline liked the Byzantine era too. And Impressionism. If he hadn't left his mother's ring she'd given to him years back, "for the one," at her house, he might've popped the question right there in the middle of the coffee shop.

He held onto the door handle to steady himself and bring his soul to earth.

Next to him, a neighbor spun his combination on the apartment mailboxes. If you could call them that. They sat in neat square rows, all decadent in metal and mini spin-combo locks.

Ideas brimmed in his skull with the possibilities for the front cover. Since Caroline liked Impressionism and Byzantine art—which used tiles and dots to form a complete picture—he could create an image made up of pieces, like a mosaic. All the broken pieces that formed a masterpiece.

When he went to spin his lock combo on mailbox 12, memories raced.

Back in college, his Art Appreciation gen ed course took them to the Cleveland Art Museum. He remembered sitting on a wooden bench in front of a Monet painting of water lilies. Blurry and delicate white flowers floated atop a lavender-hued pond.

The closer he leaned in, the more imperfections he saw. A brushstroke that went too far, a rumpled streak of white. But the farther back he inclined, the clearer the painting became.

That's what he loved about Impressionism. It turned imperfect pieces into something, well, perfect.

Nothing like the straight lines and shapes of the computer-generated illustrations that appeared on every picture book he spotted in shops. No, the kids needed something perfect and imperfect at the same time.

The lock to his mailbox clicked, and the small square door opened. By now, the neighbor had retrieved the magazine stuffed into his small spot, given him a curt nod, and headed for the stairs. Stacks of envelopes greeted Andy, and his stomach sank with rocks.

This would bring him to earth.

He used to love going to the mailbox, back in his college days when people sent him more physical checks for freelance projects. But now, with online payment methods, most of the paper in the mail presented itself in the form of bills and advertisements for local plumbers.

Sure enough, "Peter Plumber" advertised his business on neon pink cardstock. The rest of the mail, all in sad white envelopes, had red stamped on them either "second notice" or "final notice."

With a sigh, he held the heavy letters and slammed the door to his mailbox shut.

Seconds later, the aftertaste of coffee swirled over his tongue and memories from the shop flooded him once more as he traversed the stairs. Confidence surged and he bounded up the last two steps.

Once he reached his apartment and swung open the door, he squinted in the dark contrast of light.

Huh, weird. Usually by this time Elijah had returned and binged some new show on TV. Or he'd be playing a video game with friends. Instead, darkness blanketed the apartment.

Andy set the mail down on the kitchen counter and flipped on a light switch.

Dishes from earlier in the day rested in the sink. He grabbed a blue sponge and soaked it with green dish soap. Bubbles formed on his fingertips when he squeezed it.

Andy flicked on the tap and warm water seared the scrambled egg residue on the pan he held. He glanced up and into the family room and dropped the dish. The metallic bang of the vessel hitting the sink echoed in the apartment.

In the family room, the couch nearly consumed Elijah's body. A single book perched on his forehead, obscuring his face. Strange, Elijah didn't like to read.

"Sorry, bro, didn't see you there."

Elijah bolted up. The book slid to the floor and landed in a butterfly position. Elijah rubbed his eyes and peered into the kitchen. Recognition softened his features moments later.

"Hi-ya, Andy." The last syllable got caught on a yawn. Elijah stretched his arms wide as they could go, an impressive wingspan.

"You don't really seem like the kind of guy to read on weekends."

Usually, Elijah had a guys' night out with men from his church on Fridays. Andy could tell when he returned because the scent of hot wings would fill the apartment. They always had plenty of leftovers, not that Andy would complain. Hot wings dipped in ranch didn't sound like too shabby a lunch for Saturdays.

Elijah's lip sagged, and he hunched over to grab the book. Once he retrieved it, he flashed the cover at Andy. Even in the dark haze of the kitchen lighting, Andy could make out the big block letters.

50 Ways to Get a Job

Cold awareness ran down Andy's spine.

"Did you..." He set his sponge down in the sink, next to the still-eggy pan. "Did you get fired?"

"Let go." Elijah slumped into the cushion and placed the book on the carpet. This time, he ensured to close the binding. "I thought my boss had finished the cuts before Easter, but I guess he decided to hold off on the rest of the layoffs until after the holidays. 'More humane.'" He tossed up air quotes with his fingers.

Next to the couch and book sat a box full of office supplies.

Yeesh, so they'd made the workers literally pack up their desks into a single cardboard receptacle, like Andy had seen in all the movies.

Elijah braided his fingers and placed them on his abdomen. "I've been searching for jobs for the past few hours, but it seems most companies hired before Easter. Probably to beat the rush of when college students graduate and join the mix of applications."

Yowza, Andy remembered that madness from four years back.

As soon as he had a diploma, he applied for two-hundred graphic design jobs, including ones in other states, and two or three overseas. Not a single one asked him for an interview. He'd subsisted on freelance gigs.

Praise the Lord his college roommate stuck with him ever since to help him split the rent.

Until, well, now.

Andy's gaze flicked to the envelopes stacked on the counter, next to a flour stain left over from when Elijah attempted to make homemade brownies the other night. "I'm sure something will turn up. If not, you'll become a famous musician and sell platinum albums."

A one-note laugh warbled in Elijah's throat.

"Yeah. Sure. But hey, you're going to become a bestseller and make us a million dollars, right, roomie?"

Although his voice dripped with jesting, sparks of hope had filled Elijah's pupils—at least, from what Andy could tell from his position in the kitchen.

Shoot—the book.

Not only did they have to write that for the kids, but now, for his roommate as well, to cover their rent.

Besides, Clark wouldn't pay him for the job in full until they presented him with a finished product. Caroline had explained the fascinating publishing process when he'd walked her to her car.

"Most publishers only give you half of the advance up front, to have some security, in case they never get the final book. I read a publisher's blog the other day about an author who didn't deliver a final manuscript for over ten years."

He understood. Really, he did.

In fact, he remembered that his mom, during his freshman year of high school, knew of a handyman in their neighborhood looking for work. Although they couldn't even afford to put meat on the table most weeks, she paid him upfront for some services—fixing their leaky u-bend in their sink, repairing a crack in the ceiling.

But he never showed his face in their house once. Weeks later, he moved into an apartment with his girlfriend in another town.

Now every part of Andy wished he hadn't dawdled so much on the illustrations. Had he dedicated several hours each day to the project, he may have had most of the work done by now. When he wanted to, he could work fast. In fact, once in college, his art professor gave his class one hour to do an illustration.

Dr. Klimt said Andy, by far, had created the most advanced and complex image out of the entire class when the hour expired.

All because she'd put him on a timer. That ferocious beast of a clock spurred him to create well under pressure.

His glance roved from the letters, to Elijah, and then to the satchel he'd placed on the ground.

"Right, roomie." Andy dried his hands on a dishtowel and reached into his bag for his computer. "Because I'm going to finish that book, no matter what."

Chapter Fifteen

CAROLINE STARED AT THE EMAIL PULLED up on her phone.

The world around her seemed to spin as she gripped her steering wheel, sitting in the apartment's parking lot. The buoyant feeling from after the date had gone, popped like a bubble by a needle.

She knew what Helping Hope's finances looked like. It was part of her job. But she hadn't expected this solution from the board.

Helping Hope's publishing branch has created a significant drain on company resources, with little financial return on investment. Once the largest source of revenue for our charitable programs, our publishing venture now provides less than half of income, while employing our highest number of staffers.

As of next quarter, Helping Hope will begin downsizing our publishing branch and rebranding as a charity rather than a publisher. After currently contracted books are published, we will be acquiring no new titles.

The email went on to explain, in fluffy terms, that large numbers of employees would be laid off. No more spending money on publishing. Donor funding only.

Caroline's job should be safe—she mostly worked in PR and donor relations, anyway. But any chance of being moved to the publishing branch, becoming a real editor, were dashed.

She had known publishers were struggling, that the glut of half-rate self-published books and desperate authors practically shoving their free books into the hands of anyone willing to read their stories had been hurting publishers more and more for years. She knew it was hard to get anyone to actually pay for a book anymore. But for some naive reason, she'd never imagined Helping Hope *Publishing* would dump their publishing branch, their entire mission of funding charitable missions through providing hope-filled literature.

Her book with Andy would still be published, but what then? She'd come no closer to becoming a novelist, or an editor, or a publishing professional than the day she walked across the stage with her diploma.

Her mind drifted back to the coffee shop, to Andy's eyes sparkling as he told her about his favorite Impressionist artists, to him leaning forward as she mapped out the plot twists in her novel to him like a crazed conspiracy theorist. They had stayed long after finishing their drinks. For a while, like two dreamers swapping ideas, she'd forgotten the impossibility of it all.

Now reality crashed in. She was a writer with no book, and he was an artist who subsisted on random graphic design gigs that couldn't possibly be fulfilling, not with his level of talent.

Her mind went back to the email from Mom's friend Darlene Winters. She could return to New York. A job waited for her, a pathway to the New York legal scene. Starting over, going back to school for law, would be so easy, with the way paved for her. Schooling and tests certainly would pose no issue. Academics never had. Because that was her secret.

She'd bombed three SATs and two ACTs—on purpose.

It had nearly killed her high-achieving, people-pleasing heart to fill in the wrong bubbles. Not too many wrong—that would be suspicious. But she'd done plenty of research on which schools required what scores and calculated how many questions she should get wrong to score well under the twenty-fifth percentile of the least selective of her mother's preferred schools.

She hadn't intended to *continue* bombing them. Just a couple, enough to get her mother's attention. She'd only wanted to hear those words she'd been longing for all her life. *It's okay. I still love you no matter what.*

Mom never said that. Instead, as Caroline had dreaded but

predicted, Mom only grew angrier, more distant. Any words of affection dried up the moment the first scores arrived, any tenderness Mom had once shown when Caroline was the perfect daughter. Then Caroline had known.

Her mother didn't love her. She loved success, and her prize-winning daughter was only another feather in her illustrious cap.

So she bombed the tests, applied for the school *she* wanted, and walked out of the house after she turned eighteen, never to return.

Until recently.

As if summoned by thoughts of home, her phone rang. She jumped, and her heart thudded as she looked at the Caller ID. Dad.

She tapped the button and held the phone to her ear, staring at a flickering streetlight. "Hey, Dad. Is everything okay?"

"You texted and asked how your mom was earlier. I figured it would be easier to call you."

Right. She had done that. It felt like something a halfway decent daughter would do, regardless of Mom's attitude. She texted her dad every few days to check in, but the answer remained always the same. *Doing fine, just resting.* But for Kristy Penn, that was a contradictory statement. If she were fine, she wouldn't be resting. Not for a moment.

"Has something happened?" Caroline asked.

"Nothing bad. Your mom is the same, getting rest, doing fine. But we've decided to head to Ohio, like we were talking about before. Get out of New York." He hesitated. "We'll be there by next week, if you want to visit. We could even meet you halfway, for lunch or something."

She bit her lip. "I'm on deadline right now, so…"

"I understand if you can't get away. I just thought I'd let you know." She heard the smile in his voice. "And I wanted to hear your voice. It's been a while since we talked."

Her heart warmed. "It's always good to hear from you too, Dad."

"How is the book going?"

"Pretty good, actually." She fiddled with her keys, realizing that she'd been sitting in her car in the dark for longer than she intended. Liv would tell her that wasn't safe. "We have the manuscript, and the illustrator...he's good. Like, *really* good."

"That's great to hear."

A moth skittered along her windshield, probably heading for the guttering streetlight.

"Yeah." She tapped her fingertips against the steering wheel, debating. "I went on a date today."

"A date? With who?"

"The illustrator, actually."

Silence stretched for a few painful seconds. "I thought you said he was annoying and disorganized."

"Well." She winced. "Yeah, I thought so, at first. I mean, he is disorganized. But he's not annoying, and..." She remembered Andy's brilliant smile as he walked her to her car. "It was a really good date, I think."

"He's a freelancer, right? An artist? That doesn't sound like a very steady job."

"Dad..."

"Is he a Christian? Does he have a criminal record? Mom could probably dig it up—"

"Dad!"

He chuckled. "What? Only looking out for you." She could picture his smirk. "I knew it wouldn't be long after hearing how much he got under your skin."

"What?" Caroline sat up straighter. "What is that supposed to mean?"

"You told me at least ten times how much this young man drove you crazy while you were here." His voice lowered to a mock-whisper. "I'll tell you a secret. That's how I knew your mom was smitten. She wouldn't stop talking about how much she hated me." He laughed. "You're just like her."

Her stomach clenched. She was just like Mom? "Mom didn't like you?"

"She did like me. That was exactly the problem."

Caroline shoved a hand through her hair. "That makes no sense."

"Ah, Carrie-girl. This brings back memories. You're both so driven, you hate distractions. Especially of the male variety. And when someone finally does manage to distract you, it drives you crazy. Like this illustrator of yours."

She snorted, but she knew a dopey grin had spread across her face anyway. "Fine. Maybe you're right."

The grin faded. She did like Andy. A lot. But if she would be leaving soon, heading back to New York and leaving behind her disastrous attempt at a publishing career, it wasn't fair to anyone to get attached.

Only one problem with that.

"He asked me if I wanted to go with him tomorrow to an arboretum where he gets a lot of his inspiration." She plunged ahead. "I said yes, but I don't think we'll be there for too long. It shouldn't get in the way of work, and I'm ahead on things at the office, and—"

"Whoa, whoa." Dad laughed. "You don't have to make excuses to me." His tone sobered. "I want you to be happy, Caroline."

Her chest squeezed. "Thanks, Dad."

"But if he does anything wrong, you know where to find me."

Caroline laughed.

He sounded happier. Less tired. She knew everything with Mom had taken a toll on him, and hearing that heaviness gone, if only for a moment, warmed her heart.

She wouldn't tell him about Helping Hope. About her failure in publishing, or about Darlene. Right now, she wasn't even going to think about how she would need to pull away from Andy and start preparing Liv for the possibility that she might have to go back to New York.

Oh, Liv.

Tears burned behind her eyes, but she refused to let them fall.

"Don't worry," she said. "I know exactly where to find you."

Andy stifled a yawn behind the back of his hand as he and Caroline passed by some colorful red flowers at the Arboretum. Why on earth had he stayed up until four in the morning working on illustrations for the book?

And why on earth did he decide it was a good idea to proceed with the date with Caroline after getting only four hours of sleep?

He rubbed low-hanging bags underneath his eyes as he and Caroline strolled by a pond.

At one end, waterfalls cascaded over large boulders. At the center of the waters, he spotted pink-petaled flowers bobbing between lily pads. Waterlilies, like the Monet painting at the museum.

You only have yourself to blame, Andy.

Eager during yesterday's coffee date, he had asked Caroline if she wanted to meander in his favorite arboretum, a place in which he often drew inspiration for sketches and side projects. But perhaps he should've waited a few more days. Did he rush the timing? He knew she had a crazy busy schedule but figured she, like most in the corporate world, had weekends free.

Now, though, as he glimpsed her in his periphery, he noticed she kept her eyes on the winding stone path and her hand clasped around her elbow. Everything in the gesture said, "I don't want to be here."

And he couldn't blame her.

With the deadlines looming over them like a magnificent Michigan spring thundercloud, how could they have chosen—how could he have chosen—to take yet another day off to look at flowers?

Ten feet away, near a patch of bright pink tulips, a couple posed for photos. The woman on the right, who had beautiful dark skin and coiled curly hair, held up her left hand. A stunning, bright jewel twinkled in the warm afternoon sunlight.

How many bad dates did those two have before they realized they were perfect for each other?

Caroline had sunk onto a stone bench near the pond and fished into her bag. Ice jolted in his skin. He knew this move. She'd text a friend to bail her out of a mediocre date and give him some excuse for why she had to leave suddenly.

Although Andy didn't have much savvy when it came to dates, Elijah had given him all the tips on body language and red flags. "If she leans forward, she's interested in the conversation. Picks up a so-called 'phone call,' she wants to bail."

Caroline met Andy's eye and stopped her excavation for a second.

"Liv told me to check in with her every half hour or so, just to make sure I'm safe. I've heard some wacky stories from friends about their dates that went horribly wrong."

What a good friend. Whenever Elijah and Andy both went out of the apartment, they'd make sure to text the other one when they'd returned safely. Still, half an hour did seem excessive. Did Liv think he was an ax murderer or something?

She clicked a button on the side of the phone and placed an index finger on her bottom lip, as if intrigued.

"Sorry, missed a call from Liv. Better get this." Maybe it was the way her voice shot up an octave, but something told Andy that Liv did not, in fact, call. Truth or not, he couldn't tell, because Caroline bustled over to a greenhouse stationed at the end of the path. The interior held various plants and a netted butterfly exhibit, attached to the end of the house. Caroline disappeared inside the doors.

Andy's stomach plummeted, and he dropped onto the bench.

Ripples from the waterfall did little to block out his thoughts. He tried to focus on the lily pads on the water's surface to obscure the word "failure" that seemed to have been etched into his skull.

In an automatic motion, he reached into his pocket to check the notifications from his phone. Pain seared in his stomach when he saw another text from his mom.

Mom: Andy, you know I love you. Please respond.

He'd meant to respond to her email he'd received in the coffee shop on Thursday night. Even drafted a reply. But when his mouse hovered over the send button, his fingers froze.

"Oooh, could we get some pictures by the pond?" The bride-to-be from the photoshoot pointed at the lily pads. Pale pink ruffles on her dress billowed in the light breeze. Her fiancé beside her, a short man with glasses and pale skin, glanced at their photographer. Recognition filled Andy a second later when the photographer dropped the camera from his eye—Ryan, aka Mr. Hollywood, from his basketball team.

Andy slid the phone into his pocket and felt the extra weight of the device tug when he stood. "Ryan, what's up?"

Ryan squinted, and then his features softened. "Sorry, you were standing in the sunlight. Didn't recognize you, dude."

"Not a problem." Andy stepped to the side in hopes this alleviated the sun issue. "You shooting engagement photos now?"

"Yeah. The indie film stuff is more of a side job. This pays the bills." He held up the camera.

The couple posed in front of the lake, the woman lifting her heel at a ninety-degree angle. After a few shots, the fiancé wiped his forehead with his oxford sleeve. Patches of his pale skin had begun to pink. Andy hadn't realized, until now, how much the sun warmed his neck.

Michigan liked to flip from winter to spring like a spatula turning over a pancake, instantaneous and sizzling.

"Sweetheart," the man said, "mind if we take a break? We've been going for over an hour."

She nibbled on her bottom lip for a moment. "Sure. Five minutes." She rested her head on his shoulder and they sat on the bench Andy had just evacuated.

He shoved his hands in his pockets and bobbled back and forth on his heels, eyeing the greenhouse. Caroline hadn't emerged yet. Maybe Liv did actually have to talk to her about something legit, instead of ideas on how to bail the date.

Well, might as well make some new friends.

Andy introduced himself to the couple, while Ryan scanned through his film.

"Diamond." The woman pointed to her ring and herself, and sniggered, like she'd made this joke a thousand times. Then she gestured to the man beside her. "And this is Riley."

Riley gave a curt nod.

"First of all, congrats," Andy said.

Diamond's diamond ring glittered even more in the direct sunlight.

"How long have you two been together?" Andy asked.

"Hmm." Diamond pressed her finger to her lips, in the same motion Caroline had made earlier when she searched for her phone in her bag. "I think it's been a year and eight months, right, sweetie?"

"Mmm."

He took that as a yes.

"Did you two ever"—Andy shrugged to try and play the question casual—"have any rough dates at the start of the relationship?"

"Ooh, no." Diamond waved a finger with her free hand that wasn't clasping Riley's. "It was fireworks from the start." She snuggled further into his shoulder. "And we fall more and more in love each day."

Andy's chin dipped to his chest. *Oh. This date I'm experiencing with Caroline is abnormal. We probably have no chance at staying together.*

Often he had to ditch pursuing a relationship after the first date, because most girls moved too quickly… or in the case of Hadassah, wanted six children. But now, on the other end of the desk… he squeezed his eyes shut.

"Oh, darling, look at that gazebo over there. Let's get pictures under that."

When Andy's eyelids flew open, he watched Diamond help Riley to his feet, and they dashed toward a gazebo featuring Grecian columns, all wrapped in vines. Ryan smirked at them and then looped his camera strap around his shoulder.

"See you at basketball on Tuesday, Andy."

Before Andy even had a chance to nod, Ryan tore down the path toward the couple. All the way to the gazebo, Diamond and Riley held hands and skipped.

Weight from his pocket pulled him toward the bench. Right as he went to sit, he spotted Caroline exit the greenhouse. She still kept her gaze glued to the rocky path before her, all the way to Andy.

"Hey." She gripped her elbow again, shoulders hiking. "Liv really needs me to get to the apartment. There's, umm, a cleaning emergency."

Cleaning emergency? *Come on, Caroline, you're a writer. You can create a better fake excuse than that.*

"Oh, no problem." He shoved his hands into his pockets. Car keys jangled. "Do you want me to walk you to the parking lot?"

"Nope!"

This came out way too fast. Her eyes widened and she cleared her throat. "Sorry, allergies. What I mean is, Liv needs me to call her. Like, immediately. I only hung up because she had to fix a leak." She flashed the phone. "But she needs me to talk her through it. I'll be on the phone the whole time. Sorry." That somehow made even less sense than the cleaning emergency.

"Ha ha, no problem. I hope you two get it fixed."

"Thanks." She waved and then speed-walked down the path toward the parking lot.

He waited until she disappeared. Then he buried his head in his hands.

He'd blown it.

Chapter Sixteen

CAROLINE HAD DEBATED ALL EVENING AND again when she woke up in the morning whether she should call off the arboretum date. If she was giving up and going back to New York, she should nip this in the bud, right?

But she hadn't been able to bring herself to tell Liv she was giving up on publishing. Not yet. Not after Liv's evening the night before.

Caroline had come home to Liv strumming a ukulele in the near-dark, staring into the distance. When she looked up to see Caroline, she gave a forced-looking smile. "Hey, girl. How was the date?"

"It was great." Caroline's brow furrowed, thoughts of New York and Andy flying from her head as she took in Liv's red-tinged eyes. "What happened?"

Liv shrugged, strumming a chord. "Another family let me go. They're moving too, apparently."

Caroline's chest tightened. Why did all of these families need to move right now? She intended to help Liv find a new roommate, of course, someone reliable—she wouldn't up and leave her for New York without warning—but she didn't want to leave her best friend in difficult financial straits. "I'm sorry, Liv."

"I'll find another family." She set the ukulele down. "Enough about that. Tell me about the date."

And because Caroline knew it would cheer up her roommate better than anything else could, she told Liv all about it.

Recounting the evening—and Liv's enthusiastic reactions—had made it even harder to cancel on Andy. So she hadn't. Maybe Andy would turn out not to be such a good guy today or do something that sent up a red flag. Then Caroline wouldn't feel bad ending...whatever this was. She would never have to wonder "what if."

Of course, the insufferable man hadn't had the decency to be indecent.

The sky displayed a glorious shade of blue when she'd arrived at the arboretum. She had been a bit concerned when she saw the dark circles under Andy's eyes when she met him at the entrance, but once he'd explained he had been up late working on the illustrations, her heart had melted.

Sunlight reflected in sparkles off the moisture on budding leaves, while shadows danced along the paths. Andy pointed out the way colors mixed and melded, explaining how it translated to paper or canvas as she asked questions. Despite the circles under his eyes, his face lit up when he talked about art. Maybe it was because he was already telling her about colors and shadows and highlights, but she couldn't drag her eyes away from the way the dappled sunlight played over his features.

His brow suddenly furrowed. "Did you put on sunscreen?"

She thought back, then slapped a hand to her forehead. "No."

He shook his head. "Oof. The sun is out full force today. You're...looking a little red."

She smiled at the way his eyes darted in embarrassment, as if he felt awkward saying anything about her appearance. "Oh! Maybe we should find some shade for a little bit."

"There's a grove of shadier trees this way," he offered.

"Lead on." As she followed, she said, "I've always burned easily. Too pale, I guess."

He grinned. "Can't relate."

She rolled her eyes. "Yeah, yeah. Unfair."

They found a shaded stone bench beneath the trees and sat. Caroline leaned her head back, gazing up through the branches, and took a deep breath. "I don't do this enough."

"Do what?"

She closed her eyes briefly. "Go outside. Spend time away from a desk." She felt a bit of the stress start to melt away. With the rustling branches, water burbling somewhere nearby, and a cool breeze on her cheeks, she could almost forget the stress of Helping Hope shutting down publishing and her dreams of being an editor spiraling down the toilet. Maybe even forget for a moment the possible job awaiting her in New York, ready to accept her as a prodigal child finally called back to the austere halls of law and finance.

She became aware that Andy hadn't replied to that. Caroline opened her eyes and glanced toward him. He was watching her, an odd, soft look in his eyes that made her heart thump.

He saw her looking and glanced away. "I like to come at least every couple weeks, when it's open. It reminds me of the greatest Artist, especially when I'm getting overwhelmed."

Her head tilted. "Did you grow up in the church?"

"Not at first. We would only go every once in a while." He looked up at the waving branches. "But after my dad left, my mom took me all the time. Feels like I grew up there." He looked back at Caroline with a rueful half smile. "I don't know where I would be if it hadn't been for our church. A lot of my friends as a kid didn't have that sort of support, and…our lives were very different by the time high school rolled around." He sobered. "I probably wouldn't be sitting here with you."

Caroline became very aware of their hands resting near one another on the bench and barely held back from placing her hand on top of his. *No. Stop this, Caroline.* Why was she here? Why was she allowing herself to relax and enjoy the sun, enjoy spending time in the company of this man with his artist's way of looking at the world, with his calming presence that made her forget her responsibilities, especially when he looked at her like this, as if she were a Monet or Degas original he wanted to admire.

Her cheeks burned and she shot to her feet. "It looks shaded that way. Want to walk by the water?"

He rose, failing to hide the confusion in his expression. "Sure."

Caroline kept herself closed off for the next half hour. She talked when necessary to avoid rudeness. He was clearly confused, maybe a little hurt, but she couldn't forget that she might be leaving soon—if not now, then in a few months. She needed to leave everything behind—

writing, publishing, Andy. Even though she couldn't tell him yet.

She humored his attempts to ask about her writing, though it was the last thing she wanted to talk about. She gave noncommittal answers about what she would like from the future, short responses to his attempts at icebreaker questions like ice cream. When he brought up Peaches, updating her that the dog remained at the shelter, Caroline almost cracked, but she managed to remain emotionally aloof.

It was a welcome relief when Liv texted.

Liv: You alive still?
Caroline: Yup
Liv: K cool, so the toilet overflowed again, I don't know if I'll be able to fix it, so if you get home after I leave, you've been warned.

Perfect. A home emergency. Caroline pretended to miss a call from Liv, made her excuses to Andy, then headed for the exit while calling her roommate for real.

Sunlight glinted on the water, soft breezes lifting Caroline's hair, but her heart felt as heavy as one of the boulders poking up from the streambed.

"Why are you ditching him?" Liv demanded. "You said the coffee date last night was great."

"It was fine, I guess." Caroline kept her phone pressed against her ear, digging in her purse for her keys with the other hand. Luckily, she and Andy hadn't been far from the entrance.

"What did he do that was so bad you're bailing on him to help me fix a toilet? I promise you, I won't die if I have to wait a couple of hours. I'm leaving for the church soon anyway."

Thank goodness she hadn't needed to lie to Andy about that part. They did have a "cleaning emergency" of sorts. Their temperamental toilet had decided to overflow, flooding the bathroom. It was becoming a nearly biweekly occurrence.

Liv could handle that on her own. But in a special Saturday two-for-one, the flusher was also broken again, which meant Caroline needed to open up the back of the toilet and jerry-rig the chain with more paper clips. Liv had tried, but didn't seem to be able to master the technique. And they'd given up attempting to get a repairman to show up. They had been putting in a request for a broken back burner on the stove for months.

"I'd rather the apartment not flood while no one is home to stop it," Caroline said.

"You know that's not why. Spill. Do I need to beat him up for you? I have my spatula." Something crashed and clattered. "Whoops, dropped the mop."

Caroline exited the gates of the arboretum, heading across the parking lot. If only Andy *had* done something wrong. Then maybe she wouldn't be in this situation.

She sighed, pressing her key fob to unlock the doors to her car. "He didn't do anything wrong, Liv. But I think we need to keep it professional between us."

"Just didn't click?" Liv asked.

I wish. "Yeah." Thank goodness Liv couldn't see her face. Caroline was a terrible liar. "I guess some things aren't meant to work out."

Some things, like my dreams.

Elijah strummed his guitar in the family room.

Beside him, Sammy clicked his collar against the hard floor as he bent down to rest his head. Papers, warm in Andy's hand, flapped as he walked toward his bag near the counter to set them down.

"Taking a break from applying for jobs?" Andy flipped open the sleeve to his messenger bag and shoved the papers inside. He'd worked all day yesterday, with the exception of church, on the illustrations for Caroline. Never mind that they had a terrible date and that she hadn't texted him since Saturday, he still had a deadline to meet and illustrations to hand in to Clark today to set the man at ease.

Their printer had run out of ink.

He'd have to ask Maisie to borrow the church's when he completed the rest of the illustrations. And he'd pay her back, of course, for the paper and ink. But for now, Clark would have to accept three pages.

"Nah, man," Elijah said, "Maisie told me at church the other day about an opening for a worship leader position. I guess she has a niece who sings on the team."

Andy ambled to the kitchen to grab a half-eaten granola bar he'd started on that morning. He munched on a raisin and flax seed bar that health nut Ryan had handed out last basketball practice. Swirls of sweet cinnamon punched his mouth.

"Did we meet her niece during the potluck?" Andy said between bites of the bar.

"I don't think so. Remember, she did have a family celebration on the actual day of Easter. We met at her house the next day."

Andy crumpled the wrapper and tossed it into a small trash can hidden underneath their kitchen sink. The scent of mildew and spilled dish liquid overwhelmed his senses. That's what happened when a u-bend got loose and leaked, he guessed.

He lifted himself to a standing position, and his knees cracked.

"Are they making you audition, then?"

Elijah nodded, with a pick between his teeth. "There's a two-part process, an interview and an audition, to see if I play well with their group. I've been reading over the sheet music all morning." He plucked the pick and put it on a folder stand in front of him. "But before I got the email from the pastor this morning, I had more ideas for your book, aside from the illustrations you've gotten started for it."

Andy circled around the kitchen and leaned against a wall. "I'm all ears."

"You remember that fancy-schmancy charity auction you went to a while back?"

How could he forget? The line for caricatures still haunted his dreams.

"Well." Elijah scrawled something on paper with a red pen. "Maisie knows quite a few local authors, being a church librarian and all. She says they have huge launch events for their books when they come out."

Andy's leg triangled to balance his stance. "Don't those happen after the book releases, not before?"

"I think so. But you two are having a tough time with Clark, right?"

Friday seemed like ages ago, but memories of Clark flipping through his phone photos of his niece flickered across Andy's vision. He nodded.

"Maybe what you need to do to convince him is throw a launch party or auction or something. I mean, I know plenty of people who could help you out. Griffith says he could read the book in a dramatic voice at the launch. I think Ryan's partnering with the kids club for some promotional video in the next few weeks, and you know Maisie would put a hundred copies in our church library."

Probably not one hundred. Their church couldn't afford that.

Still, he hadn't considered that they had such overwhelming support for this book. His stomach wriggled. He couldn't tell if this meant he was overtaken by stress or happiness.

"And of course." Elijah jabbed a calloused thumb at himself. Guitar strings had a way of putting cuts and hard spots on Elijah's fingers. "This boy is willing to write a song for the event."

Andy palmed the back of his neck. "I appreciate the suggestion, Lij, but I'm not exactly the event planner type. You know me. For every group project, I sit back and do what I'm told."

Elijah lifted and dropped his shoulders. "Up to you, man. But I think if you want to convince Clark, you have to do more than show him some blurry images on printer paper."

All of Andy sighed when he eyed his messenger bag. It didn't really seem professional or the proper way to present illustrations to publishers. Didn't illustrators send proofs via email or something? He wished he'd taken a specialized class in college meant for this.

Maybe Clark had chosen Andy because he presented the cheapest option. Other illustrators could cost thousands, for such a rushed deadline.

The messenger bag tugged him toward the floor when he placed the strap on his shoulder.

"I'll definitely think about it. Thanks for the suggestion." He loped toward the door. Halted. "When's your audition?"

"The band's practicing tonight at five."

Andy saluted Elijah. "I'll be praying for you, man. I'm sure you'll do great."

His roommate grimaced. "I hope so."

With a wave, Andy rushed out of the door and down the stairs. On his car ride to the Helping Hope office, he listened to a playlist of worship songs Elijah had compiled. Every time he listened to the upbeat guitar strumming, everything in his body relaxed.

When he arrived and traveled to the fourth floor, once again, no receptionist greeted him at the front desk.

He ushered himself in and scanned the walls for Clark's office. Friday's memories jogged, and he recalled the exact door.

Andy marched past cubicles and the sound of fast-typing and the rumble of conversation somewhere at the other end of the room. A printer made a high-pitched din when it scanned a paper near a room he passed.

Carpet muffled his footsteps. He reached the door and his heart sunk when, through the blinds to the room, he noticed the lights had been extinguished.

Argh. He had to stop coming here during Clark's lunch breaks.

Should he try Caroline's cubicle? They didn't leave on the best note, sure, but if he handed her a few completed illustrations, maybe she'd forget about their date at the arboretum.

His advancing footsteps to Caroline's cubicle skidded to a stop when a sob struck the air.

Is Caroline crying?

Instinct took over and he dashed to the cubicle, almost knocking into a woman laden with a holder full of coffee cups. When he reached Caroline's cubicle, he stopped. It was empty, like Clark's office.

Next to her cubicle, Zinnia dabbed her eyes with a balled-up tissue. Mascara rivers had run down her cheeks.

She spotted him in her periphery and jolted. "Oh, sorry, didn't see you."

He touched his neck. Itches from uncomfortability covered it. "Sorry, Zinnia, didn't mean to barge in."

Her long-taloned fingernails waved. "Don't worry about it. Just got a rejection for an audition. Thought I'd nailed the part."

Curiosity piqued. "You're an actress?"

Zinnia tossed the tissue into a hot pink trash bag underneath her desk. "Well, I'd like to be. At least, that's what I studied in college. Glad I paid 100k for them to tell me, during my last semester, 'Yeahhh, you're going to have to work as a waitress for at least a decade before you maybe get a part in some indie films.'"

Andy knew the feeling.

In his last semester at the university, he'd also heard from a career counselor who laced her fingers together and said, "Yeah, so, basically you're gonna have to take what you can get." Didn't help that his program boasted of getting its students any job in the graphic design field they desired. He was certain all the students in the program would've sued... if they had the money.

Zinnia's thumb scoured her cheeks for any smudged makeup. "Anyway, sorry. Didn't mean to put all of that on you. Are you here to see someone?"

Papers flickered in his hands.

Printer ink smudged his fingertips when he moved them. Shoot, he should've put them in a folder or something to protect the picture's integrity.

"I was hoping to see either Clark or Caroline, to show them some completed illustrations." And to convince Clark to trust in Caroline that she could deliver a wow factor project. He didn't add the last part, however.

"Well, both are on lunch break." Zinnia had a pen in her other hand, and she bit down on the cap. "But I'm not sure when either will return. I could hand those off to one of them, though, if you'd want me to."

Perhaps he'd misjudged Zinnia. Sure, she seemed pushy but she did offer to help on two occasions he'd come here.

"Mind getting it to Clark?" He handed her the papers when she stretched out a palm. "I want to be sure he sees the progress we're making."

"Sure, sweetheart." A certain odd glint, in the dim office lighting, flickered in her pupils. "I'll make sure this gets into the right hands."

Chapter Seventeen

CAROLINE RUBBED HER TEMPLE, REFOCUSING ON her computer screen. Her fifteen-minute lunch break hadn't helped her brain feel any better.

Maybe she should have taken a longer break—she was technically allowed to take an hour—but she hadn't wanted to leave her desk for too long. Chances were, Mr. Knox would choose that moment to come back and Zinnia would make a comment to him, offering with a saccharine smile to take over whatever task Caroline was currently "neglecting."

Another reason her publishing career was hopeless. She doubted Mr. Knox would give her a glowing recommendation.

She glanced at her phone. Wasn't Andy supposed to bring in some illustrations today? Their date had ended on a bad note, but she'd swallowed her embarrassment, summoned her professionalism, and messaged him anyway asking about artwork. However, the message remained unanswered.

She marked another misused "you're" instead of "your" on the ad copy she was proofing. *Who hired this writer?* She didn't recognize the name—probably written by an intern. Colleges these days.

After sending back the proofed copy, she stretched, grabbed her water bottle, and headed for the water cooler. Had her brain taken a trip to the Caribbean without her?

Maybe her nap yesterday was still messing with her. She couldn't remember the last time she'd slept during the day. However, after pulling nearly an all-nighter Saturday night, she couldn't keep her eyes open after church.

It began with a dumb decision. Saturday evening, she opened her spreadsheet of places she'd submitted her work. Then she counted. Twenty-five rejections. Thirty-seven no replies. That made sixty-two publishers and agents who wanted nothing to do with her. Sixty-two industry professionals thought she didn't belong in publishing. That led to another spreadsheet—jobs she had applied to after college. Seventeen publishing jobs she hadn't gotten. Fourteen magazine and newspaper positions. Three copywriter gigs. Even with all her college internship credits, no one wanted her. When Helping Hope came along, she had been happy to get anything and jumped on the job offer. Clearly, she had no place in publishing. No place as an editor, definitely no place as an author. Years wasted at Helping Hope had gotten her no closer. And she doubted an in-house children's book would do anything to help her prospects.

She'd sent an email to Darlene at two in the morning, expressing interest in the position and asking about next steps. Then she spent the next two hours stalking Liv's Facebook friends, trying to find anyone who might need a roommate. Liv deserved the best roommate. Luckily, their current lease term ended in a couple months, perfect timing.

On Sunday, a notification on her phone dinged. She tapped the icon to see an email from one of the editors over in Helping Hope's publishing branch. It was a reply to the Helping Hope announcement about downsizing and layoffs.

Did you see this? I told you we wouldn't last much longer.

I've been looking at openings at other publishers, and it looks like a lot of them are downsizing or consolidating jobs too. I think I'm done with the publishing game. Publishers are dropping like flies. Too much free web content. I've found some links to internet advertising editorial and copywriting positions if you want me to send them along.

- Shannon

Two minutes later, another email came in.

Hi, Caroline,

Apologies for that email. I intended to send it to Caroline Rivers in nonfiction. Please disregard and delete.
Sincerely,
Shannon Barber
Fiction Editorial Director

After that email, Caroline had promptly taken a nap.

Now, as she strode toward the water cooler, she firmed her jaw. Maybe she'd wasted six years on publishing, with college and working at Helping Hope. But she was Caroline Penn. She did not give up. She did not fail. She would hit the New York legal scene, and she would make sure no one ever remembered she had been anything but one of the fiercest lawyers to take the bar.

A small crowd had gathered in front of the bubbling blue jug, speaking in low tones. Caroline spotted two editors, a web designer, and one of the guys from accounting. The accountant glanced at her but kept speaking.

"Cutting the publishing side isn't going to help," he was saying. "A lot of the donor funding we get is *because* of Helping Hope Publishing. People read the books and fall in love with the organization. It might not be direct ROI, but it's significant."

Caroline nodded to them and uncapped her water bottle, holding the plastic container under the spout.

One of the editors, a woman with short brown hair, tipped back a paper cup of water. The other Caroline, Caroline Rivers. "That's what I was saying to Shannon. They cut the publishing, they're toast. They'll never get enough money for all the programs."

The web designer wrinkled her small nose, round glasses falling down the bridge. "Turner said the board hasn't liked any of the books that have been coming out."

"Not our fault we've had terrible submissions to choose from," Rivers grumbled.

Water glugged in the cooler as it reached the halfway point of

Caroline's bottle.

"I heard Knox tried to save it," put in the other editor, a woman named Sandy. She planted her hands on her wide hips. "He told them he has a new writer/illustrator pair to revamp the line."

Caroline's eyes widened. *That has to be Andy and me.*

"What did they say?" the accounting guy asked. What was his name? Chuck?

"They said they might reconsider if pre-orders on the first book are high enough. If the publishing team proves they can still 'make the magic happen.'" Sandy made jazz hands.

Caroline nearly dropped her water bottle as she moved to close the lid. The entire future of Helping Hope Publishing rested on *their* book?

"How many pre-orders?" she blurted.

Her four coworkers looked at her in surprise. Sandy blinked a few times. "Oh. I just heard it through the grapevine. But at least a thousand."

Caroline's breath caught. She felt like someone had replaced her heart with a stone that plummeted to her feet. "A *thousand*?"

Sandy shrugged. "I think the point was that it wasn't going to happen. It'd take a miracle to save publishing." She shook her head and snorted. "Heard they also said they needed that book published before the end of next quarter for it to have any bearing before the layoffs."

"Before the end of June," Caroline said numbly. To have any hope of pre-orders going anywhere, they would need to start advertising months ahead. They were already behind. Two months to create the book, begin advertising, and gain a thousand orders before its release date at the end of June?

Impossible.

"It's a shame." Chuck sighed. "I like Helping Hope. Does good work. But the board's getting desperate, and I don't think it will last more than a year or two at this rate. They'll have to start cutting programs."

Caroline thought of the kids at the Hope Club, the tutoring Wyatt received there, the smiles on their faces, the lunch bags with names written on them. Where would those kids go? Who would feed them, tutor them, give them a safe place to have fun?

Her lunch felt like a lump of cardboard in her stomach.

"It isn't finished yet," she snapped. Chuck jumped at her abrupt tone. Caroline whirled and stalked toward her desk.

She may have tanked her own author career. She may have lost her chance at publishing.

But she would not let Helping Hope die on her watch.

Because she was a Penn. And if there was one thing Caroline had been bred to do, it was succeed.

Andy kicked a pile of index cards when he staggered out into the hallway of his apartment and he stumbled. Elijah hadn't turned on any lights. Good thing the rosy-fingered dawn decided to bathe the family room.

Elijah sat in the midst of an index card scatter. With his back to Andy, Elijah scratched something onto one of the white pieces of paper.

"Is it time for tornado season?"

His roommate spun around and stifled a yawn behind the back of his hand. "Sorry, couldn't sleep. After the interview yesterday, I mean."

Red rimmed Elijah's eyes. A single plate with a half-eaten toaster pastry sat on the table in the family room. That would explain the beeping oven noises Andy had heard from his room an hour or so earlier.

"Besides, I have about a billion ideas for ways you two could promote your book at the charity event thing I mentioned yesterday." Elijah leaned forward and held up one of the cards. "Maybe you could have a fun finger-painting station for kids." He flipped up another note stationed by his foot. "Or get an email list going for pre-orders of the book, so you can keep people in the loop." Another card flopped by his knees. "Or grab new printer ink at Walmart. Wait."

Elijah squinted at the card.

"Oh, whoops. I'd forgotten I'd also put a few grocery items we need on these cards. I think one of them even contains lyrics to a song." Rosy beams from the family room window lit a card that said, "Need new mayonnaise jar." Andy hoped deep inside that Elijah didn't have a ballad dedicated to their deviled egg disaster. He scooped up the plate on the table and ambled to the kitchen to wrap the pastry in plastic.

"Speaking of the interview." Andy shoved open a drawer that had gotten stuck on the corner of a tin foil container. "How did it go yesterday, since I didn't see you last night?"

Blue ink smudged the corner of Elijah's lips when he pressed the pen to them. He set the utensil down on the floor. "Not bad. But considering it just happened yesterday, I'm not sure when I'll hear back. They said the earliest was this next week." He gestured at the smattering of index cards. "We have a new hobby for the time being."

Saran wrap tore neatly down jagged metallic spikes.

Andy swaddled the plate in a few layers of plastic and stuck the dish in the fridge.

"Hey, Elijah, I appreciate you wanting to give lots of ideas, but this is technically my work task. You can't help me try to walk forever."

Memories of his business cards stuck to cork boards around town flickered across his vision.

Back in college, Elijah had mentioned he had three older brothers. All of them had pursued relatively successful careers. Because their mother had burned herself out by child number three, his parents didn't put a whole lot of effort into Elijah. Because of this, it didn't seem to matter if Elijah got a gold Olympic medal or settled for a job at a local insurance firm—his brothers had all done it before.

So Andy's roommate decided to help others' dreams succeed when possible. This included serving as wingman for a number of their friends of the basketball team—three of which were now married thanks to Elijah's matchings--getting Andy's foot in the door whenever possible, and now, planning book launches.

Wan light from the fridge illuminated a purple splotch. Maybe grape jelly? Andy shut the fridge and made a mental note to grab Clorox wipes from the store later to finish the job on that stain.

"Sorry, man." Elijah hunched forward to shove the cards into one pile. "You know I can't help it. You have so much potential."

By now Elijah had created a mountain. Andy headed to the mound to help consolidate. He sat.

Elijah's lips twitched. "Thanks. Speaking of potential, how did the date go? I forgot to ask."

A groan puffed out of Andy's nostrils. His stomach twisted. He'd spent a sleepless night, reeling the images from the arboretum over and over again to figure out how he'd messed up. Then he thought back to the coffee date. *Should I not have told her about my dad? About my family?* Caroline had said she didn't mind, but perhaps her response had been a formality.

"That bad, huh?"

"I'd rather not talk about it. I'm still not sure what I did wrong. And she hasn't messaged me since, so I guess that's going to make the rest of the project awkward."

Paper fluttering through fingertips echoed for the next few moments.

"Not to make this more awkward." Elijah clapped his index cards together. "But your mom texted me yesterday. She's beginning to get worried."

Great. One more thing he couldn't get right. He'd made a mental note to message her, right? He imagined the mental notes like a pile of index cards, as large as a mountain, about to bury him in a deadline avalanche.

Andy sighed. "I know. I feel like an awful person. Should I have gone to see her on Easter, Lij?"

Elijah clenched his jaw and stared at a brown splotch in their family room rug. Then his eyes met Andy's.

"Maybe it's not too late to visit her now."

Hope buoyed in his chest. By now the rosy morning light had

shifted to an orange.

"You know what, Lij, I think you're right. I should drive to see her." *Before I change my mind.* He'd have to go now. It took ten hours to get to his mother's house in Tennessee, barring any rest stop breaks and meals.

Andy slid his phone out of his pocket to check the time. But a white message blinked in front of his home screen photo with Sammy: *"Your account has an overdue balance. To continue your unlimited talk/text plan, click the account link below or reply PAY for mobile pay options."*

Ice filled his veins. Oh, no, how many months had he gone without paying cell phone bills? He clicked the account link and his eyes bugged at the amount. He'd have to give up groceries for three weeks to pay for that.

When his eyes met Elijah's squint, he explained the situation.

"Yikes, man. Tell you what. We may not have black printer ink, but we can print the instructions to your mom's house in purple. I think we do have cyan and magenta ink left. If you leave now, you might get there in the evening."

He hadn't even considered directions.

No way he could make it across three states without some inkling of what highways to take. Even during his childhood when his family would take road trips, they would use a large map found in the glove compartment.

Elijah bounded toward the room where they kept the printer, which happened to double as Elijah's bedroom. Minutes later, the old machine rumbled and whirred to life. His roommate emerged with a stack of paper in his fingertips. Faded purple ink dictated the various roads Andy would take.

Then Elijah held up his own phone. "I'll text your mom to let her know you're coming and about the cell phone. Don't worry about Sammy. I'll take him out for walks. It's not like I have a job to get to anyway."

After Andy changed out of his PJs into a white t-shirt and sweats, perfect travel clothes, he swirled his key ring around his index finger and flew down the steps of the apartment.

About three hours into the drive, regret and panic seized him. He had to focus on endless pastures of corn fields and cows to calm his heart rate, since the music he blasted appeared to do nothing.

Okay, Andy, relax. He puffed out a long breath and tightened his grip on the steering wheel. *Just practice what you're going to say to Mom when you get to her house.*

"Hey, sorry I haven't really spoken more than a couple sentences to you at a time since high school." Yeah, not a great start.

"So, Mom, you're looking great. Is that a new haircut?" *No. Stop right there.*

Through two rest stops and a ten-minute pause at a restaurant that served burgers, he tested different greetings and apologies. Nothing stuck.

Eventually he sipped lemon-lime soda through a straw with such force he almost choked on the beverage. He coughed and pounded on his chest with his fist.

Once he caught his breath, his body un-tensed. *Andy, it's not going to be perfect. You haven't spoken anything meaningful to her in years. Be honest, and hope she forgives you.*

Sunlight faded to purple by the time he'd reached his mother's neighborhood. Small houses, built sometime in the '50s, sported chipped paint and rusted cars on short gravel driveways. His heart jostled when he spotted his mother leaning against their front porch, underneath a glass light fixture. Mosquitos swirled around the beams like a perfect Southern spring night.

A polka-dotted apron hugged her larger, short build, like a motherly teapot. She had dark curly hair, like his.

Rocks crunched underneath his tires, and he rolled to a squeaky halt. He let in and out a long breath before he unbuckled. Here went nothing.

He swung open his car door and grimaced at her.

"Mom, I'm so sor—"

She bounded off the porch, apron strings flying. Moments later, she suffocated him with the tightest hug he'd ever felt.

"Andy, sweet Andy," she whispered, "it's so good to have you home."

Chapter Eighteen

ANDY JACKSON, FOR THE LOVE OF all things good, pick up your phone. Caroline was ready to strangle him. *You can't avoid me forever.* Just because they'd had one bad date, the immature idiot was ignoring her?

She slapped her phone back on her desktop and blew out a frustrated breath. Thank goodness Zinnia was on a late lunch break and not close enough to hear.

He hadn't called or texted her back Monday, fine. But by now, at two in the afternoon on Tuesday, it was getting out of hand.

She had spent the last few hours working on publicity for the book. She had ad copy, names of book bloggers and online influencers, social media graphics, a list of potential author endorsers, newspapers, podcasts, bookstores and libraries to ask about events...

She just needed that elusive cover so she could include the image.

Caroline knew ads and PR, considering she proofed them for the marketing team every day. She had watched dozens of book campaigns from start to finish, in the passive role of copy editor, making sure the ads, graphics, and articles all looked good. She knew what she would need for this book to succeed.

And that included a cover. Even if they didn't have a finalized manuscript, they had their main idea, pagination plans, and a rough draft—plenty to work with to create the cover.

She picked up her phone again. Five unanswered texts. Three unanswered emails. Two Facebook messages. Three calls, two voicemails. Over a dozen attempts to reach Andy, but the man appeared to have fallen off the face of the earth.

If she knew where he lived, she would march up to his doorstep and demand that he listen to her. It didn't matter if they'd had an uncomfortable date, or if he didn't like her at all, or any other ridiculous reason he might have for avoiding her. Helping Hope was depending on them.

Where he lives. Would Mr. Knox know? And would her boss hand over the information? That was probably illegal in some way, but at the moment, she didn't care.

She pushed back her chair and headed for Mr. Knox's office.

The door was open, but she could see someone standing in front of his desk. She slowed as she approached. Flawless blonde hair, stiletto heels—Zinnia. Of course Zinnia had to be the one talking to Mr. Knox.

She was about to turn away and return to her desk until Mr. Knox was available until something colorful caught her eye.

Zinnia passed inked pages to Mr. Knox, who set them on his desk and held the first one up to the light.

Caroline sucked in a breath.

From the distance, she could still make out the elegant lines and bold colors, dancing around two prominent words: "Imperfect Hope."

It was Andy's cover.

She remained rigid, speechless, until she became aware of pain radiating from her palms where she had dug in her nails. She whirled on the ball of her foot and stalked back to her desk.

Andy had abandoned her for Zinnia.

Of course he had. Caroline was a disaster to work with. She took forever to come up with the ideas. She made a fool of herself on dates. Mr. Knox clearly favored Zinnia and her competence. At some point, Mr. Knox and Andy had decided to take away the project without telling her and give it to Zinnia. What other reason could there be for him avoiding her?

Biting her cheek, Caroline copied all of her spreadsheets and files for the book's publicity and pasted the links into an email. She attached the text of the manuscript to the email as well, labeling each resource.

Then she added Zinnia's and Andy's emails to the recipient line and hit send.

There. They have everything they need.

When Zinnia returned to her cubicle, she said nothing. After a while, Caroline glanced over and saw her coworker hard at work on last-minute magazine spreads. For some reason, it made Caroline feel better to think Zinnia probably wouldn't get around to opening her email for the next few hours.

Well. That's it. With the picture book out of her hands, Caroline officially had no more ties to publishing—and soon, she would have none to Helping Hope.

It should have been a relief. The pressure no longer rested on her shoulders to save the organization. Zinnia would probably do a better job anyway, right?

At the end of the workday, Caroline numbly ducked into her car and turned the ignition. Her hands seemed to turn the wheel of their own accord, and before she knew it, she was headed in the direction of the Hope Club.

One thousand pre-orders. The number repeated in her head, bouncing around her skull like an old screensaver. Was one thousand even possible? Maybe at one of the big New York publishers, but here in Roseville?

If she was in charge, Caroline doubted *she* could do it. But Zinnia?

She wanted to think Zinnia could handle the project. She wanted to think she could walk away from Helping Hope, go to New York, and know the company would be fine.

But deep down, she sensed that Zinnia didn't care about Helping Hope for much more than just another job. Would Zinnia put in the extra hours, the extra heart, to make the book succeed?

Or would she give up and walk away, like Caroline was doing?

She stopped at the convenience store on the way to the Hope Club and picked up a couple of bags of chocolates. At the club, Linda sat behind the registration table, as usual.

"Caroline." Linda's bright smile burned away a small portion of the dark cloud hanging over Caroline's head. "It's good to see you again."

"You too." Caroline smiled as a burst of hollers and laughter floated into the hall. "I was wondering if there's anything I can help with today."

"Actually, you came on exactly the right day. Wyatt's here, and his tutor couldn't make it again. He seemed to love talking with you last time."

Her heart swelled. *Wyatt.* How was the kid doing? Had he had better success with his tests? She would be able to find out. "I would be happy to work with him. He's a brilliant kid."

"A real sweetheart, too." Linda hefted herself to her feet. "This way."

Caroline followed Linda back to the room with tables and tutors paired off with students. Like before, Wyatt sat at a table near the corner.

"Look who I brought," Linda announced.

Wyatt looked up from a lined paper covered in scrawls and grinned. "Caroline."

"Hey, there." Caroline felt some of the tension in her shoulders relax as her cheeks pulled up in a matching grin.

"Have fun." Linda waved.

Caroline pulled out a chair. "How did that test go?"

Wyatt scooted forward, leaning on his elbows. His eyebrows scrunched. "Well, I didn't get an A. But I did do a lot better. Ms. Nelson said it was a high C."

"That's awesome!" Caroline clasped her hands. "I'm so proud of you."

"Yeah." His grin returned. "I think I'm going to do even better next time. My mom said she's super thankful for the Hope Club. Coming here means I can work on homework instead of watching my sisters."

Caroline's brow furrowed. "How old are they?"

"Charlotte's eight, Mia's six, and Lily's five." He shrugged. "If we don't go to the Hope Club after school, I have to watch them until Mom gets home from work." He gestured toward the room full of shouts and laughter. "But here, someone else watches them."

So without the Hope Club, this twelve-year-old boy was stuck watching three young girls while trying to manage his own school stress?

The Hope Club that might be closing soon if publishing shuts down and revenue dies?

Zinnia, you better kill it with that book.

Caroline spent the next hour discussing literature and test strategies with Wyatt. She cracked a few bad literature puns, he showed her his comic book style drawings of characters from *Around the World in Eighty Days*, and they laughed loud enough that a couple of other pairs gave them dirty looks.

When she stood to leave, he tapped his pencil, hesitating. "Will you come back? Maybe next week?"

She bit her lip. Depending what Darlene said, how soon Mr. Knox dropped her, when she would leave, if she'd have time…

"Of course. I'll make sure to work it into my schedule." No matter how hectic life got, she couldn't let him down.

As she headed out to her car, her heart sank again, resting heavily inside her ribcage. Maybe she hadn't let him down this time, but wasn't that exactly what she was doing eventually?

There's nothing I can do about it. It's in Zinnia's hands now.

Her windshield had fogged since she'd been inside, so she sat with the defroster running while she pulled out her phone to check messages. Still nothing from Andy. Not surprising. He seemed determined to avoid confrontation and abandon her in the most abrupt way possible.

Her heart thumped at a notification in her email inbox, though. The sender read "Darlene Winters."

Thank goodness. She got back.

Caroline tapped on the email. As her eyes scanned the text, she forgot to breathe.

Dear Caroline,

I'm so sorry, I thought you were no longer interested in returning to New York.

I regret to inform you that the job has been taken.

Andy dug a spoon into a crumbling peach cobbler. Pale morning light illuminated silver strands in his mother's hair as she scooped a heaping mouthful of the treat.

Sure, this warm dish probably would've served better as a dessert the night before, instead of 7 a.m. breakfast the following morning. But they'd spent most of the night talking and catching up on the last several years. The ceramic baking vessel for the baked goods had cooled by the time Andy crashed in the guest room for some well-needed sleep.

His body ached from the ten-hour drive, and he purged away any thoughts of the same journey he'd have to make today.

Brown sugar and sweet, juicy fruit melted on his tongue. He could get used to this. Andy eyed the remains of the golden-brown pastry that took up two-thirds of the dish. Maybe he could convince his mother to send him home with leftovers.

"Before your drive." She dipped her spoon into a mound of vanilla bean ice cream she'd dolloped onto her bowl earlier. "I have some of your things here. Leftover from your college days. Mind taking them with you?"

"Sure, you cleaning house?"

"Downsizing."

The "dining area," if anyone else was generous enough to call it that, couldn't even fit a twin-sized bed. His mother had squeezed a wooden table and two chairs into the corner, but already, Andy had to scrunch his knees to make sure he didn't kick the legs of her seat.

The house boasted of two squat bedrooms, one bathroom, and a kitchen. *My apartment may even be larger than this place.*

Poor insulation from thin walls bestowed a chilly night, and loud neighbors who shouted until two in the morning, didn't help the neighborhood much. He hung his head. If only he'd tried harder in school. Maybe he could've gotten a better job, instead of working freelance, and helped his mother pay her bills.

Her dark, warm eyes analyzed his for a moment. "There's a nice condo in a good neighborhood. Been saving for years. I'll be fine. Don't you go worrying about me."

She bumped her chair an inch. It met the purple-painted wall. Then she collected his bowl and hers and moved to the kitchen. Andy stared at a mismatched salt and pepper set on the kitchen table. Moments later, splashes from sink water sounded from a few feet away.

He took in the rest of his surroundings as he allowed the warm food in his stomach to settle.

Next to the kitchen table was a family room. On a beaten wooden dresser sat an older TV his mother had scored on Facebook Marketplace a year back for a good price. Beside it a wooden bookcase with warped shelves housed a number of books collecting dust. During his childhood, Mom used to love perusing garage sales and thrift stores for hardbacks. Gilded letters from some of the books caught the sunlight from the screened door near the TV.

His mother emerged from the kitchen. She toweled off the bowls with a checkered cloth. "Meet me in the attic. There's a ladder that comes down from the ceiling."

Andy nodded and headed for the hallway. He passed his mother's room and halted when a colorful glimmer caught his periphery. She'd left the door open an inch.

Creaks sounded from the metallic hinges when he opened it wider. Drawings, watercolor pictures, and charcoal sketches covered her maroon bedroom walls. He stood at the entrance and soaked in the memories, from when he used to paint or draw after school for hours.

He didn't recall stepping into the room. But moments later, he found himself near her vanity. Painted images of sunsets crowded the mirror.

Makeup powder dusted the surface of the cabinet that held the mirror.

She'd even glued magnets he'd created in art class on the drawers and mosaics he'd formed from rocks he'd found outside their old home during his childhood.

A chuckle from the door tickled his ear. He spun on his heel and found his mom leaning against the door frame. Brown smudges of sugar splotched her gray apron.

"This doesn't look like the attic."

He'd felt as if someone had pulled him out of a pool. Brain no longer fuzzy, he winced. "Sorry. Got distracted."

She grinned, moved to the vanity, and fixed a perfume bottle that had turned over. Everything inside the room smelled of dust and the warm scent contained within that bottle.

Bright hues from a picture frame, the time in fifth grade when he experimented with acrylics, snagged his attention. The teacher, when she heard Andy had fished near dried-up watercolor palettes from the art room garbage bin to take home, bought him a set of acrylics for Christmas. She never signed the package that mysteriously appeared in their mailbox. But he knew. None of his classmates could've afforded such a gift.

"You kept all of these? All this time?" He realized, moments later, that his jaw had sunk an inch.

She didn't answer him for a moment. Instead, her gaze roved over a beat-up chair near her bed. Threads sprawled out of the cushion from years of use and wear.

"Andy, I want to show you something." She vanished from the entrance of the room. Moments later, a grunt followed by the sound of a creak came from the hallway.

He emerged from the room and watched his mother climb a ladder to the attic. When she reached the top, she flipped on a light switch that hummed. After she disappeared from his view, he followed.

Pink insulation webs greeted him when he reached the top. He made sure to give them a wide berth so as not to ruin his travel clothes.

His nostrils wrinkled. Not at the dusty attic scent, but himself.

Probably should've packed more clothing.

His mother hunched over a box. She popped off the lid and motioned him closer. "I want you to see what's inside."

She straightened and crossed her arms. Andy stepped to where she'd squatted and peered into the container full of wrinkled, yellowed papers. He pinched one sheet in the middle and held it up in the weak light to read the inscription:

"Third Grade Quarter One Report Card."

He frowned at the box and selected another sheet, a paper from his second grade English class where he got an A minus. "Are these—?"

"Grades, report cards, hallmarks of academia? Yes." She bent over him and placed the lid on the box. "You'll notice how I don't have these hanging in my room."

Wait, she ... she didn't care about the grades? About the failed class? Had he projected his disappointment with himself onto her?

Moisture pricked his eyes. He blamed this on the attic dust.

A heavy but warm hand clasped his shoulder.

"Do you know what the best part of my day was when I got back from work?" Her eyes sparkled.

He shook his head. The attic floor panels dug into his knees.

"When I'd find you at the kitchen table painting or drawing for hours." She chuckled and parked on a stepping stool. The roof slanted near the seat. "I know I should've told you to do homework, but I couldn't help it. My son was an artist, and I wasn't going to stop him."

"You." His voice snagged in his throat. He coughed to fix his vocal chords. "You didn't care about the fact I was expelled from that school?"

Her face fell. She stared at her thumbs.

"Sweetheart. Yes, I wanted you to have a good education. But it wasn't everything. Your father had gotten so obsessed with success that he left behind what really mattered."

Something large and wooly caught in Andy's throat. His mom didn't often talk about his dad.

"What if I—?"

Mist coated his eyes again.

"What if I become just like him?"

The words left him like a ten-pound weight. He'd held that burden in his stomach for so long that the question had caused ulcers to tear into his abdomen. The query that became the reason he blew the date with Caroline, even if not consciously. Because no one deserved to end up with someone like his father, especially not such a brilliant writer as her.

His mother considered the question for a moment. "You are not like him and let me tell you why." She fixed him with her gaze, and her eyes wouldn't let him go. "You came back."

Pain from his stomach subsided. Hope filled him like a light.

With that, his mother slapped her knees and rose.

"Now we need to grab your things and get you on the road. You've got a picture book to write." She patted her apron pocket, where she kept her phone. "Elijah's been keeping me in the know. Speaking of picture books."

She popped the lid off another box. Dusty spines of books from his youth sat in neat rows. His mother leaned down and fixed her hands in the box's carrying holes. "For inspiration."

With a grin, she handed him the case.

"And for my future grandchildren." She winked. "Bring that author home with you next time."

Chapter Nineteen

"OUR PROGRAMS BENEFIT NOT ONLY THOSE in need here in Roseville, but also organizations around the globe."

Caroline suppressed a yawn as she continued the donor tour. Thank goodness she'd been given this usually odious task. It kept her from having to sit next to Zinnia. She didn't think she could handle any looks Zinnia might send her, whether looks of smug triumph, or worse, pity.

No amount of makeup had been able to hide the circles under Caroline's eyes today. She hadn't been able to sleep all night after Darlene's email.

I regret to inform you that the job has been taken.

They filled the position with a bright-eyed young law student. The firm was full.

However, I will let you know if any positions open up. We may have an opening in November.

November. Could Caroline bear to watch Andy and Zinnia launch the book together, watch Helping Hope slowly crumble, for months, waiting for November?

Would she still have a job in November?

"Seventy-five percent of profit from Helping Hope's publishing branch goes directly to our programs, with only twenty-five percent reserved for internal expenses and investment in future projects," Caroline droned on to the group of six well-dressed older men and women. Mr. Knox liked it when Caroline led the tours. He said she added a certain level of professionalism and—here he snapped his fingers, thinking of the right word—*big city pizazz* that inspired confidence in wealthy donors.

She wasn't feeling any *pizazz* today.

"I heard Helping Hope might be shutting down the publishing study branch," one of the donors, a man with a large bald patch, interrupted. Caroline hesitated. "I'm part of the PR department, so I can't speak directly to publishing."

A woman in a flower-print dress clutched her three strands of pearls—literally. "Helping Hope's titles are some of the few I feel comfortable sharing with my grandchildren. It's hard to find quality books these days. I'd hate to see it go."

"We take great pride in our titles," Caroline agreed, redirecting. "If you will come this way with me…"

Caroline hadn't cried since…well, since the day she stormed out of her parents' New York apartment. But last night, she'd come closer than she had in years.

She hadn't been able to tell Liv what was wrong, so she claimed a headache and went to bed early. With nothing else to distract herself from heavy thoughts of failure and wasted years, she snuggled Rabbit and looked at pictures of Peaches on the pet shelter's website. Still, no one had adopted her. How? Such a precious pup deserved the best home. *Maybe that would be one good part of being unemployed. I could stay home with a dog.*

A dog she couldn't afford.

After the donor tour, Caroline dragged her feet back to her desk. To make the day even better, Zinnia was waiting for her.

"Hey, Carrie." Zinnia frowned, red lips turning down. "I can't seem to reach Andy. Is he okay?"

Wait, he isn't responding to Zinnia either? Maybe something really was wrong. *Except that he gave her the illustrations. That happened while he wasn't talking to me too.* Caroline shrugged. "He's disorganized." She plopped into her chair. *And that's your problem now.*

"Thanks for handing over the project, by the way. You had some good ideas. I'll probably use some of them."

"Good." Caroline couldn't bring herself to give more of a response to Zinnia's attempt to get under her skin. She paused. "Wait. What do you mean handing over—?"

"Penn!" Mr. Knox's voice carried from the office. Caroline knew better than to hope he was calling for a writing utensil.

She stood and sighed. "See you later, Zinnia."

Caroline forced one foot in front of another into Mr. Knox's office. "You called for me?"

Mr. Knox set down a stack of papers on his desk and looked up at her. His eyes were underlined with dark circles, and his squint seemed more pronounced than usual.

He sighed and rubbed his forehead. "Sit down, Caroline. And you might want to close the door."

Oh, no. She pushed the glass door shut and took a seat. "Is something wrong?"

He sat back in his chair, expression grim. "You know how passionate I am about Helping Hope Publishing. Unfortunately, the board doesn't share my vision."

Caroline's stomach clenched. "The cuts."

"I tried to convince them." The bleak expression on his face was more open than Caroline had ever seen. Like this, he almost looked like a concerned grandfather. Maybe there wasn't much bite beneath the bluster after all. "They said they'd save it if our new project had a thousand pre-orders. They might as well have laughed."

His gaze returned to her, and he seemed to pull himself together, steeling himself. "You're an excellent worker, Caroline. One of our best employees. And I know you care about Helping Hope."

"Yes, sir." *Where is this going?*

"With publishing gone, we're making other cuts. We'll need less ad copy, less PR. And with less revenue coming in. . .the board doesn't think we need two copyeditors." He folded his hands tightly on the desk. "I'm sorry, Caroline. Zinnia has been here a bit longer than you. It was a hard decision, but we're going to have to let you go."

An invisible fist punched her in the gut. She struggled to pull in a breath. "Right...right now?" she managed.

He rubbed a hand over his face. "Up to you. You can finish out the week, and the pay period, or you can leave now. We'll pay you for this week either way." His eyes shone. Was that a sheen of unshed tears? *He loves this company.* "We're out of funds. The board is pulling the plug on us. I'm sorry. I'd hoped I could convince them with a new project, something different..." He gave a wry laugh. "I guess you aren't necessarily laid off. After all, the board will save publishing if we get one thousand pre-orders. Good luck with that."

"I understand." Caroline hesitated, then stood. "I've really enjoyed working here. I believe in Helping Hope."

He nodded, and his head fell, bowed toward the papers on his desk. "I do too. I just wish the board did." He gave another mirthless chuckle under his breath. "One thousand pre-orders."

Caroline exited the office quietly, closing the door behind her. Mr. Knox could probably use some space.

She had nothing better to do, so she returned to her desk.

Her pulse raged. Blood boiled in her veins. This was it. No job anywhere. No time to look for one. Maybe, just maybe, if she'd been able to stay on the project, she and Andy could have made it happen somehow.

Instead, he'd ghosted her and turned to Zinnia instead.

She opened her work email. It was time to send one last message.

Andy,

I don't know how to say this politely, or professionally, which is pretty out of character for me. But to say I feel betrayed is an under-statement.

Her eyes burned as she pounded out the email. She knew it wasn't professionally worded. Too much emotion poured out of her. Too much brutal honesty. But she didn't truly feel her heart break until she typed the last words.

I'm going home to beg my mom to pull some strings in terms of employment. This is the lowest I've felt in a long, long time.

Have a nice life, and please do not respond to this email.

Caroline

She hit send. Then she grabbed her bag, shoved her pens and notepads into it, and scanned her desk. Nothing else personal. Four years working at Helping Hope, and she'd never bothered to put up any pictures, decorations, or personal touches. A part of her had always expected that something better would come. She never imagined the reason she'd be leaving wasn't to pursue something better, but because all of her options were exhausted as she left in disgrace.

Zinnia gave her an odd look as she stood up and walked out but didn't say anything. Good. It was better that way.

She could help Liv find a roommate from afar. She'd make rent payments until then. She pulled out her phone on the elevator.

Caroline: Hey, Dad. Text me the address of the place in Ohio?

She slipped the phone back in her purse and stared straight ahead, picturing the inevitable.

Hi, Mom. I'm so sorry.

You were right about everything.

I failed you.

Andy stared at his phone as he was hanging a picture. His mother had sent him home with a cell phone bill paid and all his drawings from her bedroom. As soon as he'd gotten home and caught a nap from his long drive, he'd gotten to work on putting up the various arts and craft projects from his youth on the walls of his apartment.

Then his phone started to buzz. Email after email, text after text poured in from Caroline.

Each glow from his phone punctured a hole in his chest until he was certain that his heart, once a balloon, sat on his ribcage in fragments.

Caroline: Hi, Andy. Haven't heard from you in a while, but just wanted to check in on picture book updates. I'm getting some scary information about the publishing branch of Helping Hope.

Caroline: I think my job is hinging on us doing extremely well in pre-orders. Ballpark is at least 1000 copies. Can we talk about plans for the launch?

He didn't know much about picture books, but Maisie had talked enough about local authors for him to know that most got lucky if they sold one hundred copies at the pre-order stage. She'd once scrunched her shoulders and said, "People like to wait until the book comes out. They want to see what reviewers have to say. By then, it's too late, and the publishers kill the next project dead in the water."

The idiot he was, he texted her before the rest of her messages rolled in. His phone, now resurrected, appeared to only accept a few messages every couple of minutes. Already the sheer amount of incoming memos had drained his battery another ten percent. He'd have to put the phone on his charger soon.

Andy: Hey! Slowly getting your messages :) Sorry, phone bill wasn't paid until now. My mom says I have to dedicate the book to her to pay her back. Wanna call to talk this over?

Right after he had clicked the blue send button, an email flashed at the top of his screen. He pressed the envelope-shaped button and his stomach clenched as he read:

Andy,

I don't know how to say this politely, or professionally, which is pretty out of character for me. But to say I feel betrayed is an understatement.

I understand we may not have the same working habits, and on our one date before the arboretum, you'd mentioned you never were the biggest fan of group projects. However, I somehow thought this would be different. When you and I were working at the soup kitchen or at the Hope Club, I sensed this synergy. As though you and I could pour soup for an eternity, and I know that sounds silly, but if that soup kitchen came with benefits and 401k I'd sign up right now.

But then you had to go and work with Zinnia.

Zinnia. That was probably the best way to tell me, "Hey, I really hate you."

He paused reading the email when he reached that name.

So she and Zinnia aren't best friends at work? The nails and dangerous, thin eyebrows should've served as a dead giveaway. He did feel his chest go tight and stomach sear around that woman. Why did he trust her with the illustrations? Clearly she didn't get them to Clark as promised. Or if she did, she pretended that Andy had asked to work with *her* instead of Caroline.

And if he said differently in a reply to Caroline, would she even trust him? Who knew what Zinnia had told her about him? He read on:

I don't know where this brutal honesty is coming from. Maybe it's the lawyer mom, the fact the industry I worked so hard to break into for six years is collapsing, or the fact that I have to type this email quickly before my work nemesis reads it.

Zinnia *read* her emails? His intestines wriggled. Man, he had a poor sense of judgment. Pounding sounded from upstairs. His neighbors often put on what Elijah called a clogs dance show. That was the only explanation for the ridiculous thumping noises that came from above. He attempted to block out the din and continued to read:

ALYSSA ROAT AND HOPE BOLINGER | 193

Anyway, I know we had a bit of a rough patch on that arboretum date, but I was hoping we could try again ... until today. I hope you're happy with working with Zinnia on this project. A heads up would've been nice. Especially since at this point, it looks like I'm losing my job over this.

I'm going home to beg my mom to pull some strings in terms of employment. This is the lowest I've felt in a long, long time.

Have a nice life, and please do not respond to this email.

Caroline

Andy slumped into the family room chair. The watercolor paintings in his other hand scattered on the floor and covered his feet. He had messed up. Badly.

He rolled his fist and knuckled his eye. Beside him, Sammy whimpered and set his head on the floor. His tail wagged.

Why hadn't Caroline told him the stakes of the book? That it had put her job on the line? Would he have churned out illustrations much faster had he known?

Charcoal drawings and papers stared at him from every corner of his apartment. The entrance door creaked open and a whoop from Elijah caused Andy to jolt in the seat.

Elijah pumped a fist in the air.

"I got the job."

The invisible weights on Andy's shoulders dissolved. "You did?"

"Yeah, I did." Elijah held up a plastic bag that smelled of broccoli cheese soup. "Met with Pastor Smith at a restaurant. It's basically what ministry people do for interviews. He'd already had his mind made up before the meal. Says that I have a very contemporary music style and it seems to fit with the church's vision for the next year."

Chest puffed out, Elijah marched to the kitchen to place the leftovers in the fridge. Pale refrigerator light bathed his beaming face. He shut the door.

"It's not going to be the same money I saw rolling in from the insurance place. Even though they're a large church, with thousands of congregants, ministry workers still don't make much. But we don't have to worry about rent. Plus, Pastor seems to love that restaurant. So we have a lot of soupy leftovers to look forward to."

A mixture of light and heaviness swirled in Andy's stomach. At least they'd solved one problem. But even with the rent paid, could he live with himself if he knew that soon Caroline would not have an income to pay hers?

"Gonna be honest, I'm a little underwhelmed by your reaction." Elijah smirked and wriggled his eyebrows. "Must be shocked. In the presence of a celebrity." He did a hair flip.

Andy's lips twitched. Then they sank.

"I'm really proud of you, Lij. But there's something else."

He showed Elijah the email and explained the mix-up with Zinnia and how he'd only given her the illustrations to transfer to either Clark or Caroline.

"Caroline said not to reply. But should I, I don't know, try to explain the situation?"

Elijah frowned at the phone screen and then handed the device back to Andy. "I think the bigger problem is the one thousand pre-orders. I don't know much about books, but Caroline sounds deflated by that number. Is it possible to get that many? And is Caroline planning to still write this book? That seems like an even bigger issue."

Did Andy even know a thousand people? Sure, he had that many friends on Facebook. But even if he posted, no way would all of them buy a children's book. Most of them didn't even have kids at this point. Even the ones who could boast of nieces and nephews couldn't always drop ten or fifteen dollars on a picture book.

Something like bricks hit Andy's shoulders when Elijah clapped his hands on them.

"Seems like you have two major problems—the miscommunication and the pre-orders. What are you going to do about both?"

Andy rested his neck on the chair head and glimpsed the artwork that surrounded them in the room. A blurred watercolor waterfall, his first attempt at drawing an eye with a charcoal pencil, a finger-painted robin on construction paper, all hopeful, all imperfect.

"I love what you've done with the place, by the way." Elijah placed a hand on his hip and admired a pipe cleaner lion Andy had placed on their bookshelf. "Looks like that Hope Club exploded in here."

Then, the idea, *the* idea, collapsed on his skull like someone had bonked him in the noggin with his ceramic vase he'd made in fifth grade art that now perched on the kitchen counter.

"Elijah." This came out in a gasp, almost like someone had deprived his lungs of all oxygen. His brain raced. "Do you still have all those index cards?"

"Yeah, why?"

He leapt from the chair. "Because we're going to make sure we sell a thousand books." A painting of a garden flickered in the gust of an air vent. "And we're going to make sure Caroline doesn't lose her job."

Chapter Twenty

CAROLINE PUNCHED IN THE FUEL GRADE with one hand while twisting off the gas cap with the other. She inserted the nozzle and waited for the hose to begin fueling.

Leaning against her car, she rubbed her eyes. In another hour, she would reach the cabin where her parents were staying. In an hour, she would make her plea.

Mom, I'm sorry. I was wrong. I couldn't do it. I'll take any job you can give me.

The dream she had pursued for six years had turned into a nightmare, and now she had awakened. Publishing was as cold and harsh of a world as law or Wall Street. She might as well go somewhere she knew she could eventually succeed.

The pump clicked off, and she returned the nozzle to its cradle.

As she slid behind the wheel, she focused on keeping her emotions in check. She turned her audiobook back on, ready to immerse herself in a world of crime and suspense. However, she was pretty sure she'd figured out whodunnit, and the book was only half done.

Books had always helped her avoid real life problems and emotions. Usually it worked, but today, her mind kept spinning. She'd even turned up the speed of the narration, hoping it would force her to focus, but memories of Mr. Knox's office and dread of seeing Mom infiltrated her thoughts.

Half an hour later, one of the lead detectives in the novel had been kidnapped—typical—and Caroline's heart raced faster with each mile closer to Mom.

Trees whizzed by on either side of her. She flicked on her headlights, traffic dwindling as she left the main highways.

A thump shook the car, a pop, then flapping, flopping *thwacks*.

The steering wheel jerked, and Caroline squeaked. She caught it, pulling her foot off the gas. *Don't hit the brake, don't do it, don't hit it.* She remembered at least that much from driver's ed.

Rocking, flapping, screeching, and thumping, the car drifted toward the shoulder. As the vehicle slowed, Caroline gently applied the brake until it jolted to a stop.

Her breath came in rapid gasps. Another car flew by, rocking her vehicle and reminding her to turn on her hazards. She braced her palms against the steering wheel, mind spinning. *I blew a tire.* She laughed once, a sharp bark. *Of course I did. I blow a tire for the first time in my life when I'm unemployed and in the middle of unfamiliar territory.*

Caroline scanned the road, making sure it was clear, then unbuckled and stepped out of the car.

She rounded the vehicle, taking in the ruptured rear left tire. *Fantastic.* She popped the trunk and ducked inside. After feeling around, she found the tire well and popped it open.

No no no no.

Empty.

She leaned back on her heels, her mind grasping for an explanation. She'd never checked for a spare tire before. There was no way she would have known if the used vehicle included one or not. She hadn't thought to ask.

Great. She pulled her phone out of her pocket, prepared to dial for help...

No signal.

No matter which way she angled it, whether she paced up and down the road, held it high in the air, no bars appeared. The sun began to sink below the horizon.

A slight hill rolled up and away from the road. She stumbled over and collapsed onto the slope, head in her hands.

This situation seemed right. Stranded, without a way to fix her own problems.

Tears squeezed out from beneath her lashes as she clenched her eyes shut. *I tried. I tried so hard.* It was one thing to fail the tests on purpose. Then, she knew she could have succeeded if she had wanted to. It was something else entirely to find herself unemployed, six years wasted, on her way home to throw herself on the mercy of the parents she had walked away from.

She looked up at the sky. "I thought this was what I was supposed to do. It felt right. Was I wrong?"

Her thoughts flashed back to her apartment. Liv's face floated into her mind, her roommate's eyes filled with unshed tears. "Caroline, you can probably pick up a job at a coffee shop or something until a more permanent job comes along. You don't have to do this."

Caroline had stuffed her last pair of pants into her suitcase and zipped it shut. "I'm done chasing a rainbow. I'm going back to something I can actually do."

"But Caroline." Liv stood in the doorway, blocking her way. "This is your dream. I don't care if you do it here or in New York or in the Czech Republic, for goodness sake—though I'd prefer here—but please don't give up. God gave you this passion for a reason."

Caroline had steeled her spine. "I love you, Liv. I'll help you find a roommate from...wherever I am. And I'll keep making rent payments until then. Besides, I'll be back this weekend to pack up my things. I just...I feel like I have to face my mom in person."

Liv threw her arms around Caroline and hugged her tight. "I know you do. And I'm not worried about roommates or the rent or anything else. I'm worried about *you*." She stepped back. "I'm praying for you, girl. Do what you need to do."

Now, head resting on her knees on the side of the road in the near-dark, she wished she had heeded Liv's advice to wait until morning to set out. But she'd been so ready to go, she'd run out without thinking.

What a metaphor.

"I get the picture, God!" she shouted to the sky. "I'm an impulsive, ungrateful disaster, and I can't do anything right. Got it." She dropped her head back into her hands.

Asphalt crunched, and headlights flowed over her. She looked up, squinting at a man stepping out of a pickup truck.

"Are you all right, ma'am?"

Caroline stood, brushing away tears and trying to pull herself together. "I'm fine."

She gripped her keys in her hand, points out, wary. *It would be my luck to get kidnapped on top of everything.*

As the man came closer, she took in his rolling gait as if from sore knees, white sneakers, loose jeans and fishing T-shirt, and the gray hair peeking out from under his tattered ball cap. *Probably not a threat.* Then a small head with pigtails poked out from the other side of the cab. "Who's that, Grandpa?" the little girl called.

"A nice lady who might need help, punkin." Headlights illuminated his affectionate smile.

Caroline relaxed. "I blew a tire, but I don't have a spare, and I can't seem to get any cell service."

"Ah." The man nodded, reaching for a phone clipped to his belt. "Happens more than you'd think around here. Use mine."

"Thank you so much." More tears slipped out as relief flooded through her.

"No worries. We'll stay with you until you can get someone out here. We're not in any hurry. We just had a big meal after a long day fishing. Isn't that right, Lucy?"

"Yeah! I caught a big fish." The girl's pigtails bounced.

Caroline smiled, taking the proffered cell phone. "How big was it?"

"This big!" Lucy stretched her arms out so far she almost fell out the window.

Her grandfather laughed. "Now that's how you tell a fishing story."

Caroline called an auto service and filled them in on the details. While she waited, Lucy and her grandfather, Don, told her all about their fishing trip. By the time the mechanic arrived, they were all laughing as Lucy showed off the way her loose tooth whistled.

"I can't thank you enough." Tears threatened to escape again.

Don swatted an invisible fly. "Don't mention it. All we did was stop for a nice chat. What's life for if not for making some new friends and helping each other out?"

His eyes twinkled. *He really means it.* With a jolt, Caroline wondered if she would have stopped to help someone on the side of the road. *Probably not. I'm always in a hurry to get somewhere.* And if Don had been the same, they never would have laughed over fishing tales, and she would probably be walking along the side of the road in the dark.

Was she missing something in all the hustle?

Half an hour later, she was back on the road, out a pretty penny from roadside assistance, but no longer stranded.

Within a few miles, service returned, and her GPS kicked back into gear. Sooner than she felt ready for, she was pulling into a gravel drive leading to a two-story log cabin with a wide front porch, windows trimmed in forest green, and water sparkling in the background, barely visible from her headlights.

This is it.

She shut off the car, got out, then climbed the porch steps. Her legs felt wobbly. She took a deep breath, raised her fist, and knocked.

A moment later, the door swung open, golden light spilling onto the porch. Kristy Penn stood in the doorway, hair loose, clad in red flannel pajamas and slippers.

Her curious expression melted into a broad smile that rivaled the light shining out into the night.

"Caroline. I'm so happy you're here."

Andy nursed a coffee cup in his hands while Griffith strode to the shop door. Griffith's left hand held a broom and the other flipped the open sign on the door to closed. Since Andy's neighbors decided to do a clog-dancing fest for several days straight, Andy sought refuge in the coffee shop to finish the illustrations to pair with the manuscript Caroline had sent to him and Zinnia.

Zinnia had somehow managed to pilfer his contact information and had been sending him nonstop emails to hammer out the details of the project. *Well, she did get his email from the message Caroline had sent to both of us.*

Hi, Andy,

So excited to be working on this with you. Carrie did such a great job, didn't she? I think kids are going to love this. Let me know a time or place to go over details together.

Cheers!

Zinnia

Hi, Andy,

I had a look at the manuscript, and I think although great, it's sort of heavy hitting for kids, don't you think? Carrie did fabulous, don't get me wrong. But I have a few ideas for changes. One word: unicorns. Let me know what you think!

Cheers!

Zinnia

Hey, Andy,

I haven't heard from you in a while, so I wanted to check in to make sure that everything is all right. Carrie had talked a few days back about you not returning phone calls. Is everything all right? Is there a family emergency?

Let me know any ways I can spearhead more of this project to take it off of your plate and hands. I'm no Da Vinci, but I can draw a pretty great unicorn (see the attachment to this email).

Sending good thoughts your way and hope to hear from you soon.

Cheers.

Zinnia

The "unicorn" attached to the email looked more like a cow with a horn surgically attached to its head. Zinnia had overamplified the legs like fat balloons in what Andy could guess was her first attempt at using a program like Illustrator.

He didn't respond to the emails and returned to his sketches on his computer. Already, in a short period of time, he'd illustrated the majority of the pictures for the book. He averaged about four hours of sleep per night and his body jittered from subsisting on coffee and any leftovers Elijah brought to the shop for him.

Thank the Lord, Griffith worked a few shifts at the shop. One of the nights he closed, he offered to let Andy stay late.

Andy thanked him and gathered all the people he could muster from Elijah's notecards to do one last planning session in the coffee shop. The group now huddled on coffee shop seats with coffee drinks that had turned watery over the past few hours from melted ice.

Griffith banged a dustpan against the trash can and vanished behind the counter with his broom. When he emerged, Andy nodded at him.

"Thanks so much for talking to your boss and letting us stay late."

The other shrugged. "I think she feels guilty for having me stay so many hours, since we're understaffed. You'd think with the number of artists in this town we wouldn't struggle to hire more baristas."

The group, made of mostly fine arts experts, gave a collective laugh and groan.

All of them had worked multiple jobs to sustain their areas of artistry.

Griffith returned to the counter with a rag and wiped down fingerprints on the glass.

"I don't want to keep any of you here too late." Andy shut the lid to his laptop. His eyes stung from staring at the screen for so many hours today. His skull pounded with a headache. "It's past ten, after all. But I wanted to go over some details before the big event in two days."

So this was the feeling of being a group project leader. A mixture of lack-of-sleep confidence *and* uncertainty slurred from his voice. As soon as the event finished, he vowed to get twenty hours of sleep in one night.

During breaks from illustrations, he had called all his contacts to help with the event. Many declined due to the time constraints, but enough agreed to play a part in the pre-orders or event festivities. Tonight's meeting included Maisie, Elijah, Griffith, and Ryan. Even though Griffith had to put to rest the pastry display case an hour before the shop closed, Maisie had brought delicious banana nut muffins to tide them over.

With a jittery arm, Andy grabbed one and pinched a sliver of the treat onto his tongue.

"Lij, since you encouraged me to spearhead this thing, why don't you get started? What are you planning to do at the event?"

Eyes a-twinkle, Elijah leaned over his seat and heaved his guitar case. "Writing music is a lot like writing a picture book ... it takes a lot of time to get all the words right. I wrote a song for the event." He reached into his pocket and unfolded a sheet of notebook paper with messy handwriting on the lines. "But I used the manuscript Caroline sent Andy and put it to music. We figure, if they get enough pre-orders, maybe we can convince Clark to put the song in an audiobook. That way parents and kids can listen to the book on the go."

Andy's roommate had been known to get carsick on road trips in college. He would always wait until they returned to the dorm to do homework, since he couldn't read in the vehicle.

Elijah frowned and added a sharp to one of the A notes marked on the sheet.

"Don't get me wrong, dude. I love the message of the story. But it's missing something."

Andy's stomach dropped. "Missing something?"

"Yeah." Elijah shoved the pen behind his ear. "Every song has at least one line that either punches you in the gut or makes you go, 'whoa, I never thought about it that way.' You've got a great message, but if you want a thousand pre-orders, you need that extra oomph."

No way he could muster a line like that on his own. Clark did *not* assign him as author to this project for a reason.

"The only reason I say this." Elijah placed the guitar case onto a small rug underneath his chair. "Is because I talked with the pastor about the book in my interview. He's really interested in giving out a copy at VBS to any kid who is five to eight years old. Especially since this year's VBS theme revolves around Hope. They charge a twenty-dollar admission price and draw about a thousand kids each year. About five hundred of those would be in the age group for the book."

Five hundred kids. Andy held back a low whistle. He'd almost forgotten that the church in which Elijah interviewed boasted congregation numbers by the thousands. The church alone could cover half the needed pre-orders.

"But the book needs to be airtight." The pen dropped from Elijah's ear into his lap. "I think if you have a line that adds an extra oomph, the pastor will be on board for VBS."

Andy bit into the muffin again and swallowed. The walnuts crunched in his teeth.

"I'll try to keep that in mind. Maybe we keep going around the circle and see how much work we have left to do."

A burnt coffee bean scent lingered in the air.

Maisie raised a hand and dropped it. "Along with stocking plenty of copies in our church library, at least ten, I've asked Pastor if we can have congregation members donate a book for our Backpack Lunches program."

Their church filled bookbags for two hundred children in the Roseville area with meals for weekends, school supplies, and other necessities. Most of the kids got free lunches at school through a government program but had nothing at home for the weekends.

Numbers crunched in Andy's fuzzy skull.

Five hundred at Elijah's church and two hundred at his. Only three hundred to go … if they had the oomph line added to the book.

Ryan pushed his glasses up the bridge of his nose and leaned into a squishy couch. The large cushion appeared to consume his legs and swallow him whole. "Although I can't guarantee any numbers, I'm planning to send the footage I film at the event to local stations. Thanks to doing a billion unpaid internships in college, I know quite a few connections in the area. And they do owe me for hundreds of hours of free labor."

Griffith returned to the circle with a dish towel wrapped on his shoulder. Hums from the machines had died. He must've finished his closing tasks. He *had* begun them about an hour prior, after all.

"I consulted the owner of the theater who puts on my plays." He dipped into a large chair and reached for a muffin. Then he peeled off the wrapper. "They said if I was willing to let them put on one of my shows gratis and with minimal set and costume requirements, they'll pay for a hundred copies and hand it to our drama camp students. *If* the publisher also allows us to have dramatic rights for the book to put on a skit for their summer performance next year."

Something caught in Andy's throat. He tried to swallow to eliminate the dryness.

"Griff, I can't make you do that, man."

His friend lifted and dropped his shoulders. "We're in our twenties, Andy. Half the time we don't get paid or paid properly, at least. Besides, I write so many plays." He pinched a walnut. "But I will probably call in a favor later."

"For a hundred copies, I'm willing to design programs, posters, anything you need for free."

That brought them to eight hundred. And hopefully with the TV publicity from Ryan and their friends and family on social media, they could get that number to the needed one thousand pre-orders. Perhaps Clark could go easy on them if he knew they'd come close to that number.

"All right, looks like we have almost everything set for the event." Andy's thumbs rubbed his droopy eyelids.

Now all they needed was the perfect line for the book.

Chapter Twenty-One

CAROLINE'S MOUTH OPENED AND CLOSED. FINALLY, she managed, "You're...happy to see me?"

Mom didn't get a chance to answer before Dad appeared in the doorway as well, grinning. "Carrie-girl. When you asked for the address, I thought you might be sending a letter."

A nervous laugh burbled from her throat. Was the porch swaying? "Here I am."

Mom stepped forward, her smile faltering, turning almost... hesitant? But Mom never hesitated. "Caroline, I'm so glad you came. Please, come in."

Caroline followed her parents into the cabin. Warm lamplight spilled across wooden floors of deep and shining red-brown and a den filled with cozy black leather easy chairs and a loveseat. A pinecone centerpiece sat on a table for six to the left, near the kitchen in the open floor plan. Stairs in the middle presumably led to bedrooms upstairs.

What truly stood out to her, though, were the lived-in touches. A newspaper—an actual, physical newspaper—on the coffee table, what looked like a half-finished crochet project, a book face down on an end table next to a mug with a tea bag hanging out of it as if someone had been drinking a hot beverage while reading before opening the door.

Nothing like the austere modernity of their New York home.

"This place is wonderful," she said.

A soft smile played on Mom's lips. "I like it a lot." She glanced at Dad, smile deepening. "I'm so glad your father suggested it."

Who are you, and what did you do with my mother?

Caroline studied Mom. She had regained color since Caroline had last seen her, and the hard planes of her face looked smoother. She might look more worn than usual, but that probably also had to do with the lack of makeup and the flannel pajamas.

It disconcerted her. She'd planned her speech, her plea for forgiveness, in the face of the cold reception she'd expected. She had her arguments crafted, her heart steeled.

But now Mom…welcomed her?

It was too much.

"I lost my job," she blurted. "I lost my job, my manuscripts have been rejected by everyone and their mother, I'm no closer to that editing job than the day I left college. Plus, the guy I thought I might like completely ghosted me."

She hadn't expected that last part to come out. Her parents' eyes widened. She pressed on. "I've failed, I give up, I'm so sorry. I'll take whatever job you can give me. You were right, Mom. All of this was stupid."

Her heart raced and her chest heaved as if she'd sprinted all the way from Michigan to Ohio. She braced herself for the "I told you so," for the criticism.

Instead, Mom's eyes filled with tears. "No, Caroline. *I'm* sorry."

Dad put his hand on Mom's shoulder and kissed her temple. "I'm going up to bed. I'll leave you two to talk." He gave Caroline a smile and a discreet thumbs up before heading for the stairs.

Mom hesitated. Again. "Why don't we sit in the living room?"

Mom settled in the seat near the abandoned mug of tea, and Caroline sat across from her. As silence stretched, Caroline broke it. "I've been so stupid. I didn't want to be a lawyer or investor or anything with that sort of pressure and competition and ruthlessness, so I ran off to write *stories*. But you know what? Publishing is exactly the same. Maybe even worse, because you throw your heart into it, only to have it flung back in your face. It's the same rat race."

A line had formed between Mom's brows, and she leaned forward. "Caroline…"

Caroline's heart was pounding too hard, her eyes stinging too much to stop. "You know what I did? I failed those tests on purpose. So

I could get out from under you and do what *I* wanted. I thought I would do something *meaningful*." She laughed sharply. "I should have known better. You were right all along."

A tear tracked down Mom's cheek, reflecting like liquid gold in the lamplight. "No, Caroline. I was so, so wrong."

Caroline sank back into the soft, dark leather. She felt like she was sinking in a sea of confusion, and the overstuffed couch wasn't helping matters. "You...what?"

Mom pushed a hand through her hair. "I wanted the best for you. I remembered what it was like as a teenager when I had big dreams. Grandma couldn't do a lot to help me, so I had to scrape everything together myself. I wanted to give you something better than what I had." She sighed. "I guess I forgot the most important part of that. The dream."

Mom leaned forward and reached for Caroline's hand. Stunned, Caroline let her take it.

"I got so lost in the success. At first, I had a passion for law. I loved the idea of justice, of fair representation, the thrill of the case, the way things came together after all the research and compiling. But then...I got caught up in being the best and forgot why I started all this in the first place. And I burned myself out."

Caroline bit her lip and squeezed Mom's hand, remembering the skeletal form she'd seen a few weeks ago.

"You and your father were the best things to happen to me." Mom gave a half smile, eyes distant. "I fought against falling for your father. He wasn't part of my twenty-year plan. But I'm glad I did." She focused back on Caroline. "I wanted so much to give you the world. And after you stormed out, threw it away—"

Caroline flinched.

"I was livid. I would have done anything for those opportunities as a young woman." Mom rubbed her temple. "But after the burnout, with nothing to do but sit with my thoughts, I realized something. A part of me had always admired you for daring to dream." She met Caroline's eyes. "But the young woman I saw a few weeks ago forgot the dream."

Caroline pulled away, throat tight. How could she say that? "I've done everything I possibly could."

"That's the problem. It's like you said. You exchanged one rat race for another. But it isn't supposed to be that way." Mom looked toward the ceiling, as if begging God for words. "You left to follow a dream and a passion that God placed on your heart, to tell stories to give people hope. But because of me, and your need to prove yourself, you forgot why you were doing it." Tears flowed in earnest. "You're a storyteller, Caroline. It doesn't matter if five people read it or five million. It doesn't matter if you're editing New York Times bestsellers or the church bulletin. If you're doing what God placed on your heart and following His leading, you're a success. And I'm so proud of you for following His call."

You're a success. I'm so proud of you. The words rang like cathedral bells, reverberating in her soul. But most of all… "You really wanted the best for me?" She could hardly force the words out. "I thought I was a status symbol. I thought you only cared so that people wouldn't think badly about us." She choked on a sob. "I thought you were mad about me failing those tests because it meant you had a failure of a daughter."

Mom sucked in a sharp breath. "Oh, my darling girl. I've made so many mistakes." She took Caroline's hands. "I love you. And *I've* been stupid. I was so angry that you weren't doing what I thought was best for you that I let it come between us. When all that really matters is that we're here for each other and love one another." She squeezed her hands. "I've always loved you. But I showed it in all the wrong ways. Please forgive me."

A sob burst from Caroline's throat, and she threw herself forward, wrapping her mother in a hug. "I understand." She laughed. "I understand a little too well. Workaholism seems to run in this family."

"Like mother, like daughter." Mom's arms held her in a way Caroline hadn't realized she ached for. Tight but gentle. Full of love and apologies and forgiveness.

Caroline spent the next day with her parents. They played games, baked cookies, snuggled under blankets by the fire, and watched a Christmas movie even though it was well past Easter. No one spoke of jobs or work or books or New York. Instead, for the first time Caroline could remember, they took a family vacation.

As the credits rolled on *Miracle on 34th Street*, Caroline's mind drifted to the picture book. She'd written words about hope in little things, about finding meaning and happiness no matter your background. But had she, unintentionally, implied that the hope came from believing a person could achieve no matter the situation? Had she, instead of giving kids encouragement, set them up to believe they had to attain something to make their lives worthy?

What kind of hope was that?

Instead, kids needed to know that they were precious and loved no matter what. And if they were following their calling, the passion God had placed upon their heart, they would end up exactly where they were meant to be.

Her eyes began to drift closed. She'd put on her pajamas already, and nestled under blankets on a couch that felt like a giant pillow, sleep called to her.

A line floated across her mind.

Andy would like that.

A groggy sort of clarity rolled through her with the thought. Andy was passionate about this project. There was no way he would drop out completely. He must have a reason for ignoring both her and Zinnia.

I trust you, Andy. Despite everything, she hoped he pulled off the best book Helping Hope had ever seen. And she would help with what she could. She'd send him the line, and he could take it or leave it, but at least she would know she'd done everything she could.

But not tonight. Tonight, I'm warm and cozy and loved.

She slipped into peaceful dreams.

For the first time in his life, Andy arrived early.

Three hours early, in fact. He and Elijah strolled into Helping Hope at 9 a.m. They emptied the trunk of Andy's car of boxes. The containers held to-be-inflated balloons, fun ceiling lanterns and strings of lights Elijah had borrowed from his church's youth leader, and Andy's illustrations. He made sure to keep the latter in a large manila folder, so none of the papers would crease.

Now in the large room that had once hosted a game of Corgi, Corgi, Chihuahua, Elijah dropped the final box of balloons and tore up the tape on top with an X-Acto knife. He pinched the neck of a balloon and strode to a pink helium container.

Letters in the shape of H O P E inflated.

"So, Andy." Elijah released the pump on the helium tank. "When are the others going to get here?"

Fuzz still filled his brain. He'd spent the last night in group messages and in his email ensuring that everyone knew when to arrive and get set up before the kick-off at noon.

He had *yet* to message Caroline. Figured that perhaps she would refuse if he gave her plenty of time to think about it. Thankfully, Elijah happened to work with Caroline's roommate at his church's new worship team—as Elijah discovered during that week's practice.

Worst case, Elijah said he could text Caroline's roommate to drag her here for the event.

Andy scaled a ladder with blue streamers and tape in one hand. "We have the coffee shop crew coming in about an hour to help us finish setting up. And the auctioneers will arrive one hour before the event to get settled into their tables."

During the auction Helping Hope had put on where Andy met Caroline, Elijah had suggested over text that Andy collect business cards from all the vendors at the event, in case they needed any help with graphic design projects. He'd spent this past week asking if they'd be willing to hold an auction for items they sold and give half the proceeds to Helping Hope charity, specifying that they wanted to support the book ... to cover the gap of one hundred more pre-orders they needed.

Most declined as they would not make a profit. But twelve vendors agreed and sent him a list of items they'd sell off.

Elijah had created a graphic design poster in Canva to help with some of the preparation work.

Although not amazing, Elijah had chosen a clean font and consistent blue color scheme. Andy approved the layout, with a few tweaks, and set Elijah loose to share the event on Facebook and other social media platforms. Elijah, who had a few thousand followers on social media from sharing songs he'd written, encouraged everyone to spread word of the pre-launch.

The post had received hundreds of shares, last Andy checked. This included some of the pages of TV stations Ryan had connections to. And even though they'd listed the event on Facebook only a few days prior, at least one hundred people said they would attend. Considering their town had a megachurch, they had thousands of contacts they reached out to. Thankfully, a small percentage of those agreed to come.

The Hope Club kids would also arrive about fifteen minutes before the event, so Andy could run them through what he needed them to do. He'd asked Linda which children often came during this day of the week, and he illustrated as many of them as possible. In three hours, they'd hold up the illustrations featuring their visages.

Although they still didn't have that killer line yet—after numerous failed attempts and one hundred filled out index cards from Andy and Elijah—perhaps the children themselves would sway Elijah's pastor to purchasing copies for his VBS.

Andy stuck a streamer on the ceiling and twisted the long paper on the way to the floor. He moved the ladder to the opposite side of the room and hung up the remaining end of the pennant.

Whew. He wiped his forehead with the back of his hand. Good thing they arrived early. It could take an hour to festoon the ceiling alone.

"Need a little help?"

He spun on his heel and squinted at the entrance to the large room. His mother, arms crossed, lips a-smirk, leaned against the doorframe.

"Mom?" His chest warmed and then a shock replaced the heat moments later. "Please tell me you haven't been driving since nine o' clock last night."

She shoved herself into a standing position and strode toward him. "No, sweetheart. I got here yesterday. Stayed in a motel. Elijah told me you might need help this morning." She outstretched her arms. He collapsed into them, and they embraced for a few moments.

Andy released her. "You didn't have to drive all this way."

"And miss this big event? I always tried to make every art show and basketball game in high school. You'd think I'd let a few hundred miles deter me?"

Mixtures of warmth and guilt stirred in his chest. Why had he taken so long to talk with her?

"Now." His mom triangled an arm on her hip. Today she'd adorned herself in a long-sleeve flowery dress. "What can I help you with?"

"I can try to see if Linda has another ladder. I'd love to get those lanterns and other decorations from Elijah's church hung."

Pink honeycomb balls, white pom-pom paper flowers, and multi-colored circular paper fans overflowed in a box near the windows on the other side of the room.

He pushed through the double doors into the kitchen and found Linda packing potato chips into a lunch bag.

"Linda, any chance that you have another ladder? We had another volunteer come early, and we can use all the help we can get."

Her gloved fingers scratched at her plastic hairnet. "Can't say that we do, sorry."

He told her "no worries" and slid his phone out of his pocket to text the group to bring extra ladders when they arrived. Two hours might cut it close, but they could try to cover as much surface area as possible.

When he opened his phone, he noticed a red notification under his texts. *Must've missed a few messages.* He clicked on the green speech bubble button, and his stomach constricted when he saw the name "Caroline Penn" in bold.

Oh, no. Had word gotten out to her about the event? Of course, he had shared about it on his Facebook page, and last he checked, she hadn't unfriended him. Yet. But she didn't strike him as the kind of person to scroll through social media all the time. Maybe she missed the post.

If she wanted to cancel now, he'd have to execute what Elijah called: "Order 66: Roommate Forces Caroline to Attend Event Anyway."

They had, after all, been a bit enigmatic when it came to convincing Clark and other members of the Helping Hope Publishing branch to attend. They may or may not have promised a pizza party for all their hard work. Andy reminded himself to call for pizza closer to the event time.

A shaky thumb tapped the message.

Caroline: Hi, Andy. I know I was a bit rash in my email to you. I assumed things and didn't give you a chance to explain what happened. Zinnia's been messaging me nonstop. And although I know you can sometimes be disorganized, I don't think you'd take days to get back to her if you were actually planning to work on the project with her.

Caroline: Anyway, I didn't want to text you about Zinnia. I recently had a chance to go home, and I'm seeing things a little differently. I know this is last-minute, and we aren't even still working on this project together …

Caroline: But I came up with a line I really think you should include in the book. It would need a beautiful illustration, of course, but let me know what you think. It came to me almost as a dream.

She'd attached an image.

The line of text was so short, so simple, and yet it conveyed everything he wished he had been able to put into words for this book. *That's it. That's the line.*

He backed into the double doors and felt the blood drain from his face. He'd need to come up with an illustration for this line, and in less than two hours.

Elijah caught his eye, mid-blue balloon inflate. His roommate frowned. "You okay?"

Andy showed him the text messages. "I think I could get an illustration done before the event." He had brought his laptop in case the drawings got damaged on the drive to the Hope Club. "It's gonna be tight. But." He scanned the empty ceiling and walls. "I don't want to leave you guys behind to do all the decorations."

Elijah's eyebrows scrunched. "You're kidding me, right? Priorities, dude. Your mom and I"—he gestured to Andy's mother, who secured a paper lantern to the ceiling with tape—"can handle ourselves while you do this drawing. Remember five hundred of the sales depend on it."

Right, half the needed pre-orders. No pressure.

With a nod, he marched out the doors and toward the parking lot to retrieve his laptop. On the way, he rattled off a text message to Caroline.

Andy: That's the most beautiful line I've ever read. Meet me at the Hope Club at noon. I have something here I think you won't want to miss.

Chapter Twenty-Two

CAROLINE TAPPED ON THE STEERING WHEEL, humming along to an upbeat tune.

It felt right to head home to Michigan after a couple of days. She still had no job, but she could at least get her affairs in order before packing up her things and moving in with her parents. And Liv had been oddly insistent that she be there by Saturday.

Only a week ago, that thought of moving back in with her parents would have filled her with horror. Now, it just made sense. Her parents would be staying in Ohio for a month-long sabbatical, and they had a lot of catching up to do. They could all spend time together while she applied for jobs.

"Of course," Mom said, "if you don't find one you like, you can always work in my office for a while until you find something you're passionate about."

Before she'd left early that morning, she had tapped out a message to Andy, sharing the line she had come up with. She had waffled on whether or not to send it for long enough. He could take it or leave it.

Now, as she exited I-90 toward a gas station, something vibrated in her purse in the passenger seat. She glanced at the clock on her dash. Nine thirty. It shouldn't be Dad checking on her already. He would know she wouldn't be home for another few hours.

She pulled up to a pump, then reached into her purse and grabbed the phone. Once the device was in her hand, she glanced at the notification.

Andy Jackson.

Her heart sped up. She tapped the message.

Andy: That's the most beautiful line I've ever read. Meet me at the

Hope Club at noon. I have something here I think you won't want to miss.

The Hope Club? And why would he want to meet her anywhere? She wasn't part of the project, or part of his life. She scrolled up. *Did I mention something about the Hope Club in my message that I forgot about?*

She noticed another bubble, one of Andy's, above her own texts. Another message? It was dated from a few days ago. She must have missed it.

Andy: Hey! Slowly getting your messages :) Sorry, phone bill wasn't paid until now. My mom says I have to dedicate the book to her to pay her back. Wanna call to talk this over?

"Your phone bill?" Caroline shrieked to no one. "You didn't answer me because you didn't pay your phone bill?"

A man passing her car headed for the convenience store shuffled away faster.

Torrents of thought rushed through her mind. Andy hadn't answered her because he hadn't paid his bill. He hadn't been ignoring her?

Her eyes widened. If he had slowly been getting her messages, he would have gotten her texts first. The texts he had responded to. And then...her email.

The email where she told him not to talk to her.

"Noooo," she moaned. Her face heated with embarrassment. Even worse, Andy probably hadn't been able to pay the bill because he'd been dedicating so much time to their project that he didn't have time for freelance gigs. She'd helped to cause this problem.

Caroline changed the input on her GPS to the Hope Club. She would be cutting it close to make it there by noon, but there was no way she wouldn't meet Andy there.

She had finished filling up and was about to pull out of the gas station when her phone buzzed again. She glanced at the message hovering above the map of the GPS.

Liv: Hey, did Andy message you?

Caroline's brow wrinkled. She typed a message with one hand while waiting for a truck to pass so she could turn onto the road.

Caroline: Yes. Why?

By the time she glanced at her phone again after merging onto the interstate, there was still no response. *Odd.*

A couple hours later, she still racked her brain trying to figure out what Andy could possibly want her to see. Maybe his spreads? But why at the Hope Club, at noon?

The clock read 11:50. The GPS gave an arrival estimate of 12:05, despite her speeding. She spoke into her phone, using voice-to-text. "Hey, Andy. I'm running a little late, but I'll be there around five after."

He didn't respond either. Just like Liv. *Is there something wrong with my phone?*

When she pulled into the entrance to Helping Hope's parking lot, her eyes widened. Every spot seemed to be taken. Vehicles were even parked on medians and the side of the road. *What on earth?*

Caroline expected to have to circle around and park somewhere else, but she spied an open spot right near the entrance, the only one in the entire lot. She hesitated, but she didn't see any cones or handicap accessibility signs, and she was already running late, so she pulled into it.

She slung her purse over her shoulder, suddenly remembering her appearance. She hadn't bothered to do her hair or makeup, since she would be driving for hours. She pulled a miniature brush from her bag and ran it through her hair. Luckily, she had opted for jeans to go with her old Helping Hope T-shirt and tennis shoes instead of the sweats she had considered. She could never walk into Helping Hope's office like this, but it was good enough for the kids at the Hope Club.

Asphalt crunched under her shoes. She stepped onto the sidewalk in front of the Hope Club and pulled open the door.

The hall was empty, the table unattended. *Okay...* Caroline stepped inside and headed for the large room where the kids played their canine version of Duck, Duck, Goose. She rounded the corner, and—

"Surprise!"

A line of children holding up colorful sheets of paper greeted her. Behind them, a crowd cheered and clapped. Caroline's mouth dropped open.

Streamers hung from the ceiling, balloons bobbing between them. Booths ringed the perimeter of the wide room, but she could barely spare them a glance with the pictures—the *illustrations*—in front of her.

Her feet carried her forward while her eyes remained glued on the first illustration—a cover. The words "Picture Imperfect" shone from the image like stained glass. *Picture Imperfect. Clever.* Andy had changed the name, and it was, indeed, perfect.

Her eyes drifted downward to the names, and her breath caught. *Written by Caroline Penn, Illustrated by Andy Jackson.* Her name was still there? What about Zinnia? All Mr. Knox had seen from Caroline was the proposed manuscript. Had he approved it?

She continued down the line. The little girl holding the next picture grinned up at her with a gap-toothed smile. Caroline managed a stunned smile back and fixed her gaze on the art.

Colorful, whimsical artwork, created with multiple tiny brushstrokes—wait. Caroline leaned closer. Hundreds of tiny *shapes*. He *illustrated* mosaics. She couldn't even imagine the depth of attention to detail that took.

She floated down the line of illustrations, the rest of the room fading away around her. Thirty-two pages. Each one with a segment of her manuscript and a rich illustration from Andy.

Then, at the end, Wyatt held up an iPad. Their eyes met and he grinned, holding the iPad higher. Her gaze drifted downward to the device, and her breath caught.

Her line, the one she had texted Andy, sprawled across the screen, surrounded by Andy's artwork.

He'd illustrated the line. In mere hours, he'd done it.

Something tickled her cheek, and she brushed it away, only to look down at her hand in surprise at the wetness. Tears.

Arms flung around her. "What do you think?" Liv squealed.

"You knew?"

Her roommate laughed. "Of course!" She pulled Caroline toward the crowd. "You'll never believe what Andy was able to pull off. He has practically half the town involved."

Liv chattered and Caroline followed in a daze. Kids laughing and playing. Leaders of organizations, schools, and churches chatting, smiling, congratulating her. As if in a dream, she watched Griffith give a dramatic reading of the book to enraptured children. Was that cameraman from a news outlet?

She peered over heads, trying to find Andy. But he seemed to be everywhere, helping set up tables, organizing snacks, and shaking hands with pastors, volunteers, and members of Helping Hope.

"Liv," Caroline whispered. "There are so many people. I knew he cared about this project, but…"

Liv whirled to face her, mouth agape. "The *project*?" She grabbed Caroline's shoulders. "Caroline. Yeah, I'm sure he cares about this project. But all this?" She waved at the venue. "This is for *you*."

Her heart turned to liquid. Those tears from earlier might make a comeback.

"I think I need to talk to him."

Liv elbowed her. "You think?" She began to stroll away. "I'm going to get some punch. Find that illustrator of yours."

After Ryan snapped a photo of all the kids holding up the illustrations, Andy glanced at Clark. The man was stationed by a window with a plate full of greasy cheese pizza. Beside Andy, Caroline was chatting with Andy's mother about the plot of her mystery book.

Time to get Caroline's job back.

Andy squeezed Caroline's shoulder. She jolted at his touch.

"Be right back," he told her. He set down the iPad that held his newest illustration with Caroline's *line* she'd messaged him a few hours prior. The iPad screen blinked to black on the auctioneer's table where he'd placed it. Blue plastic covered the surface area of the stand that advertised tickets to a Wolverines baseball game.

Andy nodded to the vendor, a woman with a baseball cap and Coke-bottle glasses. "I'll grab this device in just a moment. Watch it for me?"

She shrugged and twirled a blue pen in one of her sable curls. "I'm not going anywhere." A man, looking to be about fifty, signed his name on the silent auction sheet for that table.

With the newest illustration now safe under the watch of baseball lady, Andy strode toward Clark. Although Andy had attempted to carry the illustration around with him earlier in the event, he found it difficult to juggle plates of food while holding the drawing. Scents of grease and pepperoni drifted past. This mixed with the smells of latex balloons that crowded every single corner of the room. Perhaps his mom and the crew didn't need him there after all. While he'd illustrated the newest creation, he'd noticed his phone buzzed a lot. Probably texts from the group saying they'd arrived early and brought more ladders and tape.

Clark almost jumped an inch in the air when he spotted Andy.

"Andy, almost didn't see you." Clark dabbed the top of his pizza with a brown napkin. "That was quite the presentation you had there."

Zinnia stood off the side and gabbed loudly to a coworker about how she'd managed to do two weeks' worth of work in two days for Helping Hope. "It sure has been tough taking on the tasks of two people. But thankfully I don't crack much under pressure."

Flames heated in Andy's cheeks, but he kept his gaze focused on Clark, lips still upturned.

"Thanks, Clark, glad to hear you think that. I gotta say, Caroline really is the reason this event happened. She's driven, inspirational, and I don't think any of this could have happened without her."

Sure, Caroline hadn't met with them in the coffee shop to discuss details, nor did she string a single paper lantern to the ceiling. But it wasn't a lie. She had provided Andy the inspiration he needed, the extra push.

Color flushed a little across Clark's face. He pulled at a tight, large tie draped on his neck.

"Caroline was one of our best workers. I was sorry to have to let her go."

"But that's the brilliant thing. You might not have to."

Clark cleared his throat. "Yes, well, you see…"

An elderly woman with a cherry-red cane ambled closer. Andy smiled and nodded to Miss Evie. She winked.

"Hold on, Clark. Why don't you see what this young man has to say?"

Andy explained about his plan to acquire one thousand pre-orders. Elijah had brought along the pastor of his church. The giant of a man, 6'6" at the most modest of estimates, ducked underneath a low-hanging paper flower. Ice blond hair and sapphire eyes boasted of a Scandinavian descent.

Clark rubbed his chin and almost dropped his plate of pizza. "If Helping Hope discovers that you've secured those one thousand pre-orders, that could convince them to reinstate Caroline. Heck, I don't think any of our books have ever gotten more than two hundred pre-orders. Maybe she'd even get a raise."

Conversation from Zinnia had halted. She still had her back turned to the two of them, but Andy noticed she'd backed a few inches and angled her ear toward Clark.

"But." Clark leaned against an auction table for a romantic dinner for two at the local Italian hotspot Speranza e Bellezza. "If Pastor Smith over there falls through, no dice. He's carrying half of the pre-orders needed."

Andy's heart catapulted into his throat.

Felt like someone had trapped a bird in his esophagus. During the presentation, he'd watched the pastor's expression to see if they'd won him over. When Andy held up the iPad, he did notice Pastor Smith's eyebrows had shot up. But aside from that, the man's stone expression had not crumbled even the slightest bit.

He swallowed and nodded. "I'll go check on that right now."

Miss Evie offered a wide grin and mouthed, "You can do it."

His legs wobbled as he strode toward the pastor. Of course, Andy's mother had decided to start a conversation with the pastor as she balanced a plate of celery sticks and dip in her hand. Her pupils twinkled at Andy when she spotted him making his way toward her. As if somehow able to read his mind, she waved at Pastor Smith and backed away.

The large man swiveled and knocked the dangling paper flower with his forehead. The decor piece whirled round and round like a ceiling fan.

Andy extended his arm to shake Smith's hand. Pastor had an iron wrench grip.

"Thank you so much for coming. I know weekends can be crazy for churches."

"Not a problem." Ah, so the man had a deep voice to match that large frame. "One weekend a month we have one of our associate pastors preach. It's actually a week off for me."

"Oh." Warmth filled Andy's face. He hadn't realized he'd pulled the pastor away from a break week. Who would want to spend their time at a charity auction for books?

"I have to say, Andy." The pastor reached up to stop the paper decoration from its merry-go-round motions. "As a pastor of a large church, we have a lot of congregants who write books." He let out a low whistle. "I am happy that God has given them a heart for story. But God, it seems, has not given them a heart for copy editing."

A nervous laugh tickled Andy's throat. His memories flipped

through all the illustrations and words that accompanied them. Caroline edited the manuscript copy, right? *Please, Lord, tell me I didn't forget a comma.*

"So when Elijah came to me and told me about this book … I was skeptical. You would not believe the number of children's book writers in my congregation who want the church to buy hundreds of copies for our Vacation Bible School students."

Great. Maybe Elijah had exaggerated about the pastor's excitement for the book. So much for the five hundred copies and getting Caroline's job back.

"However." The pastor motioned toward the table with Andy's iPad. "During your presentation, that line caught my attention."

Andy had managed to hook up his iPad to a projector. During the presentation, on the wall behind him, it displayed the words from Caroline's text:

If it seems big or small,
You have already won,
If you follow your call.

"I don't know if you came up with that line recently, and that's why you hadn't printed it out, but I'm certainly glad you did. That alone sold the book for me."

All of Andy's body un-tensed. He hadn't recognized the stress-filled throbs in his shoulders until now.

The pastor clapped a heavy hand on Andy's shoulder. There was the tension again. "I look forward to ordering five hundred copies when the book becomes available." He reached into his pocket and procured a white business card with black Calibri-style font on the front. Stark and all-business. "Give me a ring once I can do so."

With that, the pastor, best he could, disappeared behind a string of dangling lights and paper fans.

All breath had left Andy. They did it.

Moments later, he regained his composure. Like a balloon, he inflated until his spine uncurled and lungs filled with oxygen once more. He caught Clark's eye from across the room and gave a thumbs up. Zinnia, beside Clark, peered at him with slit eyelids. Blotches formed around her eyes, and she swooped her bag strap around her shoulder and marched toward the exit.

He scanned the room and his eyes landed on Caroline. She high-fived a small boy who talked animatedly with his arms. Clark emerged into Andy's line of vision moments later and spoke with Caroline. Andy wanted to tear his gaze away to give her a moment of privacy, but he couldn't help it.

She clapped her hand to mouth, and she searched the room.

Look away, Andy. Look away.

Part of him felt as though he didn't deserve her. His procrastination made her lose her job. But something instinctual rose up in him that refused to hide behind a balloon tower Elijah had formed from leftover decorations and one of the ladders at the other end of the room.

Like a game of hide and seek from childhood, he did and didn't want to be found.

He lost the game moments later. She'd located him.

They should have talked earlier but he didn't have much time with the presentation and all. And as soon as *that* ended people came up to him and asked questions and shook his hand.

Caroline weaved her way through the crowd packed into that large room. They'd had a much bigger turnout than those who'd signed up on Facebook. Then again, he hadn't checked since this morning to see who all agreed to come. Many people, like him, choose to arrive at the very last minute.

When she'd reached a space about four feet away from him, she jabbed an accusing finger at him.

"You."

"Me," he admitted.

"You did all of this? To help me get my job back?"

"Well, not just the job, there were the kids too and—" He paused. "*Did* you get your job back?"

She clutched her elbows. "Clark has to run it by the board, but he says he doesn't see any reason for them not to. This book, after all, did save the publishing branch at Helping Hope."

Huh, so they *had* done it. *Thank you, Lord, for your help and for the aid of friends and family.*

"So." She stared at her flats and one side of her lip curved upward. "I think we have quite a lot to talk about. You want to try that coffee date again?"

Warmth filled his chest, as though he'd chugged a latte right at that moment.

"I'd like that."

Chapter Twenty-Three

"SHE'S ALL YOURS," the volunteer told Andy.

Caroline's heart soared. She squealed and wrapped her arms around Peaches' neck, laughing as the dog licked her chin.

Andy grinned back at her, setting the pen down as he handed the adoption papers back to the volunteer. "If Caroline doesn't run off with her first."

Caroline ruffled the dog's ears and kissed Peaches on her fuzzy snout. "Only if you don't let me see her often enough."

Fully restored to her job at Helping Hope, she wouldn't be home during the day to care for a dog—but as a freelancer, Andy would be. She had visited the shelter so many times in the past two weeks to see Peaches that Andy decided it was time to do something about it.

"Sammy needs a friend to get him moving anyway," Andy had said. "Kind of like me." Then he'd offered that slow grin she loved so much. "My place is a little closer to visit than the shelter. We even have a dog park nearby."

"I *guess* I could come take walks with you at the park," she teased back. "Strictly to see Peaches."

"Of course. Dog business only."

As Andy took Peaches' leash and they walked out of the shelter, Caroline felt like skipping. She impulsively grabbed Andy's hand. His face registered surprise, then his ears pinked. She grinned up at him. "Can I buy her bows? What about treats? I know she's a little tubby, but I think that's just her body type. Maybe we can teach her how to shake and roll over to earn treats, and—"

Andy chuckled, squeezing her hand. "Yes. Yes to all of those." Then his expression turned more hesitant. "So...it kind of sounds like you want to be around quite a bit. It takes time to train a dog."

She cocked her head. "Is that bad?"

"No! No." He shook his head vigorously. "Not at all. I just…"

They made it to where his car sat. Caroline's was parked a few spaces down. They would have to part ways, and Caroline could meet him at the dog park. She hadn't bothered to change after work, but she couldn't bring herself to care. Not when Peaches finally had a home.

Andy rubbed the back of his neck with the hand holding Peaches' leash. The dog panted up at both of them, tongue lolling from the side of her mouth. He didn't let go of Caroline's hand with the other. "I know we've only been on a few dates—well, a few dates since the book event. I didn't really count the ones before, but I mean, we could if you want to, but I—"

Caroline giggled. "I understand."

"Okay." He grinned and took a deep breath. "I'm just saying, I know it hasn't been all that long. But I was wondering, well…"

One foot fidgeted against the asphalt, and his gaze fixed downward, highlighting his long lashes. A curl fell across his forehead. Caroline reached up to push the lock aside, smirking internally as his cheeks flushed darker. "Yes?"

"Um, I was wondering if you might want to make things more, um, official?"

He's so adorable all flustered. Her smirk emerged externally. "Are you asking me to be your girlfriend?"

He looked up, meeting her gaze, worry and hope warring in his eyes. "Yeah?"

Before she lost her nerve, she stood on her tiptoes and kissed his cheek. "The answer is yes." She darted away, cheeks burning. "See you at the dog park."

His startled laugh rang out after her as she scurried to her car and hopped in the driver's seat. Peaches barked, caught up in the excitement.

Caroline sank behind the wheel and sighed, cheeks aching from smiling.

Maybe she wasn't a bestselling author. Maybe she worked for a nonprofit in Michigan instead of editing for famous authors at a New York publisher.

But she couldn't be happier with the picture imperfect life she'd been given.

Andy applied the final brushstroke to the wall of the Sunday school classroom. A white dot in the pupil of Mary Magdalene's eye as she sat at the foot of Jesus, listening to his teachings. The mural in the classroom boasted of blotches, paint splatters, and lines that curved where they shouldn't have.

In other words, it was perfect.

"Took you long enough."

Maisie hmphed but softened the words with a smile. She leaned against the door frame with a bundle of books cradled in her arms. He'd almost forgotten it was release day.

For the past few months, Caroline and Andy had marketed until their fingers about fell off. Caroline, having read tons of issues of *Publishers Weekly*, informed Andy that most books took at least a year from contract to print. But Clark didn't appear to have read any copies of PW as of late and decided that since they already had one thousand pre-orders that they wanted to rush to get the copies out to customers.

Andy plunked his small paintbrush into a cup of murky water and toweled off the paint on his hands with the drop cloths situated on the floor.

"Yeesh, Maisie, you bought enough for every kid in church."

She heaved the stack of picture books onto the bookshelf in the children's classroom. Something about the way Andy's name gleamed in small, white font on the book spine sent a shudder down Andy's backbone. He unrolled his fists and sent up a prayer.

Okay, God. You meant for this to happen. Help me to accept your plan.

Jitters had attacked both him and Caroline over the past few weeks.

Almost once a day one of them had said something along the lines of, "Do you think it's ready?"

"Should *we* have done a book together and not some industry professional?"

"What if everyone hates this thing?"

The reviews that rolled in for the book didn't help. Although many gave the book five or four stars with comments such as "beautiful," "heartwarming," and "hopeful," a few sticklers deemed the project only worth two stars with the accompanying epithets "asinine" or "even I could write this drivel."

Thankfully, one or the other of them often had sense in these moments. Several coffee dates and strolls through the arboretum helped to clear their minds.

He relaxed and warmth replaced the coldness in his chest. They'd published a book. A real, *actual* book.

Paint fumes heightened the headache at the front of his skull. He sidestepped into the hallway and Maisie followed. She'd kept one of the books and clutched it against her heart. "Speaking of every kid from the church, I know parents who are already heading to the book signing now. Why aren't you there yet?"

Ice once again replaced the blood in his veins. He slid his phone out of his pocket and gawked at the time. Why did he leave his device on silent? A slew of texts from Elijah, Caroline, and his mother flooded the screen.

Maisie snorted and tapped her fingertips against the book's cover. "Looks like someone still has to deal with procrastination."

He shrugged. "Well, I'm not perfect."

With that, he bounded down the hallway, up the stairs, and toward the parking lot. Thankfully, Caroline still managed to keep him on task through all the publicity craze. He never wanted to see another query to a book blog, podcast, or reviewer in his life. Clark, amid all the marketing craziness, already talked with them about sequels and series. The two of them would be seeing a lot more of each other this summer.

He slid into his vehicle and gunned the gas all the way to the bookstore. When he found a parking space nearby a downtown popcorn shop, he tore his keys out of the ignition, slammed the door, and a distinct whiff of caramel and cheddar followed him as he sprinted to the bookstore.

The workers, it appeared, had set up a table outside. Caroline sat underneath a large green awning. She'd already placed books on stands, had signing pens in cups, and placed a basket full of goodies wrapped in cellophane at the corner of the display.

She peered in his direction. The sun toasted the back of his shirt. Caroline shielded her eyes with her hand, but he couldn't mistake the knowing smirk.

With an exhale, he dove into the seat beside her. A line had formed, snaking along the path of shops beside the book store. "When did you get here?"

She shrugged. "Thirty minutes early."

He whistled low. "Since you set up, I'll tear down." A neon pink sign perched on the cellophane basket advertising a giveaway. A roll of blue tickets leaned against the container.

"Obviously." She smiled. "Dinner after to celebrate?"

"What? It's like you're my girlfriend or something."

They clasped hands underneath the table. The shop worker, who held up the line until the event started at two, glanced their way. Curt nod.

Okay, showtime.

Elijah and Caroline's roommates stepped up to the table first, no surprise there. They did stand awfully close, however. Something about the way their fingers gravitated toward one another, like magnets, caused Andy to furrow his brow.

Books signed, the two of them disappeared into the popcorn shop.

"Did I miss something?" Andy shook the blue pen that had appeared to already ooze the last of its ink on Liv's book.

Caroline wriggled her nose but said nothing. They signed the books of the next group in line, a family from Andy's church that he recognized from Advent time. They'd lit the candle of hope in front of the church and read a passage from Isaiah.

When they received their books and dropped a ticket into the giveaway bucket, Caroline spoke.

"I may have signed up Liv for the same cooking class that you forced Elijah to join."

After Caroline and Andy had exchanged kitchen concoction horror stories from their roommates at a local diner, Andy noticed an ad for a local cooking class on a corkboard. Because he'd taken on more freelance projects, with a manageable schedule Caroline had written for him, he had a little extra cash to spend on a birthday present for Elijah. The gift of making something other than ramen.

"What?" Caroline nibbled at her lip. "Maybe they'll bond. Liv needs a nice guy in her life who doesn't freak out about the fact she works a billion jobs. Worst case scenario, we won't have any more cabbage debacles."

He shook his head, grinned, and signed another book.

Sunlight crested the clouds of an overcast sky. As the signing progressed, the cumulus cloud withered to small white streaks in a brilliant blue sky. Hopeful weather for the most perfect of days.

The signing was over now. As the last buyers, a family with a small child, waved and turned to walk down the sidewalk, Caroline leaned back in her chair. A smile played on her lips as a gentle breeze lifted and dropped her strands of hair.

"Could anything make this day more perfect?" Caroline beamed at the blue sky and then at Andy.

He grinned. "I could think of one thing."

Andy leaned in and kissed her. There. Now it was perfect.

AUTHOR'S NOTE

Everyone in college we knew worked at least two jobs while balancing a full load of classes. And when we graduated, the situation somehow got even worse.

Most people in their twenties have to work long hours or multiple positions to pay for rent, utilities, and food for the month. We've seen so many hardworking people get burnt out or, like Andy, get overwhelmed by the sheer amount of work needed to stay afloat.

We each have worked more jobs than we could count. At one point in our college and post-college careers, we were working seven jobs, apiece.

We've both understood burnout all too well. And like Caroline, we felt a lot of pressure to succeed in a very tough field that seems to shift and downsize a lot.

We really wanted characters in a romance who understood the struggles of loud neighbors, student loan debt, kitchen experiments gone wrong, and more bills than checks coming in the mail.

And we also wanted to have characters who spoke to the perfectionism many of us face. Many schools, unintentionally, spur students to be the very best at everything. They often will crumble under the pressure and face burnout because of that. Andy and Caroline's story picks up after they've experienced that incredible strain.

They learn that it's okay that not every recipe will go according to plan, and that God can use our imperfections to create a beautiful mosaic.

Follow Hope Bolinger and Alyssa Roat on social media, their websites, or through their newsletters:

Hope's links:
Facebook: www.facebook.com/hopebolinger
Twitter: twitter.com/HopeBolinger
Instagram: www.instagram.com/hopebolinger
Amazon: www.amazon.com/Hope-Bolinger/e/B00V0VWFKQ
Pinterest: www.pinterest.com/hopebolinger
Website/Newsletter: www.hopebolinger.com
BookBub: www.bookbub.com/authors/hope-bolinger

Alyssa's Links:
Facebook: www.facebook.com/alyssawrote
Twitter: twitter.com/alyssawrote
Instagram: www.instagram.com/alyssawrote
Amazon: www.amazon.com/Alyssa-Roat/e/B08G3P1494
Website: alyssawrote.com
Newsletter: alyssawrote.com/newsletter
BookBub: www.bookbub.com/authors/alyssa-roat

Now, A Sneak Peek at Book Two

FINDING HARMONY

Releasing July 2022

Chapter One

OLIVIA WILSON CLOSED HER EYES, LETTING the music flow through her arms, her wrists, her fingers, and into the keys.

The full sound of the grand piano reverberating through the sanctuary rolled over her, filling her heart and pouring more music out through her hands.

She hit an A flat and winced. Slightly off. That was the third out-of-tune note she'd hit. Definitely time for the piano tuner to come take a look.

Her buzzing phone interrupted the rich harmonies. She sighed and glanced at the caller ID before picking up with a smile. "Hey, Caroline."

Her roommate immediately started speaking, words coming as fast as an auctioneer. "Liv! Helping Hope has an event going on in one hour, and I'm not technically going but I'm supposed to pick up the cupcakes and bring them by, but my car won't start and the icing is starting to melt and…"

Liv pressed two fingers over her lips, containing a laugh. "So you need me to come pick you up?"

"Yes, please. I'm at Charlie's Confections. Andy's doing a mural or something on the other side of town and I could try to jump my car but I think that might take too long and—"

"I got you, girl. I'll be there in ten minutes."

Liv hung up, shaking her head. Everything was always a crisis with

Caroline. Thank goodness Caroline's boyfriend, Andy, had an easygoing manner that helped keep her grounded.

Liv looked back at the piano and sighed. She would have preferred to spend a bit more time enjoying the full grand, unlike the uprights she usually got to play. The elderly woman who played on Sunday mornings had asked Liv to check if it was out of tune.

"It sounds a little out of sorts," she'd said with a chuckle. "I heard that you teach my grandkids and thought maybe you could give a listen. I can play hymns just fine, but I don't have any of that fancy training."

Liv had already taught two piano lessons to homeschooled children today, and she had a shift at the coffee shop later, but she couldn't help saying yes to the sweet woman. The congregation deserved to enjoy a tuned piano, and Liv would be out of town tomorrow for her usual first-Saturday-of-the-month visit to her dad. So, she'd squeezed it in.

It looked like she needed to squeeze in a roommate rescue as well.

She grabbed her purse, slung it over her shoulder, and headed down the aisle, her lightweight maxi skirt fluttering behind her while her sandals flip flopped. She nodded to the church secretary on her way out the door.

Outside, the summer sun paired with humidity created a dense atmosphere that reminded Liv of an ill-fated tomato soup she'd tried to make a few days ago. *Never again.* Squinting, she dug for her sunglasses in her purse, found them on top of her head, and slipped them on.

She climbed into her old sky-blue Volkswagen Beetle, nearly the same color as Caroline's car, though more faded over the years. Each time she turned the key in the ignition, she wondered if today would be the day the Bug finally went kaput, but so far it still puttered along.

She left one window down—the AC hadn't worked in over a year—and tapped her fingers to a song on the local radio station while the breeze from the moving vehicle slapped tendrils of dark hair out of her messy bun and into her face.

The song ended and a tinny voice spoke through the static of the old radio. "Calling all music aficionados! It's the fourth annual Roseville Indie Music Festival."

Liv reached over and turned up the volume knob.

"Do you think you have what it takes to be the next big artist? Come on down to the Damask County Fairgrounds and..."

A turn coming up snagged Liv's attention. She turned on her blinker, merged lanes, then tuned back in to what the radio host was saying.

"Your song could play on 92.5 FM, The Beat! Head down to the county fairgrounds."

An ad for car insurance followed the announcement. A Roseville music festival? Liv had missed most of the details, but some of her students might be interested in attending. She ran through the list of kids of all ages whom she taught piano or voice lessons. Asher seemed to like indie music, or maybe Mia...Claire only had an ear for the classics.

Her smile thinking of her students melted into a frown. The list grew smaller every day. Fewer parents seemed willing to pay for private tutors anymore.

She pulled into the parking lot of Charlie's Confections. As she stepped out of the car, a woman in slacks, heels, and a tight bun hurried out of the shop toward her.

"Liv!" Caroline threw her arms around her roommate. "Thank goodness. I had to take the cupcakes back into the shop so they would quit melting. The event is at The Vine."

The Vine? Liv had sung with the worship band at the enormous church a few times. She tilted her head. "Why there? Why not at the Hope Club?"

Caroline worked for Helping Hope Publishing, a nonprofit publishing house that specialized in helping kids. The Hope Club was the local boys and girls club run by the organization.

Caroline shook her head, tugging Liv toward the shop. "No way.

This is a *donor* event. Super fancy. Too fancy even for me. I'm just the cupcake girl. They have a big conference room rented or something."

Liv suppressed another smile. In her no-nonsense business attire, Caroline looked nothing like a "cupcake girl." Caroline could switch on her professional charm in an instant—when she wasn't panicking about life.

The bell at the door jingled and cool air washed over Liv inside the shop. She only had a few seconds to bask in the cool air and the scent of fresh baked goods before Caroline was hefting what looked like five dozen intricately frosted cupcakes in distinctive blue and white Charlie's boxes. Caroline nodded to the round-faced man behind the counter. "Thanks, Charlie."

He watched Caroline with a furrowed brow. "Careful with those."

Liv swiped two boxes off the top of Caroline's stack and backed into the door to open it. "Let's get these to the event before something happens to them."

After situating the cupcakes safely in the car with Caroline hovering over them like a mother hen with frosted chicks, Liv eased out of the parking lot, avoiding potholes.

Caroline wiped her brow. "Still no AC in the Bug, huh?"

"Sorry about that." Liv reached for the door. "I can roll down another window."

"I'm just grateful you came to get me." Caroline waved Liv off and rolled down the window herself.

Liv glanced at the clock. Still an hour until her shift. No worries. "Of course."

"No, really. I owe you iced coffee or something. Want to hit up She Brews after this?"

Liv laughed. "I work there in an hour."

"Perfect. We can hang out and relax for a while before you start."

Liv bit her lip. She'd been hoping to do a bit of lesson planning before work. "What about you?" She glanced at her roommate, still guarding the cupcakes protectively from any rogue bumps or potholes. "Don't you have to go back to work?"

Caroline smirked. "Nope. All the important people are at the event, so they gave us the rest of the day off."

Liv wanted to feel proud of her roommate. Just a few months ago, Caroline never would have treated a day off like, well, a day off. She would have been in the office anyway, doing who knew what. But Caroline had learned a lot from her mom's burnout and the events of the past few months.

Instead, a small part of Liv wished Caroline did have something else to do. But she wouldn't crush this progress in Caroline's battle against workaholism. Her lessons could wait.

"Sounds like a plan. Let's just hope Griffith isn't working today."

Caroline snorted. "I pity the person who tries one of his concoctions."

Liv had learned that the hard way.

She tried to relax. *Don't worry about the lesson prep. You can do them after work. When you send Miss Evie the link to the songs you recommended. And transpose the hymn for Cherilynn into E Major.*

How did she become an unofficial music consultant for what felt like every small neighborhood church in town? At least she didn't sing at The Vine anymore.

It may be the slightest bit possible that I've agreed to do just the tiniest bit too much.

Elijah Peterson let another person go in front of him in the line at the coffee shop. Up at the front counter of She Brews, the prime Joe-on-the-go spot in Roseville, a stocky man with a buzz cut and too loud a voice called out an order for "Sarah" for a lavender macchiato.

Elijah's nose wrinkled. Sure, he'd had his fair share of cooking fails back at his apartment—hence why his roommate Andy signed him up for a cooking class this evening—but the brewista slash local playwright, Griffith, got too experimental with the flavors sometimes.

He felt a body hover behind him. Elijah spun around. Make that two bodies. A couple with their fingers laced together in a tight grip nodded at him.

"You go ahead." Elijah motioned for them to move ahead of him in the queue.

The boyfriend of the couple—his left hand didn't appear to have a ring—shook his head. "I've seen you let five people step in front of you. We're not in a rush."

Elijah nodded and tugged a strand of long black hair behind his ear. Andy had poked fun at him for rocking the "worship leader" look, a.k.a., the need to get a haircut soon. But from what Elijah could tell from YouTube videos of the previous worship leader at The Vine Community Chapel, the church where he now worked, he'd gotten just about everything right—the long hair, often tied up in a bun, the skinny jeans, the trimmed beard.

After barista Griffith fulfilled an order for a teenager who wanted a blended drink the color of hot pink cotton candy, Elijah approached the counter. He breathed in the strong scents of coffee beans and scanned the menu for the third time for a drink.

Griffith grinned as he straightened his red apron. "Want me to surprise you again today?"

Elijah's teeth crashed onto his bottom lip. The past few times he'd come here Griffith had whipped up a few "concoctions" for him. They either left a weird, sour taste on his tongue, or if they happened to make it to Elijah's stomach, caused his abdomen to sear in pain.

But when he saw the hopeful glint in Griffith's eye, a man who lived for creating the next best "flavor" and who complained during their pickup games of basketball about how every customer ordered the same five drinks, he dropped his shoulders. Relented.

"Sure, Griffith. What do you got for me today?"

Griffith squeaked the lid off of a marker to write Elijah's name on a plastic cup. "An iced lavender matcha with a couple of pumps of vanilla syrups."

Oh, goodness, that sounded horrendous. "I'll bet it's amazing." Elijah winced so much his cheekbones blocked part of his vision. He strolled to the end of the counter and waited for Griffith to call his name.

As Griffith dumped a scoopful of ice into Elijah's cup, the door to the store dinged. In walked a towering man with ice blond hair that screamed a Scandinavian descent. Mason Smith, head pastor of Vine Community Chapel, nodded at Elijah and then selected a table near the door. Right then, Griffith slid the drink onto the counter, and Elijah scooped the cold beverage into his hands.

Here went nothing.

He swallowed hard and strode to the table. Perhaps this time in their weekly Friday coffee meeting, Pastor Smith would have something positive to say.

It would be the first time in their history since Elijah took over the worship leader position in the Spring. But like his constant agreement to try Griffith's drinks, perhaps miracles could happen.

The long red straw to the drink slipped into his mouth when he reached the table. A mouthful of sickening sweet juice that somehow tasted of grass smothered his tongue. Yikes. So much for that.

Elijah slid into the seat and noted how the plastic chair dug into his leg.

"Morning, Lij." Pastor Smith leaned against the window pane near the table. Summer sunlight dazzled his brilliant blue eyes.

Okay, his boss began the conversation with Elijah's nickname, a good start.

Smith dug into his pocket and procured a phone. Elijah's shoulders dropped. Great, the part of the meeting he hated, the emails. "Sorry to start off the meeting this way." True, they often began by talking about the latest Wolverines baseball game before they got to …the complaints. The many, many gripes from church members. "But I double-booked myself this afternoon with a couple doing premarital counseling. This shouldn't take long."

Elijah wore his best it's-kay-I-love-getting-lambasted-by-the-congregation smile.

"To be honest." Smith rubbed the corners of his eyes and placed his phone on the table. "I may just have the church secretary forward these to you. They've been filling up my inbox, and I keep losing important emails about counseling and funerals in the shuffle."

"Sure, no problem." The words lodged in Elijah's throat like the blended drink Griffith made him last week with caramel and grape. He shuddered. Never again.

"Most of the disgruntled messages are about Sarah. Her harmonies are a little experimental."

The worship team of the large church often had three of its female singers on rotation. Alexandra had to put her time on hold because since May, she'd been taking care of her mom at home. And Sarah…well, Sarah liked to do Mariah Carey types of runs, where the notes would bobble in her throat. Except, unlike Mariah, Sarah seldom found the right key.

They did have one other vocalist who knew harmony and the keyboard like she'd come out of the womb singing and playing piano at the same time. But ever since last Easter, part-time jobs and freelance gigs had swallowed her whole. He hadn't heard from her since. Pastor Smith tapped the table with his large palm. Then he scooped his phone into his hand. "Go ahead and look over the emails the secretary forwards you today. Try to change the worship set by Sunday based on their feedback."

"No problem."

Problem indeed. The band had already practiced last night, and Elijah had spent Monday through Wednesday trying to address the complaint of an elderly woman who said he made her stand too long during worship. He'd vowed to have three songs at the beginning of service and two after the sermon to accommodate.

But who knew what else he'd have to fix now?

Smith meant well, of course. From what Elijah could tell, a number of congregation members had left the church when the previous worship leader retired. "People do that," Pastor Smith had told him back in May. "Withhold giving or leave a church entirely when their favorite worship leader or pastor goes away."

A buzz from Smith's phone vibrated in his hand. He pressed the device to his ear, gave a half-hearted wave to Elijah, and disappeared out of the shop. A heavy sigh deflated Elijah. He realized, moments later, that he'd splashed bright-green liquid onto his pants. Must've gotten a splotch of Griffith's drink on his jeans when he sat.

He hopped off his seat and headed toward the restrooms at the other end of the shop. Giggles from a table with teenagers and blended drinks stung his ears on the way. When he reached the door to the men's room, he halted when he saw a bright orange sheet attached to the Community Announcements corkboard. Business cards and posters for various local businesses littered the notice board situated between the two restrooms.

Once his retinas recovered from the blazing orange, he read.

Roseville Fourth Annual Indie Music Festival

What: Performers from the city of Roseville and surrounding areas play an original song with the hopes of being chosen to be the next big musical sensation.

Where: Damask County Fairgrounds

Prizes: 1st place - $20,000, a deal with Diatonic Records, and your song will be played on local hit radio stations such as 92.5 FM, The Beat

Before he could read the second and third place prizes, his eyes scanned over the prize dollar amount again. Twenty grand? He made that over the span of a year. And even though worship leading was supposed to be "part-time," with all the changes Pastor Smith had him do, he ended up working way more.

But with that amount of money…wow, he could do a lot with that.

His heart sank when he read the "When" section. How could he ever pull together a song in less than a month? And who would he play with? The worship band, maybe? He doubted they had the time to compose lyrics or chords.

"Sorry, excuse me." A girl with black hair and bangles that clanked on her arms had tapped his shoulder. Those gorgeous dark brown eyes trapped him for a moment, like a chorus to a song that wouldn't let him go. Scarlet covered her cheeks and she motioned to the restroom.

He didn't realize he'd been blocking the entrance. "Whoops, my bad!" Elijah stepped to the side, and recognition dawned. The third girl on the worship set rotation, the one who could find the harmony. "Olivia, right?"

She moved a bracelet up and down her arm in a motion he assumed she did often and without conscious thought. "Liv, actually."

"You have one of the most beautiful voices I've ever heard." And beautiful eyes, too, but he didn't add this part. "It's too late to add you to the set this week, but any way we could work you back into the worship rotation of singers at church?" He held back a "please." Something about her woodsy perfume clouded his senses, and he couldn't get all the words out.

Having Liv on the worship set could save them. Maybe the congregation would hear her vocals and forget about their aching feet or Sarah's attempts and failures to find the right notes.

Liv chewed on her lip and dropped the armlet onto her wrist with a clank. "I'd love to, believe me." She winced. "But I just don't have enough time." With that, she ducked into the women's restroom and disappeared.

CPSIA information can be obtained
at www.ICGtesting.com
Printed in the USA
BVHW041203141021
618951BV00013B/342

9 781953 957078